THE TRAIL WEST

THE TRAIL WEST

WILLIAM W. JOHNSTONE
with J. A. Johnstone

PINNACLE BOOKS
Kensington Publishing Corp.
www.kensingtonbooks.com

PINNACLE BOOKS are published by

Kensington Publishing Corp.
119 West 40th Street
New York, NY 10018

PUBLISHER'S NOTE
Following the death of William W. Johnstone, the Johnstone family is working with a carefully selected writer to organize and complete Mr. Johnstone's outlines and many unfinished manuscripts to create additional novels in all of his series like The Last Gunfighter, Mountain Man, and Eagles, among others. This novel was inspired by Mr. Johnstone's superb storytelling.

All Kensington titles, imprints, and distributed lines are available at special quantity discounts for bulk purchases for sales promotions, premiums, fund-raising, educational, or institutional use.
Special book excerpts or customized printings can also be created to fit specific needs. For details, write or phone the office of the Kensington special sales manager: Kensington Publishing Corp., 119 West 40th Street, New York, NY 10018, attn: Special Sales Department; phone 1-800-221-2647.

PINNACLE BOOKS and the Pinnacle logo are Reg. U.S. Pat. & TM Off.
The WWJ steer head logo is a trademark of Kensington Publishing Corp.

ISBN-13: 978-0-7860-2932-7
ISBN-10: 0-7860-2932-3

First printing: February 2013

10 9 8 7 6 5

Printed in the United States of America

PROLOGUE

In the year 1850, when he was but twenty years old, young Dooley Monahan, last born and only living offspring of Janine and David Monahan, struggling Iowa farmers who had joined the first wave of pioneers, found himself fallen in with bad company.

It was a simple enough thing. Dooley had ridden south to a town near the Missouri border to pick up a new milk cow for his pa. She was a purebred Jersey—a rare breed at that time and place, and one which was renowned for producing rich milk. She was already paid for, and all he had to do to claim her was show proof of who he was. He was all set to do just that, with an introductory letter from his pa, enough chuck in his saddlebags to get him there and home again, and fifty cents emergency money in his pocket. "Just in case," David Monahan had said as he pressed the worn coins into his son's hand.

Dooley's father was always chock-full of "just-in-cases."

But Dooley—tall, handsome, and always with a twinkle in his chestnut eyes—had nodded, taken the cash, mounted up, and set off. At twenty, he was already running half of the farm. He had forty acres in corn, twenty acres in oats, twenty acres in hay, twenty acres in cattle pasture, and responsibility for all the hogs. In another year or so, he imagined he'd take over the place.

He thought about all that while riding the two days south to Corydon and half of another to reach his goal: the small farm town of Accord. There, he bartered at length with the liveryman to trade a good morning mucking out the stalls in exchange for one night's resting place for himself and his horse.

They sealed the deal with a handshake, and Dooley gave his old gelding a thorough rubdown before he grabbed his hunting rifle and the last bites of his ma's good apple pie, and headed out into the dying rays of the sun to have a look around.

There wasn't much to look at besides darkened windows and CLOSED signs until he came to the mouth of an alley, from which muted laughter and man talk burbled out onto the street along with the soft glow of lantern light. Dooley was a curious lad, and, gulping down the last of his pie, he stuck his head around the corner and peered in.

A packing crate, topped with a horse blanket and centered by a small mound of coins, sat back about a dozen feet from the street. Seated on boxes or nail kegs surrounding the crate were four men, each staring at a handful of cards.

"Damned if you didn't deal us out a mess, Usher," Dooley heard, just before the man with his back to him punched the speaker in the arm. Well, more like gave him a little shove, Dooley guessed. Leastwise, it all looked real friendly.

At least, that was what he thought then.

If he had known who they were or what they would eventually do to him, and worse, the path they would set the gangly Iowa farm boy traveling down—a path filled with pain and questions and heartbreak beyond measure, and one that would change his life forever—he wouldn't have been so eager to call out a friendly, "Hello there, fellers!" But Dooley was no fortune-teller, and so he grinned and called to them, and they waved him in.

They played poker until the morning light, though Dooley didn't remember it in much detail. They'd had a jug of homemade hooch they'd passed around too often for him to keep track. When he came into himself again, it was late the next morning and they were outside town. Old Tony, the aged chestnut gelding his father had given him on his thirteenth birthday, was safely hitched to their picket line, and Dooley was as sick to his stomach as he'd ever been. He also began to realize he'd fallen in with dangerous men.

He looked around. Usher, the one who'd been punched the night before, was a tallish fellow with oily, red hair curling into his eyes and down his back. He looked quite a bit cruder than he had in the lamplight. Dexter, the one who'd punched him, was a little shorter with close-cropped, dark brown hair and a scar running high across his forehead, like somebody had started to scalp him but got interrupted. Dexter looked like he'd skin his own mama for sneezing during Sunday service. Well, that wasn't right—Dexter looked to never have been to Sunday Service in his life—but Dooley couldn't think of anything meaner right off the top of his head.

The third man, a short blond with a droopy mustache and a permanent scowl, was across the way, angrily and jerkily stropping a knife blade back and forth across a length of leather. His name was Grubb. A fitting name if ever Dooley had heard one.

The last of the four—and the roughest, young Dooley guessed, if you took any mind of the scar on the side of his face—was another tallish fellow, his once dark hair graying already, whose name was either George Vince or Vince George. He answered to either one singly, and Dooley hadn't heard anyone call him by both names. At least, not in the correct order, whatever that was.

But despite his obvious lack of hygiene (Dooley could smell him clear across camp), he seemed the happiest that Dooley was "one of them," whoever they were. Dooley was running a little shy on the details. They seemed to be some kind of a group, and they seemed to have plans.

Later that afternoon, Dooley discovered just what their plan was: to rob the First Iowa Bank of Corydon. By the time he figured out what they were up to, he was in too deep to crawl back out.

That's how Dooley Monahan came to be one of Monty's Raiders (the original Monty having been lost in the mists of time), a gang of cheap rowdies who, before the Civil War, terrorized the central plains.

Against his will, he stayed with the raiders until late the next year, when his complaining and pleas to leave and go home finally rankled the nerves of the gang to their frazzling point. One night, Vince George (which had turned out to be his proper name), with the help of Red Usher, took it upon himself to beat Dooley senseless and leave him for dead in a ditch near a northern Missouri field.

They left him without a dime from the monies he helped them steal or his wallet, which still held the fifty cents that had been his father's final gift to him. All they left with him was Old Tony who, at twenty-five, was too old to do anybody any good. And they took his saddle.

For three days Dooley lay in the ditch, not

moving, passing in and out of fuzzy consciousness, until he was found by a passerby on her
way to a neighbor's. Battered and bruised and
barely conscious, he was saved by a woman named
Kathleen.

1

North Dakota, Fall 1869

The pot wouldn't have been considered a big one in town. In fact, it would have been laughable. But it was rich for a bunkhouse when the players were still a week and a half from payday and hurting bad for something to do. A dollar and fourteen cents, twenty-six matches, an old whorehouse token, and a train-flattened nickel sat in the center of the table. Dooley Monahan held exactly two pairs—tens and deuces.

Being unlucky at cards, it was the best hand he'd had in months. He dug deep into pockets linty with disuse and finally dug out a dime, his last. He looked across the table at Bob Smith, a summer name if he'd ever heard one, then flipped the dime onto the table. "Call, and raise you a five-cent nickel."

The other players had folded already and looked on eagerly while Smith scowled. He was the only other player left in the game, and universally disliked by the other hands.

Smith, a dull, hulking fellow with a Southern accent and a hair-trigger temper, growled, "All's I got is matches."

Everybody knew the matches would be redeemed, come payday, for a penny apiece. Monahan nodded. "Fine by me, Smith." He turned to the old codger sitting next to him. "You keepin' track, Cookie?"

Holding a folded-up piece of paper and a crooked stick of raw lead, Cookie licked the makeshift pencil. "Yup. That's five more matches for Smith. Right, Smith?"

Smith grunted and tossed five more sulphur tips on the pile. "Call," he barked. "Let's see 'em, Monahan."

Carefully, Monahan lay down the battered pasteboards to the boys' enthusiastic hum.

Smith set down his cards, but facedown. "You lose, Monahan," he growled, and started to rake in the pot.

Cookie, who was seventy-something and old enough . . . or dumb enough . . . to be brave in the face of a tough hombre like Smith—braver than Monahan was, in any case—grabbed Smith's arm. "Hold on, there. Let's have a look-see."

Monahan wasn't exactly sure what occurred over the next couple of seconds, but he recalled something about Smith calling him a cheat who lost more at cards than most men lose trying to put a size eight boot on a size ten foot! He thought he pushed Cookie out of the way right about the time Smith drew his gun, and he was a bit fuzzy about pulling his own.

But Monahan remembered the way it ended up, all right.

Smith lay dead, shot through the heart by Monahan, a man who normally couldn't hit the broad side of a barn with a handful of beans, and Monahan himself was shot in the left hip. It wasn't bad, just a graze really, but it sure hurt like hell.

And he remembered everybody whooping and hollering and cheering.

As for Monahan? He hadn't liked Smith much, but he felt awful bad about the whole mess. He'd seen far too many deaths in his life to feel marginally good about causing yet another.

A couple of weeks later the U.S. marshal came by, and from the men's description—and the wrinkled poster he carried in his wallet—he identified Smith not as Smith, but as Jason Baylor, a man wanted in three states and two territories for everything from robbery to aggravated assault to cold blooded murder. Make that multiple murders.

"The last was when him and his brothers killed a couple fellers down in Colorado." Marshal Tobin sat in the good chair on the boss's porch with the boss and all the hands—including the still-limping Monahan—all huddled around. "Wounded three more, too. Bank job gone bad." He shook his head. "If I was you, Dooley, I'd change my name and beat it out of here. Them Baylor boys is like rabid skunks. Reckon they're split up now, waitin' for the heat to die down from that Colorado job, but eventually they've got a plan to meet up. And when Jason don't show . . ."

"That's right, Dooley," said Cookie, nodding sagely. "They'll come lookin' for you, sure as anything. And that Alf Baylor? I hear he's plumb crazy!"

"Dev ain't exactly normal, either," muttered the marshal.

Monahan scrunched up his face. "Just how many brothers did the feller have, anyhow?"

Marshal Tobin frowned. "Just the two, Dooley, just the two. But you'll feel like you're in the hands of the legions of Satan if they catch you up. They're bad business. Real bad."

Monahan simply said, "Aw, crud." He was nearly forty-one and well past his prime. He'd been thinking—hoping, more like—he'd outlived what little reputation he had, and could get on with the peaceful business of living out the rest of his life and dying in relative obscurity.

Didn't seem the dice were going to roll his way, though.

Marshal Tobin scribbled on a piece of paper, and handed it to Monahan. "Reward voucher. There was plenty of paper out on Jason Baylor. Five hundred dollars' worth."

Collectively, the boys gasped and Monahan knew why. It was near two years' wages for a top cowhand.

"You can cash that in any place that has a bank and a telegraph, but I'd do it a far piece from here, if I was you. Think you know why. Hey, Charlie"—the marshal turned to the boss—"don't suppose you got anything stronger than coffee to drink around here, do you? Like to celebrate sayin' adios to at least one o' those damned Baylor boys."

Monahan left the next day, with a pillow under his left hip and the voucher in his pocket.

2

Three years later

Dooley Monahan dozed, half asleep beside his dying campfire, beneath the pewter-gray of a barely-dawn sky in the piney Arizona mountains. He'd been dreaming a warm dream twenty-some years old, dreaming of Kathy and soft quilts and that old feather bed, when he was roused by the crawling sense that somebody was staring at him.

He grabbed his Colt before his eyes were all the way open, sat bolt upright, and swung the muzzle straight into the face of the intruder.

He checked himself just in time. It was a dog. A dog was staring at him, its mouth open in a grin and its tongue lolling. A dog with blue eyes, which he had mistaken for wolf yellow.

The dog just sat there, looking at him. Panting softly, expelling faint clouds of vapor, it appeared to be smiling at him—maybe laughing at an old man for being so dad-blamed jumpy.

Monahan slowly lowered his pistol.

The dog barked softy, just once, pushing out only enough air with the utterance to flutter its lips.

"Funny," Monahan muttered. "You're a real card. Go home." He put his gun away.

The dog continued to look at him.

"Well, now that you woke me up, I gotta piss," he stated crankily, and then wondered why the hell he was talking to a dog when he didn't much like talking to people.

He stood up slowly, checking the trees ringing the old beaver meadow in which he'd made camp, and found nothing out of the ordinary. At least, there was no sign of those hounds-on-a-scent, the Baylor boys, and that was a blessing.

The morning air in the mountains was still cold and crisp, which was hard on the bones of a man who had a lot more miles behind him than in front of him. Seemed like it took forever to get his liver-spotted old body awake anymore, since it didn't wake all at one time. Aside from the general soreness he attributed to too many years of sleeping on hard ground, there were his old wounds.

His left shoulder woke first with a sharp, quick stab fading to a dull, lingering ache, where he'd taken two Mescalero arrows about fifteen or sixteen years back. A man would have thought there was a tiny little bull's-eye painted on his shirt, those arrows were so dang close together.

At least, that was what the doc had said when he was digging them out.

The way Monahan figured it, that sawbones had

dug out about half his shoulder joint while he was in there. Least, it had felt like that was what he was doing. The son of a gun had enjoyed it, too!

Monahan's shoulder had never worked all that good again, but at least it was on his left side. He would have been out of work and down to sweeping saloons and emptying spittoons if it had been on his right.

His legs woke next. His right thigh complained with throbs in the places where he'd broken it, once by sailing ass-over-teakettle off a raw bronc, and once by falling down a ravine when he was out after strays.

Last to wake up was his head. Too many insults had left him with a permanent throb and ache. Sometimes it robbed him of his memory, other times, just part of it. But either way, it hurt worse in the mornings.

As he walked toward the trees, Monahan gave thought to his left hip. He'd never turned in the voucher from Marshal Tobin, although he still carried it in his hip pocket on the side that still ached from Jason Baylor's bullet. He figured it'd be bad luck—in more ways than one—to mess with bounty money. He'd been right, too. He'd worked all over the west since then, and hadn't heard a blessed word about the Baylor boys since the shooting.

Until six months past, leastwise. It had come to him that Dev and Alf Baylor were looking for him. Fortunately, he heard they were looking in Utah. But recently, he'd got word they were headed south into Arizona. He'd quit his job soon after and moved on, taking his cramps and his throbs and his soreness and his old hurts with him.

And so, on that crisp mountain morning while the dog watched, he took inventory of his aches and pains, and waited for them to stop their hollering.

At least half the time his left foot woke up numb, and he hadn't a clue why, although stomping on it for two or three minutes seemed to bring it around. And his neck always had a crick in it, from the time he took a bad fall off a bronc up in Wyoming.

He managed to hobble off a few feet and relieve himself, buttoned up, and had another look around at the trees, just in case. Another look at the dog revealed it hadn't moved more than an inch.

If that.

Monahan knew dogs like that one. He'd seen them, here and there, on cattle spreads. Well, on a few sheep operations, too, but sheep weren't something he liked to think about, at least not before he'd had his coffee. Old Billy Toomey at the B-Bar-T had a pair, an odd-eyed red merle and a brown-eyed black and tan, and he used them to work cows up from the range.

"Stand up," he said to the dog.

It yawned and lay down, stretching itself beside the fire.

"Well-trained, ain't you?"

Sighing happily—or perhaps with exhaustion—the dog closed its eyes.

The dog was a male, and bobtailed. Probably born that way, if it was what he thought it was. Its coat was longish and rough and as wild-colored as a jar full of jawbreakers. Even in the thin, early light, he could tell that much. The color was called merle: a bluish gray broken with patches of black, like somebody had slopped watery bleach over a black dog. Additionally, it had white feet and a white chest. Bright coppery markings covered its lower legs and muzzle, and a thumbprint-size smudge of copper hung over each eye.

He'd heard dogs like this called Spanish Shepherds or Australian Shepherds, or California or Arizona Shepherds, or Whatever-State-or-Territory-They-Happened-to-Be-In Shepherds. The folks calling them by any one of those names got awful touchy if somebody happened to call them by the wrong place.

He played it safe, and stuck with calling them plain old cow dogs. Of course, the Indians didn't call them that. They called them ghost dogs, the ones that had blue eyes, anyhow. Folks said as how Indians steered clear of those who had even one.

It struck him that this particular dog must belong to somebody. It looked like somebody had been feeding it regular, anyhow. He should have thought of it before.

"Where's your people?" Monahan asked, stomping his left foot on the ground rhythmically. The feeling was starting to come back. "Ain't you got no people?"

The dog opened his eyes and yawned, then went back to panting softly.

"Seems queer, you out here by your lonesome," he muttered, and his eyes flicked once again to the trees. Nothing. He was getting as spooky as an old woman.

Slowly, he walked through the tall, dewy, meadow grass toward a pine at the edge of the clearing, pausing to pat the neck of his hobbled bay gelding, General Grant. "Good mornin' to you, old son," he said softly. The horse looked up from his grazing just long enough to snort softly.

At the pine, Monahan untied his rope from the trunk and lowered his chuck bag, which he'd stashed up the tree in case of bears. He made his way back to the fire—and the cow dog—and slowly eased himself down again in his place across from the fire.

He added a few twigs to the embers and gave them a stir. "Ain't heard no folks. You run off from somebody?"

The dog sat up again and just looked at him.

In no time, Monahan had bacon sizzling in one skillet and biscuits baking in another.

The dog drooled steadily, watching his every move, but it didn't offer to snatch any from the pan.

"You got decent table manners, anyhow," Monahan muttered, and started the coffee.

When the biscuits were done, he broke one in two, the long way, and as the steam and that good smell rose on the cool morning air, he poked a piece of bacon inside it and made ready to pop it in his mouth.

Softy, the dog whined.

"Wait your turn." Monahan inched the biscuit closer to his mouth.

The dog's gaze followed that biscuit like a man's eyes, when he's fresh off a long trail, will watch a pretty woman.

"Oh, hell," Monahan grumbled, and tossed the little sandwich arcing over the fire. The dog caught it in his mouth, chewed twice, then swallowed. He licked his chops and stared again at Monahan.

"Don't try to fool me," Monahan said sternly. "I know how you dogs are. Even if you'd just ate a whole steer, you'd still be beggin' for cake."

The dog stared at him expectantly across the fire, a string of the ever-present drool slowly dripping from one corner of its mouth.

Monahan fixed a second biscuit, then averted his eyes and ate it himself . . . and damned if he didn't feel guilty!

"I just got enough for two more, dog." He looked at its face more closely. The light had come up enough that he could see faint grizzle on the dog's muzzle. It was old, or at least middle-aged . . . kind of like him. He figured it had to belong to somebody.

"They're little!" he said in his defense for wanting to eat both sandwiches when the dog lifted a paw and whined. "What do you weigh, anyhow? Can't be more 'n fifty, sixty pound. I'm three times bigger 'n you!"

He fixed a third biscuit with bacon and ate it, at which point the dog sat straight up on his haunches and waved his front paws in the air. Monahan heaved a sigh, fixed the last one, and tossed it to the dog, who caught it in midair.

"Happy now?"

Two chews and a gulp and the biscuit was gone. Its front feet on the ground again, the dog looked at him expectantly.

"Ain't no more." Monahan poured himself a cup of coffee.

The dog whined softly in anticipation and shifted its weight from one front foot to the other.

"That's all there is," Monahan said more firmly.

The dog whined again, a high-pitched sound winding down three or four octaves to a low, rumbling groan.

Monahan shook his head. "I ain't never heard anything so pitiful! Dang it, anyhow! If I feed you full, will you go on home and let an old man be?"

Ever since his old yellow dog Two-Bits died, Monahan hadn't had the urge to own another. Two-Bits had got something terrible wrong with his hindquarters. First it was just a little limping now and then, but over time the poor critter howled every time he so much as stood up or took a step.

One morning, Two-Bits couldn't get up at all, anymore. Monahan had to shoot him to put the poor thing out of his misery. A whole decade later, he still felt awful bad about it. He couldn't remember what he'd been calling himself then, or what state or territory they'd been in, but he still dreamed about it sometimes. Those brown eyes had stared up at him right until the end, full of trust and terrible pain. He didn't want to go through that again. "Will you leave?" he asked the blue dog again.

The dog huffed quietly and waited.

"Hell's bells!" Monahan muttered, and dug into his grub sack for more biscuit-makings and bacon.

After he'd fried up and fed the dog nearly a pound of bacon and a full pan of biscuits—good ones, whose dough had been rising all night beside the fire—and the dog showed no signs of decreasing hunger, Monahan finally threw up his hands. "You're a bottomless pit, that's what you are, dog. I believe you'd like me to fry up General Grant and serve him on cornbread! Well, I ain't gonna waste no more vittles on you."

He drank his final cup of coffee and dumped the last of the pot on the fire, then walked down to the stream cutting through the center of the meadow. He rubbed the skillets clean with cold, clear water and a handful of weeds, packed up his cooking things, and moved on to General Grant, who'd been grazing quietly. In the clear light of full morning, he brushed down, then tacked up the horse, and made ready to leave.

The dog had followed him from the ashy remains of the dead fire to the creek and back. He stood a short distance away, watching as Monahan worked.

"You can just go on home, now," Monahan said as he gave General Grant's cinch strap a final tug and let down the stirrup. The dog's rump wiggled. "This here kitchen's closed. Me and General Grant, we got business down Phoenix way."

Actually, the "business" was north of Phoenix at

Tom Sykes's ranch, where he hoped to find work through the summer. Monahan had been employed for the past year up near Flagstaff at the Rocking J, but when old man Jensen had up and died, his good-for-nothing son sold off all the cattle directly after spring roundup, put the land up for sale, and headed for San Francisco right about the same time Monahan had heard about the Baylor brothers heading south.

However, none of that was worth saying to the bobtailed, biscuit- and bacon-eating cow dog.

"I'm askin' you again, dog. You leavin'?"

The dog studied him, cocking its head. Its blue eyes were more startling now that the sky was fully light.

Monahan stepped up on General Grant. "Suit yourself, then." He gave the horse a nudge with his knees, and General Grant moved out at a slow jog, across the meadow and into the trees.

The dog followed.

3

Two hours later, Monahan was nearly out of the thinning pines when he came to an old stagecoach road.

The dog had traveled quietly twenty to thirty yards off Monahan's left flank, nosing at deer droppings or pausing for a moment to mark a tree. But he raised a commotion at the precise moment Monahan reined General Grant onto the rutted road and started south.

Swiftly, Monahan reined General Grant 180 degrees, certain the Baylor boys were closing in fast, but saw exactly nothing. He checked the tree line. Nothing but trunks. He took a deep breath and waited for his heart to settle back in his chest, then leaned the back of his wrist on the saddle horn.

He looked down at the dog. "What? Iffen you live that a way, go on home and quit talking' about it. Quit givin' people apoplexies." Then he added coaxingly, "Reckon you'll get a second breakfast."

The dog ran about twenty feet to the west, then

turned and faced Monahan again. He barked out several yips, sounding for all the world like questions, or maybe pleas.

"Get goin'," Monahan yelled. "Crazy fool of a dog, scaring me half to death like that! Go back to your folks!" He checked the road one more time, then clucked to General Grant and started south at a soft trot.

Immediately, the dog charged to a point square in front of Monahan and stopped right in his path.

Monahan reined General Grant to the side, and the dog moved, too. Monahan moved the horse another step to the right and the dog did the same. Every time the horse moved, the dog followed suit. Finally running out of moving room, Monahan reined General Grant to a stop, lest he run smack over the furry no-tail cur.

"You quit that!" Monahan shouted, shaking a fist. "Consarned beast! Just 'cause I fed you some breakfast don't give you no call to go bossin' my General Grant around. Me, neither!"

The dog stood still, staring at him intently.

In frustration, Monahan reined his horse to the left with the intention of simply going around the fool critter. No sense in getting himself worked up about a dang dog, and a crazy one at that.

General Grant had taken no more than two steps when the dog leaped to the side and faced him off again.

Belatedly, Monahan recognized the dog's posture—head lowered, eyes riveted to the horse, legs tensely splayed in preparation to jump in any direction at a split-second's notice. That crazy dog was trying to work General Grant like a balky steer that wouldn't go through the chute!

General Grant stopped on his own quickly and flung his head in the air with a dull clank of bit against teeth. Monahan had to grab for the saddle horn as the horse's head nearly smacked him in the face.

Whether it made any sense to get worked up over the situation or not, Monahan reckoned he was. His jaw set, he reined General Grant over to the right, sternly pointing his finger at the dog. "You stay there, gol-dang it!" he shouted. "I've had about enough o' your foolishness. You just stay right the hell over there!"

Again, the dog moved to block his path, and General Grant came to another sudden halt. Monahan sat there and steamed for a minute, then scratched the back of his neck. Angrily, he said, "What am I gonna have to do, dog? Shoot you?"

The dog just stood there, head low, his tongue lolling, his eyes intent.

Staring at the cur, it dawned on Monahan that the dog hadn't nipped at General Grant as if it were pushing livestock. It was sure as shooting pushing him, but it hadn't so much as growled or lifted a lip. It wanted to go west and take him along with it— dead set on it, as a matter of fact—and was trying to convince him as friendly as it knew how. But west wasn't where Monahan was going.

In a calmer but still firm voice, he said, "Listen here, blue dog. You're gonna make me late for my business appointment." There didn't seem to be any sin in making it sound fancier than it was. After all, only the dog and the horse were there to hear him. "You just go on back to your folks and leave me and General Grant alone. Be a good ol' blue dog. Go on home, now." Monahan swung his arm toward the west. "Git!"

At last the dog moved grudgingly to the side and out of his path.

With some degree of self-satisfaction, Monahan said, "There. That's a good fella. That's the idea, boy. Your people are probably missin' you somethin' fierce by now." He gave General Grant a nudge, and before they had taken three steps down the road, the dog all of a sudden jumped at the horse and snagged Monahan's right rein in his teeth, ripping it right out of his hand!

Monahan was so shocked he couldn't think of a dad-blasted thing to yell—nothing that was evil enough—until the dog had backed nearly ten feet toward the west, leading the confused General Grant off the road by a taut rein.

"Hold up, you bilious bag o' bones 'n' fangs!" Monahan shouted at last, leaping down from the saddle like he had a bawling calf on the end of his rope. It was still pretty fast, despite his years.

"Of all the sneakin', scrofulous, mule-headed tricks!" he ranted as he marched out in front of

General Grant. He snatched his rein back from the dog, shouting, "Leave go!"

If he'd been thinking, he would have been ready for a fight, but the dog didn't offer one. It released the rein, turned, and ran about twenty feet to the west before stopping and barking twice. Trotting back, the dog came right up to Monahan—who hadn't so much as offered to pet it during their acquaintance, let alone get within arms' reach—and snagged his pants leg, tugging for all it was worth.

"Hey!" Monahan shouted, hopping on one leg and leaning backward. "Stop that!"

But the dog kept on yanking, and nearly pulled Monahan's leg right out from under him before Monahan threw his hands into the air and cried, "All right, for cripe's sake! I ain't gonna shoot you, and you won't give me no peace till I go with you, so I'm goin'! You hear me? I said I'm goin', so let go!"

The dog let go with no warning, which caused Monahan to sit down hard and fast. He watched as it trotted off about ten feet, then paused and looked over its shoulder, waiting.

"It just better not be far, that's all I gotta say," Monahan muttered as he fingered his trouser knee. "I'm gonna dun your folks for a new pair of britches, that's what I'm gonna do."

The dog had bitten right through the cloth, leaving four small puncture marks. Monahan poked his pinkie finger through one and out another. "Dang it, anyhow! These is practically new! I only had 'em a year, you no-account excuse for a hound."

The dog barked at him again.

"All right, all right, don't get yourself in a tizzy!" Monahan climbed creakily to his feet, which was easier said than done. Any more, his knees felt like they were filled up with gravel.

He brushed himself off, gave his sitting place a hard rub, and stepped back up on General Grant. The moment he started the horse moving off the road and toward the west, the dog took off at a dead run. It stopped about fifty yards out and turned, staring back through the sparse trees to make certain Monahan was following, then turned and ran again.

"I ain't never seen a hound so gol-danged single-minded, General," Monahan muttered, and pushed the gelding into an easy lope. "Ain't seen many people that mule-headed, 'less it's them Baylor brothers. 'Course, I ain't exactly seen 'em yet, either."

As he left the trees behind and headed out through the low scrub, he kept thinking he was going to ask—demand—those folks for new britches money, and then he was going to have them tether that dad-blamed, wild-colored, blue-eyed dog to a tree until he was in the next county.

But he also thought something must be awful wrong, somewhere, for the dog to act the way he was acting.

And that surely did nag at Monahan.

By the time he had covered six or eight miles and the dog showed no signs of stopping, Monahan had invented all sorts of dire reasons for the dog's behavior. Some miner owned the dog, he reasoned, and was trapped in a cave-in. Or somebody was in a gully with his leg broke. Mayhap it was some rancher's wife, stuck in a creek tryin' to save a spring calf from drowning!

Dogs could be awful loyal. He'd heard of heroic dogs pulling children from rushing flood waters, heard stories of dogs saving folks from house fires and such. Of course, old Two-Bits had been with him the spring he broke his leg for the second time, and he'd tried and tried to send that dog back to the ranch to get somebody. But the old fool wouldn't leave him, and finally they'd just huddled together for warmth till another hand came looking for them.

It seemed like the old cow dog was more the go-for-help type, although why the dog had settled on Monahan as its provider was a mystery.

"You'da thought he'd find somebody younger," Monahan muttered. "I can still pull a calf out of an arroyo. Might take me longer than some, but I can still do it. But I sure ain't up to diggin' some feller out of a mine all by my lonesome."

Although the dog had slowed its pace somewhat, going quickly from a dead run to an extended trot eating up the ground like nobody's business, it just kept on steadily heading someplace specific. It was single-minded, he'd give it that. Keeping General Grant to a moderate trot about twenty or thirty feet back, Monahan shouted, "This had best be important, you mangy old blue dog! I ain't got no time for sightseein'! I'm a busy man, and I ain't gettin' no younger!"

The blue dog twisted an ear back toward him, so Monahan knew it had heard. But it didn't seem impressed by a man's pressing appointments, and it didn't slow down.

Another two miles or so sped by under paw and hoof and Monahan thought he'd best bring General Grant down to a walk for a while, then break out the water. It wasn't all that hot, yet. It was too early in the season for the man-cooking heat that came to the flats around late May and stayed till September. Monahan, however, was of the opinion it was best for man and beast alike to drink before they felt the thirst come over them.

He'd give that dog a drink, too, if he could only get it to stop for a minute. The blasted thing must have legs made out of cast iron was all he could figure.

They'd traveled over gently rolling hills all morning, going slowly but steadily down in altitude, and had come into a hilly landscape devoid of trees, but thick with spring-green grasses and the occasional thicket of plump prickly pear. He was just about to rein in the General for a well-deserved break when the dog barked excitedly, picked up speed again, and disappeared over the crest of a hill.

"Aw, cripes," Monahan muttered under his breath. "Well, we've come this far, General. I reckon we'd best see what's got his knickers in such an all-fired twist." He nudged the horse into a lope.

Less than ten seconds later, he found out.

Breasting the hill, Monahan heard the dog barking, wild and rapid. It was far ahead and down the other slope, racing along the wide flatland below and heading for a distant cluster of buildings at a flat-out run.

Not much was left of the buildings. As General Grant skidded down the hill and hurried closer, Monahan could see wisps of smoke coming from what was left of the barn and a shed. They had fallen in on themselves in a black, smoky rubble.

The house was only partially burnt, with a blackened hole in the roof. A dead longhorn shot full of arrows lay in the yard and a spring calf with a spear in its side had fallen just in front of the barn. It was already beginning to bloat.

"Aw, damn," Monahan whispered as he slouched in the saddle and slowed the General to a walk. There was no need to hurry, no matter what the dog thought. Monahan knew he wasn't going to find anybody alive.

The dog had disappeared by the time Monahan rode into the yard and dismounted. "Hello!" he shouted, just in case. "Anybody here?"

No one answered but the breeze.

He ground tied General Grant and reluctantly walked toward the corral. His boots scuffed the dust, raising little clouds. "Hello!" he called again. "Dog? Where'd you get to?"

No answer.

He found another cow—a milker—partially butchered on the other side of the barn, and a more grisly discovery out back.

It was a man, or what was left of one. The rancher's face had been mutilated beyond recognition, and his private parts and fingers had been cut off. Monahan swallowed hard and turned his head away, a surge of ancient hatred mixed with sorrow flooding his veins.

The poor sod. Monahan hoped he'd been dead when those heathen bastards started whittling on him.

He left the body where it was and started back toward the house, calling, "Dog? Blue dog!"

A soft whine came to his ears when he was halfway across the yard, and he followed the sound into the house. It had been ransacked. Broken crockery crunched beneath his boots along with shards of dishes, bowls, and the pretty little things women liked to set around just for show.

Blue gingham curtains had been ripped from their moorings and clothes had been scattered from their dresser drawers. Furniture was overturned and smashed. A pot of stew had burned to a solid cinder in the fireplace. Fueled by a straw mattress, fire had swept up one corner of the place and burned a hole in the roof, but it had gone no farther. Unlike the barn or the shed, the house was made of adobe and pretty near impossible to burn.

In the opposite corner, the dog pawed gently at something behind an overturned easy chair, still whining softly. Monahan clenched and unclenched his fists for a moment. He had a good idea what the dog was fussing at, but he hated like hell to look. He'd lived west of the Mississippi for most of his grown life, almost forty-four years and he'd seen more than enough of what was left after Indians came marauding.

Eventually, he took a deep breath and made his way through the rubble.

A woman was hidden behind the chair. She was on the floor with her back pressed hard against the wall. There was a pistol in her hand and an arrow deep in her breast. She hadn't been messed with, and that was a blessing, but her lifeless arm was curled about a little boy, maybe seven, maybe eight.

His throat had been cut.

The dog nudged the child with his nose and looked up at Monahan with a plea in his icy eyes.

"I'm right sorry, feller." Monahan's words came out choked. "Hell of a thing." He knelt beside the dog and, for the first time, put a hand on him. Unconsciously, he began to stroke the dog's coat, comforting him the best he could. "Ain't nothin' to do now but bury 'em, boy," he said softly.

The dog turned slightly and licked Monahan's hand. Then, with an enormous sigh, he stretched out his neck and rested his muzzle gently on the little boy's chest.

Monahan rose to find a shovel, his throat thick, his face hot, and his knees complaining loudly.

4

Several hours later, Monahan stood beside the three mounds he had made on the far side of the corral. Two were normal-sized, and one so small it broke his heart. The dog lay on top of it. He had not moved, not even to take the water in a pan Monahan had carried up from the well for him.

Wearily, his shoulders and back aching something terrible, Monahan laid down his shovel, then took off his hat and held it over his chest. "Lord, I can't rightly tell you these folks' names, but I reckon you already know who they were. Seems to me they was good people. They had a right nice spread here, anyhow, and the dog sure liked 'em. Ain't nothin like a dog for judging human nature, 'ceptin' maybe you. I sure hope you'll gather 'em into your arms and make 'em welcome on those streets o' gold, and that you'll take the hides off the ones what killed 'em so cruel. That's all for now, I guess. Amen."

He settled his hat back on his head, and addressed

the graves. "Hope you folks think I done right by you. I done what I could, anyhow."

He dipped two fingers into his pocket and tipped out his watch. Four o'clock. No wonder his belly was growling, for he'd forgotten lunch entirely.

He bent and retrieved the shovel, his sore back complaining, and turned toward the dog. "You hungry?"

When the dog didn't move other than to twitch its ear, Monahan gave a little shrug and started for the house to scare up a butcher knife. He figured the dead steer in the yard wasn't so far gone a man wouldn't want to eat any of it. Shame to see it go to waste.

He built a small fire in the wide, dusty yard about ten feet from the porch—didn't seem fitting to make himself to home inside—and set his beans to soak. Then he made his way to the longhorn and carved out the tenderloin from one side. He rigged up a spit for the meat and set it aside while he seasoned his beans, set them on the fire, and made up a batch of biscuits.

He sat back, staring across the yard and the corral at the graves and the sorrowful dog. The poor critter had stopped whining, anyway. He'd put up a holy fuss when Monahan had carried the child's body outside, and put up a worse one when he'd gently lowered the little boy into the ground and started covering his blanketed form with dirt. He'd let out a weak moan when the other two bodies had been dragged out and buried, but that was all.

"It's all right, fella," he'd said in an attempt to comfort the beast. "Stop your fussin'. Ain't no other way."

The dog had been lying on the mound ever since the last shovelful had slapped into place.

After a few minutes, Monahan went into the house. It bothered him, not having any markers. He figured maybe, if he searched deep enough, he could find a Bible with their names in it. That, or maybe a letter or a bill would tell him who they were. He would have settled for a surname.

After some scavenging, he found what was left of the Bible. It was near the mattress, and the lists of names and dates of birth and death were burned up. Back behind the wash basket, where it had likely been shoved during the fracas, he found one unbroken bowl. It was chipped and glazed yellow and white, and somebody—a child's hand, to look at it—had laboriously printed *Blue* on the side.

It brought tears to his eyes, which he brusquely wiped away.

He set the Bible on the window ledge, and carried the dog's bowl outside with him, figuring to split the tenderloin with the dog once it was roasted.

But he didn't see the dog. It had left the grave. Monahan's first thought was that it had swiped that big hunk of raw meat. But the meat was still on the spit right where he'd left it.

"Blue?" Monahan called, scratching at his ear with the hand that didn't have a yellow dog bowl dangling from it. "Blue dog! Where'd you get to, fella?"

There was no sign of him, not even a puff of dust on the horizon. Monahan shouted toward the corral, "Where'd that consarned dog get to, General?"

The horse just stomped a hoof lazily and shook the flies from his neck.

Monahan frowned in frustration. "Well, I'll be jiggered."

An hour or so later, it was just starting to get dark. He was ladling beans onto his old tin plate beside a healthy slab of beef and a steaming biscuit, when he heard riders coming in.

His first thought was the Baylors. But he heard too many horses, and jumped to the conclusion it must be Apaches, come back to get him, too. In the half second it took him to think those thoughts, he umped up and spilled hot beans down his leg.

Silently cursing the burn, he scurried to the shelter of the house's outer wall and pressed himself flat against it, his pistol drawn.

Slowly, as the sound of slowing hoofbeats drew nearer, he inched toward the far corner and peeked around it. "Cripes," he whispered in disgust, and holstered his gun. He brushed the last few beans off his britches, then stepped out and waved an arm at the riders.

There were seven of them, and as far as he could tell, none of them looked like Baylors. Not that he knew what Dev or Alf looked like. But the man in the lead, a stocky fellow riding a flashy sorrel mare, wore a badge glinting softly in the late afternoon light. Monahan didn't reckon that a Baylor—even a disguised Baylor using a summer name—would choose to ride with the law.

The sheriff jogged out ahead of the others and stopped about ten feet from Monahan, surveying the scene. He took in the burned buildings, the dead steer, and the speared calf, and a frown came over his lined face. "Aw, hell and damnation," were the first pained words out of his mouth.

"That's about the size of 'er," Monahan said stoically.

The sheriff dismounted, and Monahan offered his hand. "Monahan, Dooley Monahan. Just passin' through. On my way to Phoenix."

The sheriff shook Monahan's hand while the other men in his party rode into the yard, and stepped down off their horses. "Milton J. Carmichael," he said wearily, momentarily doffing his hat to run thick fingers through his graying hair. "Sheriff over at Iron Creek. We got word a raiding party skipped the reservation. Army would take two, three days to get here, so we lit out of town. Been to four other spreads already and sent the folks to town." He slid his hat back on. "This was the last one. Don't suppose anybody's alive."

It wasn't a question and Monahan didn't much like the way Carmichael had said it, but he answered anyway. "Wish like anything I could tell you different. I buried 'em out past the corral." He pointed, scanning the distance once again for the dog. It was nowhere in sight.

A young man, tall and slender, stepped up and squinted at him. "Mister Monahan?"

It took him a moment to recognize the red-headed youngster as a fellow he'd worked with three or four winters past, up in Utah on the Circle D. The boy had hired on about two days before Monahan had gone up to the line camp and had moved on before he came down in the spring. He racked his brain for a name, finally saying, "Sweeney, was it?"

"Yes sir, that's me." The boy seemed pleased Monahan had remembered. He stuck out his hand. "Butch Sweeney. Thought it was you, Mr. Monahan. Sure is fine to see you again. I'm just sorry it had to be . . . like this. If you know what I mean."

Monahan nodded curtly and shook the young man's hand. "If you boys are hungry, I got plenty of vittles cookin' if you don't mind bein' short of beans. Took the whole tenderloin outta that long-horn over yonder. 'Course, I was gonna give a chunk of it to the dog . . ."

"Dog!" Sheriff Carmichael barked out derisively. "You mean to tell me that damned dog of Morgan's lived through this?"

Monahan found himself a tad ticked off, but he dug in his heels. "I reckon he did, though I'll be skinned if I know how. Leastwise, he come lookin' for help. Found me."

Carmichael stared at him like he'd lost his mind.

"Brought me ten, maybe eleven miles down outta them mountains," Monahan continued stubbornly, poking a finger over his shoulder. "Dang near bulldogged my horse to get me to follow him."

Carmichael crossed his arms. "Where's he now?"

Monahan shrugged. "Don't rightly know. He was lyin' over there on the little tyke's grave. He's gone now."

Quietly, Sweeney said, "He was just goin' out to round up the yearlings." They turned to follow his pointing finger.

Sure enough, a small herd of six fat, half-grown, shorthorn steers was headed their way at a dust-churning trot. The dog was at their heels, barking. As they watched, the dog herded the cattle into the yard and tried to put them in the corral. Monahan had shut the gate when he'd put General Grant in there—and had hauled over some bales of half-burned straw to block the part that was busted down. He hollered to one of Carmichael's men to open it and haul his horse out.

The dog pushed the cattle through, waited till the gate was shut again, then went back to his post on the child's grave.

"I'll be jiggered," said Carmichael grudgingly.

"Ray Morgan told me just last week how every afternoon, long about five, Blue would go out and get them shorthorns. Didn't have to tell him or nothin', just regular as clockwork." Sweeney turned back toward Monahan. "He was feeding up these six, grainin' 'em for some fancy restaurant down to Tempe."

Monahan was thinking it'd be a new one on him if Tempe even had a restaurant, let alone a fancy one, but he held his tongue. It had been a good while since he'd been down that way.

"If that pet steer of Morgan's was still fresh enough for you to butcher it out," Sweeney went on, "I reckon the Apache swarmed 'em late in the day. The dog woulda been out after the shorthorns then. Don't know as how they woulda even rode in here with that old shepherd-dog around."

Carmichael, who was still staring at the dog, scowled. "Damn thing's meaner than a cornered wolverine. Should'a been shot years ago."

Monahan opened his mouth to say something in the dog's defense, but Sweeney beat him to it. With a sad half smile, the boy said, "Old Blue ain't mean, Sheriff, just picky. He was awful fond o' that young'un."

Carmichael sniffed. "Still say he's a dangerous old cur. Ain't to be trusted." Absently, he gave a rub to his butt. "Well, I reckon we oughta get some markers made for Ray and Lizzie and little Adam. Any lumber left that ain't burned?"

"Reckon there's a few pieces of the barn worth usin'," Monahan replied. "Pulled them bales o' straw out, anyhow. The ones blockadin' the corral." Carmichael, a man to whom he'd already taken a solid dislike, was beginning to wear awfully thin.

"Monahan?" the sheriff said. "If you can get near that dog without gettin' bit, you'd best move it off a ways while the boys work."

5

It was dark before Butch Sweeney had a chance to settle beside the fire and wolf down some grub. The Hopkins brothers and Sheriff Carmichael had finished off Monahan's tenderloin between the three of them, but Pete Jenks had sliced off a decent cut of meat for himself and Sweeney. There was plenty to go around.

It felt kind of funny, eating Ray Morgan's pet steer like that. Ray had named the old longhorn Freddie, and kept him in the near pen. He was tame as a house cat. But the steer had been fat enough, all right, and was dead and past caring. Freddie was also tender to the tooth, having been shut in the pen for so long with no need to exercise. Sweeney ate heartily, despite his misgivings.

While he ate, he watched Dooley Monahan. The man sat close enough to the others so as not to seem outright antisocial, but far enough away that he didn't have to listen to them, or engage in conversation. He was older and leaner and more bent than Sweeney remembered him, but just as tough. He'd only spoken to Monahan twice, and that had been three and a half years ago. However, he wasn't a man you could easily forget.

He was a long drink of water, maybe two or three inches taller than Sweeney's six feet. His short, sandy hair had more gray than color, his coffee-brown eyes had a watery look to them, and the miles showed on his liver-spotted hands and face. Cowboying surely put extra years on a man.

Monahan had been a tough old bird when they met on the Circle D. The first time Sweeney had laid eyes on him, the man had saved his life.

Sweeney shoveled another bite of old Freddie into his mouth, then shook his head. Monahan didn't appear to remember pulling him out of that long-ago corral, and out from under the hooves of a crazy, fresh-caught bronc that was dead set on killing him. Sweeney supposed when a man got to be Monahan's age—which was, in itself, a feat for any cow man, what with busted bones and the cold and the heat and the sheer cussedness of the profession—he'd probably already pulled so many idiot kids' fat out of the fire that one more didn't stand out.

But Sweeney remembered, all right.

He looked toward Monahan again. After carrying a bowl of meat to the dog once they were finished with the markers, he'd sat down, ignoring them all and staring into the darkness. Old Blue was still out near the graves. His eyes—two small, glowing dots of pale red in the gloom—showed every once in a while, when he turned his head toward the campfire and the men. It sort of gave a man the spooks.

Sweeney shuddered and turned his attention to what Sheriff Carmichael was saying. "Morgan had a brother over to New Mexico, near as I can recall. Come morning, I figure we should go out and round up what's left of Morgan's herd. Push 'em closer to Farley Delaney's place. Delaney can watch 'em till I hear what the brother wants done with 'em."

Oscar Wilkes spoke around a mouthful of meat. "What about them Apache, boss?"

Carmichael snorted derisively. "Them cowards are long gone. Probably halfway to Mexico by now. We won't see no more trouble from 'em."

Sweeney was thinking the great Milton J. Carmichael hadn't seen *any* Apache trouble, large or small, in all the time he'd been in Arizona. No real trouble, just its aftermath. He was a coward . . . and a clever one. But Sweeney knew better than to mention it, and instead asked, "What about the dog?"

The sheriff frowned. "If I can get a rope on him, I s'pose Nils'll take him. He's been wantin' a mean dog to chain out back of his store to keep the kids and rowdies away, ain't he? If we can't haul him back, I reckon we'll just shoot him. I got half a mind to shoot him now. Don't much like the idea of havin' him in town."

Sweeney rested his fork on his plate. He'd seen that dog only a few times, but he liked the critter and it put up with him. He didn't much cater to the notion of that old weasel, Nils Gunderson, keeping the dog on a short chain for the rest of his life, let alone the sheriff putting a bullet through his head.

Sweeney cleared his throat. "Why not let Monahan take him? I mean, the two of 'em seem to get along good enough."

Carmichael flicked a glance out toward Monahan's figure and sniffed. "Sure," he said with a shrug. "No skin off my butt."

One of the Hopkins brothers snorted out a laugh. Sweeney didn't notice which one.

"Be a treat to see the old man try to convince that stupid dog to go along," the sheriff said with a grin bordering on nasty.

One of the Hopkins boys said, "Bet you a buck you'll still end up shootin' him."

Sweeney ignored Hopkins and the sheriff's snide tone. "Reckon I'll ride out with him, too, if nobody minds."

"Don't know why you rode out with us in the first place, Sweeney," Carmichael said with a wrinkled forehead. He helped himself to more beef. "Woulda been a whole lot safer if you'd just kept on sweepin' Gunderson's floors."

Both Hopkins brothers laughed. Dutch Grosvenor and Oscar Wilkes, too.

Sweeney didn't say the obvious: nothing was safer than riding with Milton J. Carmichael. If

Carmichael had been paying attention to business instead of lollygagging at the Robbard's spread for half a day, then jawing so long at the Delaney's that they'd had to bed down there for the night, they would have reached the Morgan place a day earlier, maybe sooner.

They could have arrived in time to save Ray and Lizzie Morgan and their little boy.

According to the telegram Carmichael had received, there were only five or six braves in that raiding party. There were seven men in the posse, and they were heavily armed. They could have handled six braves who, by the looks of things, hadn't owned a single rifle between them.

"Fine, then." Sweeney set his plate on the ground, assuming the absence of a direct answer was as good as a yes. "I already gave my notice to Gunderson." He stood up.

"You what?" Carmichael thundered.

"Gunderson said I was even," Sweeney said calmly. "I only came along on this shindig so you couldn't find something new I owed you for. Seems like every time I got close to even, you and Mordecai Clancy would come up with another mirror I'd broke over to his saloon."

There was laughter again. Carmichael twisted toward the perpetrators, and growled, "Shut up!"

Sweeney took advantage of the momentary distraction and stepped away. All he had to do was convince Monahan to let him tag along.

As he left the light of the fire and made his way

over to the old man sitting on his heels in the dark, Sweeney was thinking Monahan was a loner if ever he'd seen one. He hadn't said more than a handful of words to Sweeney after he'd pulled him out of that corral, and he'd been just as closemouthed with the other men.

Of course, the hands were full of a million Monahan stories, which he heard over and over again all that winter long when Monahan was up at the line camp and couldn't defend himself.

They'd been good stories, though. A man couldn't cowboy for twenty years without becoming something of a legend, even if he wasn't aware of it himself. Monahan didn't seem to have the slightest notion he was practically famous.

Sweeney stopped a few feet from the cowboy. "Mind if I pull up some ground?"

Monahan shrugged without looking up. "Ain't my dirt."

The minute Sweeney started to sit down, Monahan got up and ambled toward the corral. Sweeney rolled his eyes, came out of his half crouch, and trailed along. Monahan stopped at the corral fence and looped his elbows over the top rail. Sweeney aped his position.

"Helluva thing, what those Apache done," Sweeney began.

"It was that," Monahan said, still watching the dog. "Far as I can see, nobody over there seems real upset about it."

"Carmichael's a horse's butt."

Monahan grunted.

"That's sure some kinda dog," Sweeney offered after a moment.

"Yup," said Monahan.

They stood in silence for a few minutes, the only sounds the distant murmur of conversation from the yard, and the soft sounds of cattle drowsing.

"You'd best take him along when you go," Sweeney finally said.

Monahan looked over at him for the first time. "Got no use for a dog."

Sweeney slouched against the rail. "Well, Sheriff Carmichael's gonna shoot him if you don't. He can't stand that dog. Blue bit him real good in the backside a couple years back—least, that's what they tell me—and nobody holds a grudge like old Milton J. Carmichael." He scowled. "I should know. I got into a saloon brawl six months back, and he's had me slavin' at his brother-in-law's store ever since, paying off the damage. Just cleared my debt. Figure I paid it about double."

"Carmichael's a horse's rear end, all right. Coulda told you that after I'd knowed him thirty seconds." The old man's face quirked up in a smile. "That ol' Blue dog bit him in the ass, did he? Lucky he didn't get the hydrophobics."

"Carmichael?"

"The dog."

Sweeney smiled.

Monahan squinted at his hands in the moonlight, studying them. "I don't know as how he'd go along with me even if I was to say I'd have him. 'Sides, folks don't like it much when a hand comes in with his own dog. Not all ranchers believe in 'em. I've knowed some fellers what would shoot a dog on sight, same as they'd shoot a coyote or wolf."

Sweeney nodded. "That's sure true, Mr. Monahan. Might just as well let Carmichael use him for target practice."

Monahan snorted. "You're chappin' my butt, boy. And knock off that 'mister' business."

Sweeney didn't say anything, but he smiled to himself. If he was any judge, Monahan would take the dog.

"You mind a little company in the mornin'?" Sweeney asked, careful to keep his tone casual. He wanted like the dickens to ride a ways with the cantankerous old cowboy, if only in the hopes that he'd share a story or two.

If he ever had any kids, he'd admire to tell them he rode a piece with Dooley Monahan, who was once upon a time the slickest hand to ever saddle a bronc or throw a loop; the man who'd shot it out with the Worth boys back in '67, and who'd known Black Jack Flannery and the James boys and Wild Bill Hickok, to name a few.

He knew getting Monahan to open up, just a little, would be harder than pulling teeth, but he didn't mind. He had nothing else pressing to attend to. Besides, he had everything he owned in his saddlebags. He was ready to go.

"You said you was goin' south, and that's as good a direction as any to me," Sweeney added.

Monahan frowned. Softly, he said, "I got some fellers after me. You'd best stay clear."

Fellows after him? It was music to Sweeney's ears! They were bound to be famous. "Who are they? Are they rough customers?"

Monahan turned toward him and without expression said, "Dev and Alf Baylor."

The Baylor gang? Sweeney's breath caught in his throat. "I heard of 'em, all right. Heard their brother Jason got himself killed a year or two ago. He was a mean one, all right, but not as mean as Dev or as crazy as Alf. I heard Alf shot a piano player up to Denver last year 'cause he played the same song twice. I seen paper on 'em back in town. Why they after you, anyhow?"

With a bemused shake of his head, the old man turned away again. He muttered, "Crimeny, boy. You ask too many questions."

Sweeney pulled himself up. "I'd admire to come along, anyhow. If they're trailin' one man, they won't suspect the track of two men and a dog. Hell, we'll probably lose 'em altogether."

"Suit yourself," the old man replied with a shrug.

"Thanks," said Sweeney. "It'd suit me fine."

Monahan woke in the middle of the night to make water, and found that Blue had moved. He was lying in the yard between Monahan and the others, and was watching Carmichael. It didn't appear to be a real friendly watch. Whatever grudge was between the sheriff and that dog ran deep.

When Monahan stood up and walked over to the pen for some privacy, the dog followed him and sat down, waiting for him to finish his business.

"I'm leavin' in the mornin'," he said as he buttoned up his trousers.

The dog stood and began to wiggle his furry butt a mile a minute. Monahan figured it was a good thing Blue didn't have more than a nub of a tail, or the force of its enthusiasm would have knocked down half the corral.

He stooped slightly to pat the dog's head. The fur was like speckled eiderdown under his fingers, and he wondered that anything could be so soft on so tough a beast. Blue pushed up against his leg and groaned softly.

"Reckon you can come along if you like. Grabbin' my rein like that," he muttered with a shake of his head. "Danged if you don't beat all."

And thus, Dooley Monahan, worn-out, beat up, forty-four summers old, and winding down into old age, fleeing for his life before invisible enemies and who hadn't wanted any more burdens than the multitude he already carried, came to own the blue dog.

6

Monahan and Sweeney rode out at first light with Blue trailing behind, while Carmichael's men were still yawning in their blankets. They left without incident, except when they topped the hill over which Monahan had ridden the day before. The dog turned one last time and paused, lifting his head in a single long mournful howl.

It set the hair on the back of Monahan's neck to prickling.

"C'mon, Blue," Monahan said kindly. "Come along, fella."

After a moment the dog turned away from the ruined place it had lived and known good, hard work and love, and followed them.

All that day they traveled south, with an occasional bob or weave to the west or east to avoid climbing a hill too high or skidding down a gorge too steep. It seemed to Monahan the farther south they went, the faster the calendar was pushed along. Spring roundup had just finished in the mountains, and he could still feel the recent memory of snowy climes and icy creeks chilling his old joints.

But the Christmas smell of the high country had gone out of his nose entirely. The fellows around Phoenix would have finished their spring roundup a good month past. They'd get enough heat to bake a buffalo come summer, but they rarely saw more than a brief dusting of snow, and it never smelled like Christmas.

He was beginning to think he'd best cowboy on the flats for a while, maybe forever. For old men with cranky old wounds, life was a good bit easier close to sea level than it was at seven or eight thousand feet. A good bit warmer, too.

He'd managed to push thoughts of Dev Baylor pinning him to a pine with a rusty baling hook—and Alf twisting it—from his mind. Sweeney had had a point. If the Baylor boys were tracking him, and if they knew anything about him—which they probably did—they'd know he always traveled alone when he was between jobs. They wouldn't follow the prints of two men and a dog.

The young man was turning out to be a halfway decent traveling companion. At least, he was quiet enough after Monahan ignored four or five attempts to get a conversation going. Sweeney gave up and seemed content to ride in silence, and that was all right with Monahan, who figured he'd used up about all his talking back at the Morgan ranch.

* * *

But he wasn't deaf or stupid as Carmichael and the other others thought. He'd heard every word, when they were talking around their campfire the night before. He wasn't as lackadaisical as Carmichael about those Apaches, either. He'd kept his ears cocked and his eyes open all day long.

But the Apaches didn't show.

Monahan and Sweeney made camp for the night in a little hollow lush with paloverde just thinking about bringing up some yellow buds. Sweeney shot a big buck jackrabbit for their supper and was skewing it on a makeshift spit when his talking muscles all of a sudden kicked into high gear again. "Back up at the Circle D, those hands yammered about you all winter."

Monahan put the bean pot on the fire and sat back, shaking his head at the dog tossing the rabbit hide up into the air and catching it over and over. "Reckon we'd best find that dog somethin' to herd. Trampin' the trail all day, and he's still got enough energy for twins."

Sweeney wasn't easily dissuaded. "They said as how you knew the James boys. That true, Monahan? They said as how you rode with Jesse." He leaned forward and lowered his voice. "They said you rode with Quantrill."

Monahan snorted. "Hog squirt." He poured himself a cup of coffee.

"Which?" Sweeney insisted. "That you rode with Quantrill or that you rode with Jesse?"

"You just don't give up, do you, son?"

Sweeney smiled. "No sir, I don't."

Behind him, the dog threw the rabbit pelt high in the air with a snap of his neck, then leaped up to catch it in midair. He gave it a good shaking, and then another toss.

Sweeney didn't see any of it, but Monahan did, and it put him in a pretty fair mood to see the critter finally enjoying itself. After a moment, he said, "I'm from the great state of Iowa, boy, and I fought for the Union . . . I think." He took a sip of his coffee. "If I'da ever run into Quantrill, I wouldn'ta stopped to say howdy, that's for dang sure. I probably woulda put a lead ball between the crazy man's eyes. And I wouldn't know Jesse Woodson James if he was to walk in here and ask for a plate of rabbit and beans."

A puzzled look crossed Sweeney's face, and Monahan added cryptically, "Now, his brother Frank? That's another matter."

Sweeney leaned forward, his face eager as a pup's. "How'd you come to know him then, if you fought for the North? Did you ride together? I mean, after the war?"

"Nope." Monahan took another sip of coffee. "The backstabbin', bank-robbin', rebel coward married up with my second cousin."

That seemed to stun Sweeney into silence, and Monahan took advantage of the lull to give the beans a stir and add four pinches of salt and three of pepper. He couldn't stand flat beans. While he was at it, he adjusted the rabbit's spit, giving it a half turn. It was starting to get a little too done on one side to suit him.

Monahan gave the beans another stir and said, "It was a long time back. Reckon I've got over the worst of the mad."

"F-Frank James is your second cousin?" Sweeney finally stuttered.

Monahan shook the bean spoon at him, and a couple of beans hissed when they hit the fire. "Only by marriage. Don't you get to blamin' that pestilential James clan on me!"

"Well, did you go to the wedding?"

Monahan snorted. He had gotten over the worst of his mad at Frank James, all right. That was, he was past the point of uprooting trees over it. But he was still plenty doggone ticked.

"I should say I didn't! I was up to Minnesota when my old neighbor wrote me about it, and I was so disgusted I up and burned that letter right then and there. And I'm through talking about that rebel trash, iffen you don't mind. And even if you do."

"Yes, sir," said Sweeney. "Sorry."

"Well." Monahan supposed he'd snapped at the boy. Young Sweeney couldn't help it if a bunch of bored bunkhouse cowhands had talked his ear off. "Just don't believe everything you hear."

"No sir, I won't."

"And quit that 'sir' business."

"Yes sir. I mean, okay."

Monahan tried to mash a bean against the side of the pot, but it was still a little stony. He topped off his coffee and leaned back against his saddle.

"When you was a kid, did you ever play a game called Town Gossip?"

Sweeney shook his head.

"Well, Missus Frye—she was the parson's wife, up at our church back home—had us play it when we was kids, to teach us against the sin of repeatin' tales. It was a right good lesson, and I ain't never forgot it. She'd start out with a long line of young'uns, and the first one gets somethin' whispered in his ear. Say, for instance, 'Sally went to town and bought a green dress.' Somethin' simple like that. And then that kid whispers it to the next kid and so on, right on down the row. By the time it's gone through that long line, it'd end up 'Sally caught herself a greased pig and barbecued it with Mayor Woolard' or some such."

Monahan hadn't thought about that old game in years, and danged if it didn't make him feel kind of sentimental. He didn't know whether he liked the feeling or not, but he put it down on the side of not, just in case.

Sweeney said, "I reckon it's a good thing you told me the truth of it, then. Just to clear things up."

"Maybe."

"What about Bill Hickok, then?" Sweeney asked. "Or Clooney Portnoy or Arapaho Jones or Cole Younger, or these Baylor boys that are followin' us? What about the Kalikaks or Charlie Goodnight or Joaquin Murietta or—"

Monahan barked out a laugh, couldn't hold it in. "Joaquin Murietta? By gum, those boys surely did talk, didn't they? Joaquin Murietta was beheaded in the Golden State almost twenty years ago, boy, back when California was a place where donkey-headed fools went to scratch in the dirt for gold. Well," he added thoughtfully with a scratch of his chin, "suppose they wasn't all donkey-headed. Some of 'em actually found somethin'."

"But—"

"That's enough," Monahan said crisply, signaling a halt to the proceedings, and Sweeney stilled his tongue. Monahan dug a hand into his possibles bag and pulled out his own dinged tin plate and a fork, as well as Blue's chipped bowl. "Iffen them beans ain't ready, I'm gonna eat 'em anyway," he muttered, scooping a soupy ladleful into the dog's bowl to cool.

Blue had given up tossing his rabbit skin around—which was just as well so far as Monahan could tell, for the hide had become a tattered, unrecognizable, muddy lump—and came to sit beside the fire. He eyed his bowl and hungrily licked his chops.

Monahan shook the spoon at him. "You just hold off until I say," he warned. "That there's too hot for dogs. 'Sides, I'm gonna put some rabbit in it for you." He turned toward Sweeney. "You got a plate?"

"Guess I know where I rank around here," Sweeney said sheepishly. With a smile, he held out his dish.

* * *

Long after Monahan was asleep with the dog stretched out beside him and snoring softy, Sweeney stared up at the stars. Damned if it wasn't something, his meeting up with Dooley Monahan and actually riding along with him! He was Frank James's cousin! All right, it was a second cousin and by marriage to boot, but Sweeney didn't much worry about the details.

He'd tried to pump Monahan for more information about the Baylor brothers, and why they were dogging him. After all, if those mean no-accounts were on Monahan's trail, he wanted to know the reason why. Not that he actually wanted to tangle with them, no sir. But it would be an interesting story to add to Monahan's legend. Sweeney was all for interesting stories.

However, every single time he broached the subject, Monahan either changed it or ignored him. It seemed the old cowboy was embarrassed by talking about the Baylors. Any man who had done the things he had done and known the people he had known ought to be more convivial. Why, he ought to be downright eager to share stories! At least, that's the way Sweeney looked at it.

He hoped Monahan would open up after they got to know each other a little better. Riding with a famous man who knew celebrated people—and was sort of related to at least one of them—was a long stretch from growing up an orphaned kid, kept practically a slave by fat old Fess Wattlesborg at his lonely place up in the mountains.

Sweeney could picture the sign out front of the shack. HOOCH AND EATS AND TRADE—WATTLESBORG'S ROAD.

The "road" was a narrow trail not wide enough for two horses abreast, and it was snowed in three-quarters of the year. Oh, he could just hear Wattlesborg. "Clean them stalls again, you lazy little peckerwood, and do it right or you'll get a right proper lickin'! Here I took you in outta the kindness o' my heart, and you ain't once showed me the proper gratitude!"

It had seemed to Sweeney, still heartsick over the loss of his folks, that he could never clean the stalls right. Nor did he rub down Wattlesborg's roan mare good enough to suit him, or cut enough firewood, or treat the customers right—when they had customers for the rank mash Wattlesborg brewed and the venison steaks he sold to trappers and the occasional passerby at two bits a plate, or in trade for pelts. Wattlesborg was a hard man indeed, fat and tall and strong and nearly always sozzled and looking for trouble.

Sweeney had spent four long years, from the age of twelve until just after his sixteenth birthday, either bloody and bruised and curled on his pallet from one of Wattlesborg's punishments. Either that, or facing up to a new beating.

But come his sixteenth year, Sweeney had been blessed with a growing spurt, going from five-foot-six to six feet tall in less than eight months, and one day he'd finally owned the courage to hit Wattlesborg back.

He guessed he'd been madder—and Wattlesborg drunker—than he thought, because the man didn't hit him back. When Sweeney up and slugged him, he went down in the straw in a surprised three hundred and fifty pound heap.

And Sweeney had kept on slugging.

Wattlesborg was still breathing when Sweeney left the barn. He supposed he'd given the fat man no better or worse than he'd ever given him. Better, maybe, because the beating was administered with his own righteous bare knuckles instead of a rake handle or a harness strap or a club plucked from the woodpile, the instruments of punishment Wattlesborg usually favored.

Worse, perhaps, because Sweeney had huffed and puffed and finally managed to drag the senseless Wattlesborg right up behind that old mare of his. The roan had obliged by lifting her tail and dropping a steaming pile of fresh manure right on Wattlesborg's chest, and she followed it up with a long hot stream of piss. He guessed the roan had a few scores to settle with Wattlesborg, too.

Afterwards, he took off through the snow on foot. Not the best idea for a kid whose britches hit him mid-calf and whose sleeves didn't come close to his wrists. Not the best idea when it was still winter in the mountains, and the snowdrifts were deeper than he was tall. But he hadn't wanted to steal Wattlesborg's horse and give the man a solid excuse to follow him.

He had made it to civilization with a little help from a crusty old rock-breaker who found him near the base of the San Francisco Peaks, half frozen to death and mewling for his long-dead mama. At least, that was what the rock-breaker had told him once he thawed out.

Sweeney spent the next few years on the wander, sweeping floors and clerking, emptying spittoons, and delivering telegrams. The pay wasn't much and the jobs were boring, but nobody tried to beat him senseless, and Wattlesborg had never come looking for him. Leastwise, not that he knew of.

When he was nineteen and working at Trimble's Mercantile up in Bonny Fir, he all of a sudden got it into his head that he was born to be a cowboy. It was a dang fool notion. He'd never been close enough to a live cow to put his hand on it, and he'd never been able to afford a horse, let alone ride one. At least, not since he was twelve.

But he'd had an empty place in him, a vacancy created by parents gone to Jesus, or perhaps by those four lonely, aching years with that stinking pile of suet, Wattlesborg. That empty place had needed filling. In retrospect, he supposed it was the romance of the sound of spurs that finally did it, the manly jingle and clank of them on Trimble's scarred wood floor.

Exactly three weeks later, Monahan had pulled him out from under that bronc.

Oh, he'd learned to ride and rope, all right, but he hadn't filled the empty place. And since then, nearly four years of drifting hadn't filled it, either. He supposed he'd always feel the hollowness.

Sweeney turned on his side and studied Monahan and the dog. Monahan slept tidily, with his arms folded over his chest, his hat pulled over his eyes, and the blanket all tucked in around him, neat as a pin. Not Blue. The dog had rolled over on its back and lay belly-up, its feathery legs spread, its lower jaw and throat turned skyward, its lips flopped back to reveal pink gums and teeth broken long ago, probably by some cow's well-placed kick.

"If that ain't a picture of comfort, I ain't never seen one," Sweeney whispered, his eyelids drooping.

He'd never imagined Ray Morgan's old cow dog would go with anybody else, no matter that Ray was dead. Ray had told him Blue had wandered into his place a few years back and made himself to home. Morgans never knew where he came from.

"Bet that dog could tell me a few good stories, too," he muttered, and pulled his blanket closer, hunkering into it against the cold. "Everybody around here's so damn closemouthed you'd think they was statues," he grumbled, and let his eyes drift closed.

7

"He camped here, all right." Dev Baylor stood up and brushed at his knees, scowling at the fresh grass stains. Unlike his brother, he was careful about his clothes, and tried to keep them clean and pressed, a difficult task when a fellow was on the trail of a murdering, back-shooting coward. Keeping his duds tidy would be even more difficult when they finally caught up to Monahan.

He imagined there would be quite a lot of blood.

Dev paused to run a finger down one side of his well-groomed mustache, and curled his fingers to follow the line of the goatee, trimmed perfectly that morning, as it was every morning. The man admired himself above all else, and didn't skimp on self-grooming.

Sweeping back a black duster, he cocked a fist on his hip and speculated, "A night ago. Maybe two. Hard to tell on accounta all this grass."

"Jason woulda knowed," said Alf, by far the

slower of the duo. In his stained overcoat, he stood a few yards away, bent at the waist and sweeping the deep, dewy grass from side to side with long, scarecrow arms.

"Jason's dead," said Dev.

"I knowed it. You don't need to go remindin' me all the time." Alf peered down into the grass again. "I'm still thinkin' it's a wolf," he muttered before he stood erect and smiled.

Something was intrinsically wrong with Alf's smile, always had been. Even after so many years, Dev wasn't used to it. Probably never would be.

"I'da liked to see that! Him all tore apart and screamin' and such." Alf continued as if all their problems were solved and the slate was wiped clean. He dug two fingers into a pocket of his filthy vest, happily announcing, "This calls for a tune!"

Before Alf had blown two wavering notes on his harmonica, Dev snapped, "Put that stinkin' thing away, Alf!" The poor idiot could be downright moronic, even on his good days.

Dev was thinking he never should've broken him out of that asylum back in Arkansas. He should have just left him there to rot to a ripe old age, with three squares a day.

After all, Alf had said he kind of liked it there. Somebody had taught him to play the mouth organ.

Dev sighed, wishing he could get his hands on the music teacher for five minutes.

He hadn't been able to bear the thought of his brother in the loony bin and had busted Alf out. Back then, he had another brother to help keep an eye on Alf. Another brother some peckerwood cowhand named Dooley Monahan had seen fit to cruelly murder while the brothers had split up, waiting for the uproar to die down over that unpleasantness outside Salt Lake. Now he was stuck with Alf, God help him.

With a pained expression on his narrow face, Alf lowered the harmonica. "You just ain't got no joy in you, Dev."

"Listen, Alf," Dev said slowly, waiting a moment until he was certain he had his brother's full attention. "It weren't no wolf. It was a dog. Them tracks are too round for a wolf. Plus which"—he pulled himself up slightly—"the dog was here at the same time Monahan was."

"Was too a wolf," Alf said stubbornly.

Dev ignored him, knowing if he didn't he would go as batty as Alf. "And here. See? Some of Monahan's boot marks are right on top of that dog's, overlappin' like. And sometimes it's vice versa."

Alf started to raise a question, and Dev hurriedly added, "Means the other way round."

Alf's face wadded into the same expression—*you're not gonna tell me no different or I'll get me a blade and carve up your mama*—that had been his trademark since he was five. "You think you're real smart, don't you, Mr. Smarty?" Alf's eyes narrowed and fists clenched.

He had already carved up and killed their mother—and daddy—some years ago. The way the brothers had seen it, it wasn't that much of a loss.

In another minute he'd start stomping his feet. Either that, or pull a blade.

Dev closed his eyes for a moment and muttered, "Give me strength." He turned toward Alf again with forced cheeriness. "Why, you woulda seen it yourself, Alf, if you'd been over here! You was just lookin' in the wrong spot, that's all."

"Oh," Alf said slowly, drawing the word out to three syllables. He brightened. "A little mouth organ music, then!" He began to blow out "Camptown Races." It was the only tune he knew, and he played it very badly. For some reason, he couldn't play the high note at the end of the phrase, "Gonna run all night," and had to stop and sing out the word *night* instead, every time.

The reason for this eluded Dev, but then, a lot of things about Alf eluded him, even the name of the song. He could never remember the name. "Camptown Races" or "Camptown Ladies." Jason had been better with him.

Squinting against the assault on his ears, Dev shouted, "Let's move out!"

Alf nodded, never taking the harmonica away from his lips, and hopped from foot to foot, dancing a jig over to his horse. As they rode out of the beaver meadow, birds fled the sound of that caterwauling mouth organ in great, rising flocks.

Dev hoped the dog stayed with Monahan. A man and a dog would be a whole lot easier to track than a man alone. His tracking skills weren't the best, anyhow. He needed all the help he could get. Hand-to-hand fights, a little rustling, a little stage robbery:

those were his strong suits. A hand-to-hand fight with a knife was the best. It stirred a man's blood, especially when he knew from the start that he was going to win.

Despite his less than superior tracking skills, it was the closest they'd been to Monahan. At least, he hoped it was Monahan. He hoped he hadn't got off the track somewhere, and they hadn't taken to trailing a whole different fellow entirely. It had happened about six or eight months ago, up in Utah.

When they'd finally found the man they'd killed him anyway, just because they were so damn mad about wasting two whole months. Well, he was, anyway. Alf had killed him just for the sport of it.

What if the trail turned out to be a wrong one? Hell, Dev reckoned he'd let Alf kill whomever it was they'd trailed, and his dog, as well. The gall of some people, making him think they were somebody else and wasting his precious time!

He mounted his horse, straightened his jacket, smoothed his trousers, and rode at a lope into the trees, catching up with Alf. Sometimes he lost the track but always miraculously—to his mind, leastwise—Alf found it again. Things were better when Jason was alive, a lot better. He wasn't the sharpest tool in the shed, but he'd tracked like a goddamned bloodhound.

Slowly, they picked their way down the mountain, with Alf enthusiastically playing that sorry harmonica—and stopping far too often to sing a high, cracked, "Night!"

Dev hunched in his saddle and scouted the

trail, fretting over the new wrinkles he was putting
in his shirt.

Far to the south, the panting dog waited pa-
tiently on a rocky creek bank at the bottom of the
steep-sided canyon. The morning was clear and
bright and crisp, the canyon was wide, and the
creek was shallow and fast and sparkling.

Monahan and Sweeney were only halfway down
from the northern rim, leaning back in their saddles and hanging on for dear life as their horses
skittishly navigated a rocky slide, leaving their path
something less than vertical, but not much. There
hadn't been another way around—not unless they
wanted to waste a day.

Monahan and General Grant hit the bottom at
last, and the horse came up out of the half squat
he'd assumed for the entire trip. He snorted in complaint and shook his head, his bridle jingling.
Sweeney and the strawberry roan weren't far behind.

"Seems to me somebody real smart oughta build
a bridge over this thing," Sweeney complained. "I
wouldn't mind payin' a toll."

Monahan dismounted to make sure General
Grant hadn't skinned his hocks on the slide down,
and Sweeney got down to check his roan, whose
name, he had informed Monahan, was Chili. The
General still had all of his hide, and Monahan
patted him on the rump. "Good fella."

"Chili's fine, too, in case anybody's interested."
Sweeney pulled down his canteen and took a long

drink. "Where was I? I mean, when I got interrupted by this here mountain we had to skitter down?"

Monahan grimaced. "Ain't you tired of talkin', boy? Seems to me you'd want to give your throat a rest." He knew if they followed the canyon for about four miles, there was an easy place to get out along the southern rim. Another day in the saddle, and they'd be at Tom Sykes's place, and the kid could use up his jawing at the other hands.

If somebody didn't shoot him first.

Monahan clucked to the General and led him down to the river to drink. Sweeney and Chili followed. The dog stood up, barked, and wiggled his butt at Monahan's approach. He sure was an eager cuss, all right. He'd made it down that slope in slap time, and seemed to enjoy every minute of it, like it was a game made up just for him.

In fact, Monahan didn't believe he'd ever known a dog to be so dad-blamed joyous about everything. Except for the time when they'd been at the ranch, of course. Blue had been downright pitiful back there, and Monahan couldn't fault him for it, not a bit. But he'd be skinned if that critter didn't have a natural smile on his chops most all the time!

Sweeney's roan had finished drinking, and after he refilled his canteen, he ruffled the dog's fur and mounted up with a creak of leather. He looked down at Monahan. "Don't know why you're still lookin' for those Apache. And don't tell me you ain't. I got eyes, and I see you lookin' behind every bush. Carmichael figured they took off with half a butchered steer in their packs, and leadin' a live milk cow to boot."

Monahan suddenly found himself thinking about milk cows. His ma's milk cow, to be exact. The one he was supposed to bring home so many years ago. Had she ever gotten it, he wondered. As quickly as it had come, the thought vanished from his mind.

"Took the horses in the barn, too, three of 'em," Sweeney was going on. "They're halfway to Mexico by now."

"Maybe." Monahan stepped up into his saddle with a complaint of saddle leather and joints, the joints being his. Actually, he'd pretty much decided those Apache had headed south, and in a considerable hurry. He was more worried about the Baylor brothers. He had one of those crawling feelings again.

"Well, then, why're we taking this roundabout way?" Sweeney insisted. "We coulda gone through a town or something by now, for cryin' out loud! I coulda had me a beer!"

Monahan clucked to the General and started along the riverbed with a soft, "C'mon, Blue dog." To Sweeney, he said, "This here's the straightest route to old Tom Sykes's ranch. You don't like it, there's a town about twenty-some miles thataway." He jabbed his thumb back toward the east.

"Real funny," grumbled Sweeney.

"Didn't mean to be," said Monahan.

As he had done all morning long, the dog raced out ahead of them, scaring up flocks of Mexican doves and coveys of California quail, nosing briskly after kangaroo rats, and giving a halfhearted chase to the occasional jackrabbit that broke cover. Earlier, Blue had spied a lone coyote and given chase, but Monahan had called him off. Coyotes were crafty. Sometimes, one would lead a dog off, and all of a sudden that dog would find itself faced with a whole family of coyotes, just lying in wait to rip him up. A dog in that situation didn't stand a Chinaman's chance.

"Well, I done told you about the time I was working in that saloon up to Kramer and shook the hand of Morgan Earp himself," Sweeney rattled on.

There was no rest from it.

"'Course, he's not a real famous Earp brother. His brother Wyatt's a famous marshal over to Kansas or someplace. Could be Tombstone now, but that's only a rumor I heard. But Morgan's writ up in some o' them dime novels they write about his brother. And I told you about the time I was working in that livery and held the reins of a chestnut mare for the one and only Darrell Duppa. Now, if you ain't heard of Morgan Earp, mayhap you heard about him!"

Monahan muttered, "That old gasbag . . ." He'd spent more time than he cared to remember listening to Lord Darrell Duppa spout off nonstop in English, German, French, and Latin.

Sweeney, who hadn't heard him, went on, "So I figure now's about the time for you to be telling me somethin' about Treacherous Ted Romanoff or Wild Bill Hickok. Or about the Baylor brothers, which have a pretty good chance of being on our trail right now."

Monahan's eyes were searching the ground ahead. He'd lost the dog, couldn't spot him anywhere. Most like, he was around the next bend in the canyon, but the hairs on the back of Monahan's neck were pricking, and that wasn't a good sign. Distracted by his warily itching neck, Monahan lied. "They likely ain't followin' no more. Reckon you and the dog threw 'em off." He nudged General Grant into a trot.

Sweeney kept pace. "You change your mind on that every fifteen minutes, Monahan!" They had almost reached the bend.

"So do you. One minute they're murderin' us in our sleep, and the next they're somewhere in up Canada." That, at least, was the truth. Monahan swore Sweeney talked just for the pleasure of hearing himself orate. He wasn't going to let the kid spook him about those Baylor boys any more than he was already spooked.

He reined in the General abruptly and pointed to a cliff in the distance. "Now what the devil you suppose that dang dog's doin?"

Sweeney reined in Chili next to Monahan and looked in the direction his friend pointed. Halfway up a cliff face, Blue stood at an opening in the rock, either a full-blown cave or a wind-eroded hollow. Monahan wouldn't have spied him at all if he hadn't been wagging that shaggy butt of his like nobody's business. It was the only thing sticking out or moving, and his mottled coat tended to blend in with the surroundings.

"Danged if I know. He's wigglin' like it's another critter, though. I swan, that dog's scared up half the varmints in the territory this mornin'!"

Monahan got that prickly feeling again. "Aw, cripes," he muttered, sliding his rifle from its boot. Sure as anything, the dog had found a den—either a coyote's or a cougar's—and Mama wasn't to home, by the looks of things.

But her babies were, if Monahan was any judge at all. He forded the rocky shallows of the creek and crossed to the other bank, stopping just a few yards northeast of the place where Blue's wiggling butt stuck out of the cave, high above.

"What're you gonna do, shoot him?" an alarmed Sweeney asked.

Monahan craned his head up. "Blue!" he called firmly. "Get on down here, Blue!"

The dog turned around so his head was sticking out of the hollow. He barked rapidly several times in succession before he whirled round again and showed them his tail feathers.

Monahan hollered again, but the only thing he got for his trouble was a repeat performance.

"Dad-gum it!" Monahan swore loudly. There was no immediate danger, and he slid his rifle home again. "Get down right now, you rapscallious villain!"

Sweeney swallowed hard. "You figure a cougar's got its young'uns in there?"

Monahan looked up the wall. He'd be blamed

if he could figure how that fool dog had climbed up there in the first place! Of course, he was half mountain goat, if the way he'd taken that slide was any indication.

"I'm goin' on without you!" he called up to the dog. "I ain't got time to shilly-shally, and I ain't gettin' no younger!" He reined General Grant away and set out at a trot.

Sweeney quickly followed. "You just gonna leave him there, with a she-cat coming back any second? Mayhap a wolf?" He twisted his head back and forth between Monahan and the dog, who was rapidly disappearing in the distance. "How can you just leave him?"

"Oh, he'll be along." Monahan figured the dog would just give up on whatever it had found and follow.

So he wasn't surprised when, not three minutes later, the dog came galloping up from behind them. However, it did surprise him a good bit when the dog raced about ten yards ahead and faced off the horses, barking. Sweeney made the mistake of trying to ride on past him, and Monahan, who had held up General Grant right off—having been through such antics before—laughed right out loud when old Blue went to work on that Chili horse of Sweeney's.

"Got an eye, don't he?" he called, still chuckling.

"Jesus Christ!" shouted Sweeney, who had nearly been thrown when Chili made an unexpected stop followed by a half rear. The horse was tense as a fiddle string, reminding Monahan for all the world of a rabbit caught in the headlamp of an oncoming train. Blue stood there, head low, legs splayed, ready to keep that horse from going one step farther, let alone right or left.

"Dog, is this gonna be a habit with you?" Monahan called. Then he added to Sweeney, "Just rein that roan back this way, son."

The moment Sweeney turned Chili back, the dog raced around him and back to Monahan, barked twice, and took off back down the canyon.

"What the hell's wrong with him?" Sweeney asked angrily. He mopped sweat from his brow although the morning was still cool. "He spooked Chili so bad he near to dumped me! What in tarnation's givin' him fits?"

"Couldn't guess," Monahan said. "Reckon I shoulda thrown a rope over him while I could. But I didn't, so I reckon we'd best take a look, after all."

"And I suppose I'm the lucky one who'll have to go climbin' up there after him," Sweeney groused. "You bein' old and all."

Monahan frowned. "After that crack, I reckon you're elected, all right."

Blue had stopped about fifty yards away, and was barking furiously.

"All right, all right!" Monahan shouted with a shake of his head. "Don't go gettin' yourself in an uproar!" He showed the General some knee and followed the dog, Sweeney on his heels.

By the time they were within a hundred yards of the place, Blue was scaling the cliff. Monahan could see a steep path he hadn't noticed before. As they rode closer, he began to make out steps, crudely cut into the stone and worn by time. He figured the place to be an old Indian hideout, long deserted.

At least, he hoped it was.

"Put a loop on him from here," Sweeney suggested. He was eyeing the cliff as if he hadn't remembered it being so tall or so steep.

"How long you think my rope is anyway, boy?" Monahan asked.

Blue had disappeared into the cave entirely by the time they reined in the horses and Sweeney got down. He slung his rope over his arm and grumbled, "If I get up there and find a bunch of pretty kitties aspittin' and ahissin' at me, I'm gonna have that dog for my dinner."

"Thought you wanted adventure," Monahan said, holding back a smile.

"I like hearin' about it," muttered Sweeney. "Not so much havin' it."

"Don't worry." Monahan pulled his rifle from the boot once more. "I see anything with fangs comin' your way, I'll shoot."

Scowling, Sweeney began to make his way up the crumbling steps. He was about halfway up when he stopped and stood stock-still.

Monahan heard it and his eyes suddenly left the canyon rims, abruptly coming to focus on the opening above.

The dog backed slowly out of the cave, growling.

8

"What the hell you gone and turned up, you mangy ol' cow dog?" Monahan muttered to himself as Sweeney began to slowly climb higher.

Nobody heard him, so nobody answered.

All he could do was watch Sweeney make his way up the cliff and pray. Mostly, he prayed for that damn fool dog, although he'd never have admitted it.

Sweeney climbed higher and higher, sometimes missing a step or two, sometimes coming to a clear spot where he could take four or five steps in a row with nothing crumbling or breaking off underfoot, until he was even with the dog's backside.

Monahan held his breath. Just as he began to whisper, "Let him know you're there." he saw Sweeney's mouth move and his hand lift to stroke the dog's leg. "Atta boy, Butch," he heard himself whisper as Sweeney hoisted himself up the last few steps and stood next to the dog, peering into the cave.

Sweeney took a few steps forward and spoke

again. It was louder than before, but still not loud enough for Monahan to make out any words. In fact, Monahan was swearing at the younger man and himself when Sweeney suddenly turned around, looked down at him with a grin as wide as Christmas morning, and hollered, "You ain't gonna believe this!" He let out a hoot and disappeared into the cave before Monahan had a chance to ask—let alone formulate—any questions.

The cowboy sat his horse, his hands trembling, while echoed murmurs of Sweeney's voice drifted down to him. Not that he could tell what the kid was saying, and not that he could explain why snatches of it sounded for all the world like he had a gal up there, or maybe a child.

He chided himself for making up tales as a voice—definitely female—shouted, "I said to leave go o' me!" Sweeney emerged from the cave . . . with his arms full of skirts and a blanket and within them, a flailing female figure. "Leave me go! Do it now, you side-steppin' piss-drizzler!" the girl shouted again.

Sweeney stopped walking. He twisted up his mouth and said loud enough for Monahan to hear, "You close up that nasty gob o' your'n, missy, or I'll drop you right here and now, all thirty feet down!"

A pretty, freckled face surrounded by billows of russet curls parted the blanket, took a look downward over Sweeney's arm, and gasped. The woman threw her arms around his neck, and ducked her head into his chest with a strangled shout. "Don't you *dare* drop me!"

Monahan held back a chuckle as Sweeney made a slow and careful descent with Blue leading the way—and stopping every four or five steps to look up and check on him. "That's right, buddy," Monahan whispered as his grin burst forth in a soft bubble of laughter. "Like you wouldn't hear him hollerin' bloody murder if he fell."

After a few false steps that sent him skidding, Sweeney finally reached the bottom of the makeshift staircase and swung the girl's legs to the ground. She shrieked at the movement, terrified she was being hurled over the cliff, but as soon as her toes touched the earth, she slugged Sweeney in the chest, nearly knocking all the air out of him.

She wheeled toward Monahan, still seated on his horse. "And who are you?" she demanded. "His daddy? This your idea of family doin's? Ridin' after little girls and rapin' 'em? What do you do? Take turns holdin' 'em down?"

Her words were bold, but her jaw trembled. Fear crept into her eyes.

Monahan growled out, "I don't molest no girl children whose name I don't even know, missy. Or who appear to be too tender to spell it."

That last part got her dander up, all right, and she hollered at him, "It's Julia. Julia Alice Cooperman. You want me to spell it out for you?"

Behind her, Sweeney had finally caught his breath. "Where the devil's your horse, Julie?"

"It's Julia," she snapped. "And I don't have one."

"How in tarnation did you get out here, then?" Monahan asked, perplexed.

"Flyin' carpet?" asked Sweeney snidely.

Ignoring Sweeney, she twisted back toward Monahan. "Had one. He up and died 'bout a half mile due west of here."

Monahan gave a nod and a grunt. "You et lately?"

When she didn't answer—too proud, he guessed—he swung down off General Grant and immediately searched around in his saddlebags until his fingers found what he wanted. "You like bacon?" he asked as he pulled out the last of it— just enough for a meal.

Julia's stomach growled at that moment and she sheepishly nodded. "Butch, fetch us some kindlin', would you?"

Sweeney turned and walked back to the brush. Once the boy was out of earshot, Monahan said, "That there's Butch Sweeney. He's the one what saved your life."

The girl's face wadded up like a dried apple. "That's real funny. He didn't do nothin' for me that I couldn't've done for my own self."

"You got water?"

She hesitated. "'Course I do."

Monahan paused before he said, "Sure you do. Just like you got a fancy sit-down dinner for six in your hip pocket." He'd lost track of the dog, but heard a soft woof coming from his left side. Quickly he added, "Sorry. Dinner for seven."

Miss Julia Cooperman crossed her arms firmly across her flat chest, blew out a huffing snort, then sat down directly where she stood. "I ain't sharin' my lunch with no dog."

Her statement only served to remind him that he and Sweeney ought to have something to eat, too. He turned once again toward his saddlebags and began to dig. Beside him, Blue licked his lips.

"Just a minute, old son," Monahan muttered, and kept on digging.

Butch Sweeney licked his fingers. "Got any more o' that bacon?" His begging look almost out-pitifulled that of the blue dog's, and Monahan tossed them each a thick strip.

The last two, as a matter of fact.

"All the beggin' in the whole wide world ain't gonna do you no good now, Blue," he said to the pleading cow dog. "Ain't no more of it, period. You can have the last a' the grease with a biscuit, but that's all I got."

The dog leaned toward him and whimpered softly, jealously eyeing the empty pan. It glistened with melted fat.

"All right, all right," Monahan muttered. He gave his head a shake, then snatched the last biscuit out of its pan and broke in into chunks, which he then dropped into the bacon fat. He gave it a stir, tested it with his finger to make sure it had cooled enough for the tender mouth of a greedy dog, then shoved the pan toward Blue.

Shaking and trembling as if he hadn't just eaten half a pound of bacon and half a dozen biscuits already, Blue didn't move an inch closer to the pan until Monahan said, "Okay."

The old man shook his head and chuckled. Butch Sweeney broke his own silence to mumble, "Whoever trained that dog sure weren't no slacker."

Across the small fire, the girl—who wasn't much past twelve—asked, "Where are you fellers headed, anyhow?"

"South," said Sweeney at the same time Monahan said, "West."

The girl's face twisted up before she said, "Which is it?"

They spoke again and the answers were the same. Monahan turned toward Sweeney and repeated himself more firmly. "West. Why the hell would we go any other way? She comes from the west and she belongs there. You said so yourself, didn't you?"

Suddenly, the girl shot to her feet. "I thought you looked familiar! You been workin' in the store. For Mr. Nils Gunderson. You busted up the saloon and been workin' it off in trade." Her tone was accusatory, but at the same time, a little admiration seeped through.

"Yeah, that's me." Sweeney looked at Monahan and explained. "The whole town's in an' outta there. Can't expect me to remember everybody. And what you mean, I told you where she was from? I never said no such thing!"

Monahan nodded. "Never said you did. Only asked if you did or didn't."

Unexpectedly, Sweeney laughed. "Well, damn. You did, didn't you?"

But the girl didn't. Little Miss Julia gave her

head a haughty shake and said, "If you think I'm goin' back there, you're sore mistook. I never want to see that lousy excuse for a town again so long as I live. Been a lot done to me, and I done bad back when I had me a chance, but now I want a whole new life. Want it where nobody knows me, where I can start fresh without my uncle's reputation colorin' the way folks act an' what they say. Wanna go somewhere fresh that's just startin' out so's I can start out with it."

Monahan folded his arms across his chest and leaned back against a rock. "And how you plan to earn your way whilst you're doin' all this startin' over?"

"Anything I can," she said right out. "Keep books or wait on ladies in a store. Work slingin' hash or mixin' drinks. I ain't even opposed to . . . you know, makin' my livin' on my back if I gotta."

The offer was made more boldly than Monahan believed she intended it, but he simply nodded his head. "Attitude like that's gonna draw the fellers in like bees to honey."

"Oh, shut your pie hole, old-timer."

He took momentary umbrage to the word *old-timer* until it dawned on him that she was right. He let it pass.

Sweeney, on the other hand, wasn't so forgiving. "Who you callin' names, you baby she-cat?"

Just like that, she pounced on him, letting loose with a barrage of unaimed and unanswered blows and kicks. As she pounded, she shouted, "Don't you go callin' me names!"

Despite his occasional shocked look when she contrived to land a blow that actually hurt him, Sweeney managed a big grin and taunted, "Here, kitty, kitty, kitty . . ."

"You peckerwood idiot!" she screamed, hitting and kicking as hard and wild as she could—which was growing pretty danged wild and hard.

More in order to save the young cowboy some face than anything else, Monahan climbed to his feet and stood over the girl. "That'll be about enough, Miss Julia." Grabbing the back of her shirt and the waistband of her skirts, he lifted her straight off Sweeney, still kicking like an airborne bronc and trying to punch the living daylights out of him. She landed a good, sound slap to his cheek, then spat in his face.

Monahan had turned around and was setting the girl on the ground, feet first, when the air behind him moved with a little localized *whoosh*. He planted a hand on Julia's shoulder and held her away at arm's length, then twisted his head toward Sweeney. He was on his feet and looked very angry. Maybe not angry enough to kill her, but Monahan wasn't taking any chances. He stretched out his other arm and planted it in the center of Sweeney's chest, stopping him as he stepped forward.

"Let me have at her," Sweeney muttered, never taking his eyes off the girl's. "Just lemme at her for five lousy minutes."

Monahan noted that the girl had stopped pushing forward. Most of the pressure was coming from Sweeney "Butch, ease up. She's just a kid."

Sweeney growled, "Yeah, just a smart-mouthed, sassy little wench askin' for a whippin' kinda kid!" He put pressure on Monahan's arm.

"Maybe you're right, Butch, but it's not up to you or me to decide. It's up to her folks. That is, if anybody claims her."

He felt her jerk toward him again and he snarled, "Now, knock it off, the both o' you, or you're both gonna see some whompin' like you ain't never dreamed to see afore!" With that, he pulled them toward him an inch or so, then thrust them apart.

Sweeney was unaffected, but Julia landed on her fanny in the weeds. *Well, at least I can still push a little girl down,* Monahan thought ruefully. He staggered, and felt Sweeney catch his arm.

"Careful, there, Monahan."

The old cowboy shook him off like a dog shakes off pond water. He didn't want sympathetic words. He wanted twenty years back, that's what he wanted. He couldn't for the life of him figure out where to complain, though. He'd tried the Lord, tried him a lot, but nobody ever answered. "I'm alright, dammit! Now, let's get this lunch mess cleaned up and be on our way."

Sweeney stepped right up, getting his tin plate, utensils, and cup scrubbed out with sand, wiped down, and packed away. Monahan, who cleaned up after the dog as well as himself, was ready a few minutes later.

The girl hadn't moved an inch.

"C'mon, Julia," Sweeney said. "Shake a leg."

"Ain't goin'."

Incredulous, Sweeney stopped fiddling with his horse's bridle and turned toward her. "You ain't goin'? Why not?"

Monahan watched the girl, waiting for her response. When none was forthcoming, he finally said, "Julia, you're goin' with us whether you aim to or not. Now, get up on your feet and get crackin'."

She looked up directly at him. "Said, I ain't goin'. You can't make me. I know my rights."

Despite himself, Monahan grinned. "An' just what makes you think you got rights?"

She looked even more annoyed with him. "Mr. President Lincoln freed the slaves, didn't he? I figure that includes me, since I feel like a slave mosta the time."

"Don't matter a whit how you feel," Monahan said, trying to rein himself back to reasonability. "You're a minor and a girl to boot. And it ain't 'Mr. President Lincoln'. It's Mr. Lincoln or Mr. President, if you're talkin to him direct. And Mr. Lincoln or President Lincoln if he ain't there but you're just talkin about him."

"What about him?" she demanded, shooting her finger toward Sweeney and confusing Monahan. "He can't be more 'n eighteen!"

Sweeney threw a leg over his saddle. "First off, I'm twenty-three. Second, you can call me Mr. Sweeney or you can call me Butch, but you got no call to be sayin' a word about Mr. Abraham Lincoln, former President of these here United States and its territories, on account of he's murdered, dead, and buried. Understood?"

Julia lowered her finger, but didn't speak. She kept staring at Sweeney, and it wasn't a happy stare, not by a long shot.

"C'mon, missy," said Monahan, hauling her up to her feet. To Sweeney he added, "Well, I don't think they would've buried him if he wasn't dead," before he stepped up on General Grant and pulled his boot back from the stirrup. He held down his hand. "C'mon, girl. We ain't got all day."

At last she took his hand, although grudgingly, and climbed up behind him. "I ain't stupid," she muttered into his shoulder so only he could hear. "I know President Lincoln got assassinated at a play. It was *Our American Cousin* and at it was at Ford's Theatre. So I ain't stupid."

Monahan didn't turn round, but asked, "And why're you tellin' me?"

"'Cause I ain't speakin' to *him*."

9

That evening, they made camp later than usual. Monahan had wanted to get to a wide open area where, if the girl decided to run, she couldn't get out of sight before they noticed she was gone. According to Sweeney, they were about a day and a half from the town of Iron Creek.

Monahan was disappointed. He was in a toot to get to the ranch he'd been aiming toward in the first place, eager for the immediate prospect of money coming in on a regular basis, and eager for a cot to sleep on most every night. The business with the girl had him all knotted up inside. The nagging feeling that something bad was on its way, and heading straight for him wouldn't go away.

About seven miles north and five, maybe six miles east of Monahan's camp, the Baylor brothers had finally camped for the night after aimlessly wandering a sloppy zigzag through trees and scrub that took them back to within a mile of their starting point. Dev was suddenly jolted awake by his brother's wild thrashing, creating a racket. As usual, Alf had forgotten to take off his spurs before he hunkered down for the night, and the rowels had gotten hung up in his thin blanket.

Over all the noise of ripping blanket and clanking spurs and his brother's unintelligible shouts, Dev hollered, "Alf! Alf! Put the cat down! Put the gaw-damn kitty down!" When Alf didn't respond, Dev dragged himself around the embers of their dying fire and shook his brother by the shoulder. "Let go of ol' Fluffy, Alf. You know he's Ma's favorite!"

Usually, that was enough to bring Alf out of it, but it didn't work. He just started kicking harder, which created more sounds of ripping blanket.

Dev tried again. "You're dreamin', Alf," he said gently. "You're dreamin'. Now stop kickin' and fussin', Alphonse. Settle down. Settle . . . calm down. Shhh, shhh, shhhhh," he finished, and Alf finally quieted to a loud but regular snore.

Figuring things had settled to a safe decibel level, Dev slouched back to his own side of the fire.

But he had just closed his eyes again when Alf began talking. At first, he thought it was going to be like the night before when Alf had mumbled for an hour or so before finally sinking into a deep and silent sleep. But it was not so. Sleeping Alf—who was very different from Waking Alf, Dev had discovered—was in a talkative mood. He wasn't making any more sense than usual, but his words were crisp and clear.

"G'day, mite," Alf said rather quickly, and in a voice at least a register lower than his usual confused and cracking tenor.

Dev hadn't figured out what kind of accent it was, exactly, on those occasions when he paid it any mind at all. But Alf was consistent, anyway. He used the same slang often enough that Dev thought it sounded sort of British. But if it came from some part of the British Empire, Dev didn't know where.

". . . said he'd be diddled iffen that ol' Papa Croc didn't carry off 'is leg, the blasted idiot. Oh, he was bleedin' an' yellin' to beat the band, he was. Didn't last long, rest 'im. Owen, he couldn't get the gushin' blood to stop and neither could ol' Cods. And the guards, they wasn't no bloody 'elp atall, atall . . ."

Dev frowned at the dash of Cockney. He'd met a Cockney sailor, once—in some waterfront dive back in Boston. Of course, everybody there sounded funny, but the sailor? Everything rhymed, for one thing. "Plates o' meat, that's your feet." Dev recalled that one, because it had taken him so long to figure out.

But the jabbering Alf did when he was sleeping? It was only part Cockney—and part something completely different. Something that came from a place far away from the British Isles or the United States. Or even Canada!

For the millionth time, he told himself that he and Jason never should have taken Alf out of that loony bin.

* * *

The next morning, Monahan was up before the dawn, stomping on numb feet and moaning while he rubbed at his head and his neck, and made the other assorted creaks and groans he made every morning. Sweeney, who was just beginning to get accustomed to Monahan's pre-light uproar, was awakened not by Monahan's ritual, but by the girl's reaction to it.

She screamed.

And it wasn't your everyday, garden variety 'Help, help, I saw a mouse' scream, either. It was a 'Help, help, a whole passel of raping, murdering, wild-eyed Apache just broke through my door with mayhem on their minds, slaying in their hearts, and a whole arsenal of tomahawks and assorted deadly blades tucked in their belts' kind of screech, with bone-shattering, bloodcurdling, gut-wrenching overtones.

At least, that's what it sounded like to Sweeney. After a quick look around to make sure there weren't really any rapacious Apache, he muttered a muted, "Lord have mercy," and yanked his blanket over his head.

Monahan's reaction to Julia's scream was a little different. He spun around on his heel—a real feat, considering he'd barely stomped any blood into it yet—and hissed, "What the *hell* is wrong with you now?!"

"Are you crazy? You're makin' too much noise!" the girl said, her hands clasped over her ears.

"Not as much as you," Monahan mumbled. He began stamping his foot again. "I think you already spooked the bejesus outta Butch, there." He pointed a finger at Sweeney's huddled form, barely discernible in the pre-dawn light.

He had seen the young cowboy flinch when the girl screamed, and watched him tunnel down into his blankets a few seconds later. "No use tryin' to hide, boy. Now that she's woke up everythin' within five miles what can kill an' eat us, we might as well get on with it."

A grumble came from Sweeney's general direction, and Monahan took it as an acknowledgement. He turned back to the girl. "Well, Miss Julia, hop to it."

She glared at him—and he glared right back— until at last she stood up and went into the brush to relieve herself. Or so he guessed. His hands moved to his knee, which was crying out for second place on his "ouch list." To the slowly moving lump that was the blanketed Butch, he said, "You up, kid?"

"I'm up," was Sweeney's muffled reply.

"Well, get a move on. I got a feelin' we ain't got time to take breakfast, least not here and now."

The blanket-man shifted. "Why?"

"Just got a feelin', that's all." Monahan put his hands in the small of his back and began to knead it as best he could.

"Okay." Sweeney made a small move to indicate he understood.

Monahan went on with his morning ministrations. He had yet to get to his shoulder, and was grateful for no further questions.

By full morning, they had moved on about three miles. Pleased enough with their progress, Monahan let Sweeney shoot a couple of rabbits. But he made them put another four miles under their horses' hooves before they could stop and rest.

As relieved—and as hungry—as anyone, Sweeney made a small fire as fast as Julia could tote sticks, and quickly skinned, cleaned, and roasted the jackrabbits. The dog occupied his time by tossing the pelts high into the air, then leaping to catch them. And Monahan kept busy by tying out their horses in the knee-high grass until lunch was ready.

It wasn't that he was antisocial. Well, he was, but most especially, he was putting off seeing the girl again. For some reason, she left a bad taste in his mouth. She had ridden behind his saddle for the most of the morning, and she hadn't said one word to him. Or to General Grant, for that matter. A person would at least figure she'd thank an old horse for going above and beyond the call of duty.

"They're ready," Sweeney announced as Monahan walked back into camp. He held out a roasted rabbit on a stick.

"You got a plate for that?"

Sweeney sighed and handed him a plate, then the roasted rabbit.

Monahan took it and sat, cross-legged in the

grass beside him. He pulled out his pocketknife and cut the roasted buck or doe in half, and then in quarters. "Heads up," he said, and when the girl turned his way, he tossed one of the front quarters to her. He threw one of the back quarters to Blue before he let himself sink his teeth into the other.

The juice ran down his chin, and he smiled. "Good jackrabbit, Butch," he managed while he chewed. He'd swear it tasted almost as good as those old cottontails back in Missouri.

Now, why on earth had he thought of that?

About the same time Sweeney had a change of heart . . . and a pang of conscience . . . and began slicing up his jackrabbit to share with the girl and the dog, too, the Baylor brothers were riding into the meadow where Dooley and his crew had camped the night before.

Alf thumbed back his hat and slouched forward, his forearms folded on the saddle horn. He stared intently at the ground before them.

Dev let a few seconds pass before he let out a snort. "What?" he asked derisively.

Alf made no attempt to defend himself. He simply shook his head slowly, raised his head, and looked at his brother. "I's flummoxed."

"Well, of course you are. You always are." Then he thought better of it and in a friendlier tone, Dev asked, "What's botherin' you this time, Alf?"

"Well, first we was followin' one man, then all of a sudden he turned into two fellers an' a dog. And now there's a kid with 'em." Alf shook his head. "I just can't . . ."

"Fathom it?" Dev asked. To tell the truth, he was perplexed, too, but it wouldn't pay to let on to Alf. The only things *he* remembered with any surety were that he couldn't play that high note in "Camptown Races" and his brother's mistakes. He had a tendency to bring up those with alarming frequency.

Well, Dev thought so, anyway.

"Yeah, that's good, Dev. *Fathom.*" Alf's face brightened. "I like that word." As was his habit, he repeated the word over and over, beneath his breath. But Dev heard and, as always, it pissed him off.

Alf didn't notice, though. He stuck out an arm, pointing to the garbled story left by footprints in the earth. "Those look like a kid's to you?"

Dev took a long time and a deep breath before he said, "No. Looks like the tracks of a girl's shoe." They were short and narrow, with too thin a heel and too finely chiseled a toe for a boy's boot. But why would that brother-murdering Monahan be carrying so many people? Dev wondered. He figured the other man must be good with a gun, and perhaps the dog was his. But now Monahan had added a girl to the mix?

"I just don't get it," Dev said, giving his head a slow shake.

"Mayhap she's a fairy," Alf whispered.

She didn't have a horse, Dev was thinking. That was for certain. Only two horses had ridden in, and only two sets of tracks led out. He'd been right, then. He'd told Alf the faint noise that had woken them before the dawn wasn't any owl's hoot. He smirked. He'd bet they were messin' with her. Otherwise, why would she holler so loud they'd heard her clear back up at their own camp?

Beside him, Alf was still staring at the ground, muttering, "She could be a haunt, 'cept haunts don't leave no footprints, I doesn't think. Dev, do haunts leave footprints?"

Dev took the course of least resistance and smacked Alf across the face with his hat. "C'mon." He rode west out of the camp, following the trail of bent and broken grass.

Alf was right behind him. "But Dev . . ."

"Of course ghosts don't leave footprints," Dev said without bothering to turn toward him. "Did you ever see a ghost with feet?"

"Ain't never seen no haunt," a dejected Alf replied.

"Well, then don't bother me with stupid questions." Dev checked his pocket watch. "And we'll be stopping for lunch in about a half hour."

There was relief in Alf's voice. "All right, Dev. Good thinkin'."

But Dev didn't hear him. He was thinking . . . and busy pushing his horse into a slow lope. They hadn't lit a breakfast fire, which meant they'd cut out early, and with a purpose. They were headed for Iron Creek. He'd lay cash money on it.

10

Monahan had hurried them the rest of that day, hurried them to the point of exhaustion. But to his mind it had been worth it. He couldn't see much of the town as they rode in. Just that it wasn't much of a town. Naturally, Julia didn't say a word. At nightfall, he had taken over ferrying her, much to Butch's delight, and he swore, it was like riding double with a big sandbag.

But he'd been thinking she was acting the way he would've acted if he'd been in her situation, if he'd been just a little snip of a girl and all, and had been picked up and bossed around by Sweeney—who was at least a foot taller than her—and himself. And he was even taller than Sweeney, especially with his boots on. He wondered who had legal charge of her. He'd never thought to ask.

Sweeney stopped in front of a dark building, which, by its scent and size, could only be the livery. Lost in his thoughts, Monahan stopped just in time to avoid riding right over the top of him.

From behind, the girl said a cranky, "Hey!" She slid down, then looked back up at Monahan. "I'm gonna have me enough trouble tonight without you crashin' me in the middle of the street!"

"Didn't mean nothin' by it," he muttered as he stepped down off General Grant. He rubbed the gelding's neck. "Sorry, big fella."

Sweeney dismounted and walked ahead a bit, peering into the building's one visible window. "Don't look like anybody's to home."

"Well, best turn 'em out into the corral, then." Monahan began to uncinch his saddle. He kept an eye on the girl, but it wasn't necessary. She leaned back against the corral's fence like she was nailed to it, which made him worry all the more about just what, exactly, they had brought her back to face.

Once they had stripped the tack off their mounts, slung their saddles over the top rail, and collected their saddlebags, Sweeney spoke. "Well, I reckon gettin' the gal home's at the top of our list."

"Let's think about that for a second there, Butch," Monahan said.

Sweeney cocked his brows.

"We don't even know where we're takin' her, first off. Second, it's near ten at night, and her kin's bound to be sleepin'. And third, I say we take her to the hotel and get her a room. On my nickel, boy, don't be lookin' so thunderstruck."

The girl smiled wide for the first time since their acquaintance, and Monahan started ahead before he realized that he didn't have a clue where the hotel was. "Julia?"

She ran the extra two steps to his side and grabbed his arm. "This way. " She gave him a tug to the right.

"Julia, does your Uncle Kirby know you're out at all hours with these strangers?" the clerk asked, squinting at the two men across from him. He turned up the lamp a little and took a closer look at Sweeney. "Sorry, Butch. Didn't recognize you. What you doin' back in town so soon?"

Sweeney smiled and turned the big book on the counter toward himself. He took the pen from its well and signed *Butch Sweeney* firmly and with a flourish. "Tryin' to rent a bed with a roof over it, Abner."

He handed the pen to Monahan, who took it, dipped it in the well, and signed his name beneath Sweeney's. In turn, he handed the pen to Julia.

But the clerk snatched the pen from her hand. "She don't need to sign. Not unless she's aged a few years since I last saw her."

Monahan gave a quick nod. "Butch and me need a double, and a single for the girl."

"With a pass-through connect, right?"

Monahan's face scrunched up in offense. "You askin' do I want a connecting door to Julia's room?"

The blanching clerk scuffled back and visually gulped.

Monahan figured he must look more imposing

than he felt. Either that, or the clerk was feeling guiltier about something than he was letting on. The more he thought about it, Monahan put his money on the latter. He shot a quick look in Sweeney's direction, and read much the same thing on his face.

He figured he could push the clerk for more details, but it was late and he was tired. He didn't want to get into anything. Not at the moment, anyway. All he wanted—besides making sure the girl was tucked up safe and sound—was a soft bed . . . and to be left alone.

As he was mulling things over, the clerk slid keys atop the desk and pushed them toward him. Monahan picked up the one marked 2A and asked, "Second floor?"

"Yes, sir," came the nervous answer.

Monahan nodded in reply, then handed the key to the girl. As an afterthought, he gave her his sidearm, making certain the clerk saw the transfer. "You know how to use this?" At her slight nod, he gave further instructions. "We'll be down to give you a chance at breakfast around 8:00, all right?"

The girl smiled, her shoulders slack with relief. "Yes, sir, and yes, sir." She gave a stronger nod of satisfaction. "See you fellers in the morning."

She looked at the clerk, who pointed toward the door beside the stairs. "To the left. Number's on the door."

She nodded and headed to her room, leaving the three of them—two tired and one terrified— standing in the lobby staring at each other.

"Where's our room?" Sweeney asked, more to cut the tension than anything else.

Monahan fingered the other key. "Upstairs, I reckon."

The desk clerk appeared to have been struck deaf and dumb, but mustered the strength to poke his thumb toward the stairs.

Noticing the motion, Monahan muttered, "Yeah, upstairs." Leaning over the counter he spoke in a lower tone. "The gal best be fit as a fiddle come mornin', you got me, Abner?"

The quivering desk clerk managed a "Yes, sir," then leaned back against the wall and slowly slid downward until he came into contact with the floor.

Monahan nodded curtly. "Night, then." He followed Sweeney up the stairs.

Outside town a couple of miles to the north, a wooden shack surrounded by smaller shacks and a lean-to sat along the dry, rocky creek bed. The usual soft scuttling of tiny animals moving across the forest floor had stilled, leaving the night quiet. No insect song came from the trees, no stomps or rustles, lows or whinnies wafted up from the barn. Only silence filled the air.

The interior of the shack was dark, so dark the moon beamed like a searchlight as it shined through the small parlor window. Julia felt engulfed by the silence—as if it were a predator who had found its prey. Her.

Not again.

Then, as if somebody somewhere had thrown an enormous switch, noise and hubbub and cacophony came at her, flooding over her like a wall of thick mucus, engulfing her in its too-familiar stickiness and stench at the same time calming her with its familiarity.

She heard a new sound.

Someone was coming.

She whimpered. *Not again.*

Julia whirled toward the front door just as it burst inward and revealed—

She woke abruptly. Stiff, sweating, and terrified, her scream was muffled by the pillow.

Across town, Sheriff Milton J. Carmichael sat in the saloon, nursing a beer. It had been a long day. A long week, come to think about it. Making it longer was Kirby Smithers, who had come waltzing into the office to report his niece missing. It would have been nice if he'd bothered to report it the first day she was gone.

That would have been Tuesday, Carmichael reckoned, taking another long draw on his beer. The day the posse finally made it out to the Morgan's spread and found what those murderous Apache had left behind.

His lips pursed with horror and distaste while he gave his head a slow shake. *Foul things, Apache. The government ought to raise the premium on their scalps.* He never should have come West. He should have listened to Martha and gone into business at her father's hardware. He'd probably have at least four kids by now—maybe six! She had always looked like sound breeding stock.

Had he listened to Martha, he'd probably be the sole proprietor of Gary, Indiana's oldest and finest hardware, too.

His thoughts continued in the dark vein. Some other feller had probably already stepped into his role. Some other feller had taken his place and was living his life. Some other feller was the Hardware King of Indiana.

Well, God bless him, whoever he is. The thought was halfhearted.

He brightened. *Hope the poor sod is takin' good care o' Martha's bunions.* And he laughed out loud.

"Somebody write a joke in the bottom of your beer mug?"

Carmichael looked up to find Butch Sweeney standing beside him, and immediately frowned. "Ain't you supposed to be someplace else? Like, somewhere far off?"

Sweeney tipped his hat. Without expression, he said, "Thanks for the welcome. 'Preciate it."

Carmichael unceremoniously drained his beer and stood up, which put his nose directly level with Sweeney's armpit. He made a foul face. "You stink like a horse what's rolled in the manure pile, Sweeney!"

Sweeney, still expressionless, looked down at him. "Beg your pardon, Sheriff Carmichael?"

Carmichael opened his mouth, but closed it without uttering a word. It was too late, he was too tired, and he plain just wasn't up to it. He pushed past Sweeney and silently started the short walk toward home.

Sweeney had waited until Monahan nodded off before he'd let his jumpy nerves take over and headed to the saloon. He watched the sheriff leave, then helped himself to the chair the man had just vacated. He signaled the barkeep for a whiskey. He figured to wash it down with a beer, which he ordered when the first drink was delivered.

As the bartender clomped back toward the bar, Sweeney raised his glass. "To Iron Creek—the town I hoped I'd never have to see again." He gulped down the shot and was immediately sorry. It went down the wrong way, and he couldn't stop coughing. Tears came to his eyes and he bent at the waist, hands flat on the table, when somebody began to pound him on the back without mercy.

"Hey!" he managed, still coughing. He tried speaking again. "Stop . . . it . . . dagnab . . . you!" The words came out separated by whoops and gasps for air. He whirled around.

"*Dagnab* me?" Deborah laughed. "Who you been hangin' 'round with, Big Butch?"

He flushed and returned her grin, shrugging. "I'm awful damn glad to see you, Deborah."

"I was beginnin' to think I'd have to get used to life without you." She pursed her lips into a pout. "Sheriff Carmichael was just in here . . ." She twisted her head, looking for him. "Well, he was in here a minute ago. Anyhow, he said you rode off west with some feller they found out to the Morgans' spread." She wrapped her shoulders in her arms, pointing her index fingers out to the side. "Oh, those Apache! They're so horrible!"

With the sinking feeling he was about to be taken advantage of yet again, Sweeney pulled out the chair next to him. "Sit down, Deborah."

She grinned and quickly sat next to him. Without asking or looking, she raised an arm over her head and began to lazily circle her hand.

Sweeney knew the drill. She would be served room temperature tea in a whiskey glass, for which he would be charged a premium whiskey price. He figured by the time he'd gotten that one puzzled out, he could've bought a whole damn tea plantation. He reached over, took hold of her arm, and pulled it back down to her side. "None of that, if you don't mind. If I'm rememberin' right, it was those weak tea whiskeys that got me in trouble in the first place."

She had the sense to look a little guilty, and let out a long breath before she said, "Yeah. I told you before, Butch, it was just that—"

He held up his hands. "I know, Deb, I know." He became aware of someone standing on the other side of him. He turned and discovered it was the bartender, with his beer in his hand. "That was fast, Emmitt."

The barkeep set down the beer glass. "Two bits."

"Oh, I been fine, too," Sweeney said as he dug a

hand into his pocket for change. He found the right coins and placed the money in Emmitt's palm.

Without any comment except a quick glance at his hand to make certain his money was all there, the barkeep left them.

"Chatty as always, I see." Sweeney took a long, grateful draw on his beer, then turned back to the girl, who was following Emmitt's retreat with her eyes. To the side of her face, he said, "I see Emmitt's still workin' nights. Mordecai ain't found nobody to replace him, yet?"

Languidly, Deborah turned back toward him. "Didn't know he was lookin' to."

Well, she probably didn't, now that he thought about it. She'd always been a little shy on brains. In fact, he was surprised she was still working at Clancy's Bar.

Sweeney had been away nearly a week and couldn't believe Mordecai Clancy—that penny pinching son of a shanty Irishman who owned the place, and who had been the recipient of the sweat of Sweeney's brow these past six months—hadn't come up with an excuse yet!

Some people, he thought, taking another pull on his beer.

11

On the trail leading to Iron Creek, the two Baylor brothers arose with the dawn. Dev stoked the fire, took a piss, and rooted through the saddlebags for breakfast before he woke Alf. Even then, he didn't touch him. "Sun's up. Rise and greet the day."

Alf came awake and gave him a good-natured grin—always Alf's first lie of the day, Dev often thought—then stepped a few feet away from the fire.

Thank God he'd picked the downhill side, Dev thought with a roll of his eyes. He set their bacon on the fire, then started the biscuits baking. He didn't look up when Alf asked, "You makin' coffee this mornin', Dev?"

Face twisting with aggravation, Dev replied, "I always do, don't I, Alf?"

A moment passed before Alf grudgingly allowed that he did. "Almost always."

Dev shot to his feet, shouting, "Jesus! One time! One lousy time in more 'n fifteen years on the trail together!" Briefly, Dev clamped his eyelids closed and sucked in a big breath of air. It helped—just enough. More calmly, he continued. "Eight years ago on the morning of March fourteenth, I didn't make coffee because we didn't *have* any coffee. Somebody lost it when he was fordin' Arapaho Creek the night before. Remember?"

Slowly, the veil seemed to lift from Alf's eyes. Then, quite suddenly, he grinned. "That creek was *cold,* Dev!" His hands rose to grip his shoulders in the memory of it, and his feet danced a little jig.

"Jason warned you," Dev said.

Alf nodded. "Spring runoff, he said. There was chunks o' ice in that creek!"

"And one big chunk o' you. And one little chunk of our total coffee fixin's."

"Yes, sir, that's right, Dev. And you ain't let me carry it since. Ain't let me carry nothin' important."

"That's right, Alf." Dev turned his attention to the fire, gave it a stir, and added a few more twigs.

"Coffee's real important, ain't it, Dev?"

"Real important."

The bacon was cooking up fine. Carefully, Dev cracked open and added in the bird's eggs they'd found the day before. . "We're in luck. The mama just laid 'em, fresh." There was nothing he hated more than having his mouth all set for a clear, clean egg, then cracking it open to find nothing but a ready-to-hatch chick. He didn't see any miracle in it, or hold any pity for the dazed and motherless chick, which was more than often thoughtlessly cast aside.

"When you figger we'll catch 'em up?" Alf asked. At least he'd changed the subject.

Dev shrugged. "When we do, I reckon." He kept his eyes focused on the skillet.

Fortunately, it was enough of an answer to suit Alf, who simply stuck his empty plate forward. "Them eggs ready, Dev?"

Monahan woke slightly after nine o'clock—very late for him—figuring he could cut himself a little slack. After all, the last few days had been bone battering. He took his time performing the usual stomping and rubbing of his broken parts, amazed Sweeney slept clean through it. By the time he made his exit with Blue the sun was up so high in the cloudless sky it nearly blinded him.

There weren't many people out and about, so nobody paid any attention when he said, "I'm goin' to the livery." He started toward the small corral across the road, then thought better of it and turned around to give instructions to Blue. "You find Julia, you best bring her to me, you hear?"

The dog let out a low bark in agreement.

Satisfied, Monahan turned back in the direction of the livery. From in front of the hotel, he could see several horses in the corral. General Grant trotted to the fence and whinnied.

"I'm comin', I'm comin'," he muttered as he gained the paddock fence.

General Grant waited on the other side of the boards, his neck stretched over the top rail as far as it would go. His upper lip twitched out a few inches farther. Monahan chuckled under his breath as he reached the old gelding and scratched at the few scattered white hairs on his forehead, imitating a star.

"All right, old son," he muttered, digging into a hip pocket. He thought he had a lemon drop somewhere in there.

He did find one, and managed to slip it between General Grant's greedy choppers before the horse could swallow his sleeve's frayed cuff. The horse's attention diverted, he made a quick beeline for the office. But before he could grab the latch, let alone open the door, it swung open under the power of a gangly, teenaged, dark-headed boy. *Part Indian,* Monahan thought.

The boy spoke. "Thought I heard a little ruckus out here." He stuck out a wide, bony hand. "Tommy Hawk's the name. I'm in charge whenever Mr. Pearl ain't around, that bein' most of the time. And you're . . . ?"

"Dooley Monahan." He took the boy's hand and gave it a shake. "We come in late last night, and there weren't nobody here, so we left the horses—"

"In the corral." Tommy Hawk nodded and grinned. "Figured they had to belong to somebody." He poked a thumb back over his shoulder, toward the interior of the livery. "Brought your saddles inside this mornin'. Ain't safe to just leave 'em out like that, at least, not 'round here."

Monahan nodded. He'd met the law and was pretty sure the kid knew what he was talking about.

He dug in his pocket for his wallet. It slid easily from its hiding place—too easily—indicating it wasn't exactly fat with money. "What do we owe you so far?"

The boy scratched his head. "Well, you wanna just leave 'em out in the stock pen, or you figurin' on a roof over their heads?"

"Got a good cross breeze?"

"Each stall's got its own winder!" the kid replied huffily.

"Don't get your dander up. Just askin'. How much for that, with a turnout two or three times a day? And water and feed."

Tommy Hawk's face smoothed out into its former, more kindly state at just about the same moment Monahan got the joke of the boy's name. Trying not to laugh, Monahan peeked into his wallet, saw green, and again asked, "How much?"

"Two bits a day for each one. And we won't count last night. We'll just agree that you fellas rode in early this morning, all right? And we feed alfalfa hay, full-grain corn, and oat bran mash."

Monahan nodded. General Grant was going to think he'd died and gone to horse heaven! "Sounds just grand, Tommy." He slid a worn dollar bill from his wallet, loosening something else in the process. "Here's for today and tomorrow," he muttered as he held the money out to Tommy with one hand and thumbed free the scrap of paper from his wallet with the other.

He recognized it almost immediately. "Alaska," he whispered almost reverently.

"What'd you say?"

He looked up. "Oh. Alaska! That's where I'm goin'."

"Why'd anybody wanna go up there?" Tommy said, his face flooded with disbelief. "I hear the whole place is froze over practically the whole dang time!"

"No, it ain't. Says so right here."

Monahan held the clipping up, then farther away until it came into focus. "Says the climate is salubrious."

The boy's brow furrowed. "What's that mean?"

"Means it don't snow all the time," Monahan said, a bit more gruffly than he intended. He quickly stuffed the clipping back inside his wallet.

"Didn't mean no offense." Tommy was obviously concerned about the board money. He knew travelers passing through town could just as easily leave their mounts tied to the rail . . . and usually did. He needed the business.

"None taken," Monahan replied. Thank God he'd found the clipping! Hell, he might have wandered around the southwest for years without remembering where the heck he had set out for in the first place. "Did I pay you?"

Tommy dug his toe in the dirt for a second before he said, "Yes sir, two day's worth." The money was clenched tightly behind his back, and they both knew it.

"Well, I'll leave you to get to it." Monahan smiled a little, thinking he'd best go roust that Julia gal out of bed or it'd be time for lunch!

He had no sooner said his piece and turned about when he spied a man across the street.

The man gulped at the sight of the old cowboy, but held his ground. "Monahan!" he cried, and his feet did a little jig that was completely out of character with his expression.

To Monahan's thinking nothing about the fellow matched up, including the giggle that made its way out of his mouth directly after Monahan's name.

Monahan cocked his brow. "What?" he hollered back.

Across the street, the artless grin faded just a little. "I says, is you Dooley Monahan?"

Where was the damned dog when you needed him? Monahan thought, without allowing himself a look-round. "Who's askin'?"

The stranger pulled himself up a little taller. "Alf Baylor, and you gunned down my brother over cards." His fingers began to twitch.

Without taking his eyes from the stranger's, Monahan hissed, "Get inside and lay low, Tommy." Behind him, he heard scrambling boots, then the hollow boom and dull click as the door closed and the latch dropped.

Monahan had failed to notice the hotel's front entrance, a simple thing at best, where the door briefly opened just a crack, then closed. On the other side of the door stood Julia, suddenly wide-eyed and shaking with terror.

The desk clerk sat forward and lowered his

newspaper, the two front legs of his chair hitting the wood plank floor with a smart tap. "What's the matter with you?"

Julia didn't dillydally. "The men I came in with yesterday. The younger one—Sweeney, he's called. He come down yet?"

"Been here since seven, and I ain't seen him." He leaned back dismissively and pulled up his paper again.

Julia fairly vaulted up the stairs and down the hall.

Monahan had done his best to delay the inevitable. But Alf, who he was quickly learning wasn't exactly the sharpest tool in the shed, seemed to be tiring of it.

"Now, you listen here, Monahan—"

"Shouldn't we wait for your brother?" Monahan interrupted, not giving him a chance to finish. He couldn't recall the name, but knew there was one.

Annoyed, Alf snapped, "He'll get here when he comes! Now, let's get on with it!" Alf went for his gun, forcing the old cowboy into action.

The Colt slid easily from its holster, felt right in Monahan's hand. He fired at the very instant Alf did. And they both missed.

Rage overtook Alf's features and he shouted, "You hold still, you liver-spotted ol' hop toad!" He fired again, and duly missed.

Before Alf had a chance to accuse him of dodging and weaving again, Monahan opened fire, fanning his gun for all he was worth—which wasn't much, to his thinking. Every single bullet missed, although he put a hole through the post Alf was standing beside and blew out a little stained glass windowpane on his right. He sighed, thinking he might as well let Alf kill him because he could never afford to replace it, when Alf drew his attention again.

He sneered and called out, "You outta lead, Monahan?"

"I am that," he reluctantly replied. "Don't suppose you'd mind if I took a walk over to my saddlebags for bullets?"

Unbelievably, Alf seemed to consider it for a moment, but then shook his head. "Nope, Monahan. You already had your shots, used 'em all up." Slowly, he lifted his arm and leveled his pistol at Monahan. "You're a dead man."

12

Monahan stared at Alf. Nothing else registered. Everything had faded into the background until the very last second when it came out of nowhere like a blurry, gray cannonball, colliding with Alf's gun hand as the percussive explosion split the morning air.

Monahan hit the ground, scrambling quickly toward his saddlebags and the half-full box of ammunition he knew was there. But his old legs didn't carry him as fast as he wanted, no matter how strongly he willed them to. Another shot rang out and apparently hit General Grant, for out in the center of the paddock, the gelding immediately started bucking.

"Damn you, Alf Baylor!" Monahan shouted as he dug into his saddlebag and—miracle of miracles!— his fingers landed directly on the cartridge box. Without further thought, he wheeled around, dropped into a squat, loaded the pistol, and took careful aim at Alf Baylor.

But Alf had dropped his gun and was staring down stupidly at his wrist, which he cradled before him. Blood dripped down and spattered on the boards at his feet. "Not fair!" Alf shouted at Monahan.

"What you talkin' 'bout, fool?"

"Not fair, you sendin' some fancy trick dog out here to bite me! Near to took my hand off, he did!" Alf turned his attention back to his wounded wrist and began to sniffle.

Confused, Monahan frowned. Some fancy trick dog? Could he be talking about—

"Blue?" Butch Sweeney stepped out of the mouth of an alley down the way. His rifle was out and pointed square at Alf Baylor's head. He called, "You shot up, Dooley?"

"Nope," Monahan answered, silently thanking God his opponent was as bad a marksman as he was. Before he could form a word to ask Sweeney where the hell Alf's brother was, he had a face full of wagging, wriggling, whimpering and licking Blue dog.

As he tried to pry fifty pounds of happy-beyond-measure dog off, he heard new voices. Hopefully some of the locals had seen it was Alf who'd started the ruckus.

Once he finally got the dog peeled off him and climbed back up to his feet, he saw that the sheriff had taken Alf into custody. He was cuffed, anyway. One of the men who'd been in the posse the other day—a deputy, Monahan was pretty sure—had taken possession of Alf's gun and was marching the shooter toward the jailhouse. The sheriff turned toward the little crowd that had gathered. He was trying to calm them down, Monahan thought, although he couldn't hear anything over the crowd's hum. He continued watching as Sweeney reached the mob across the street and had words with the sheriff. They didn't exactly look friendly.

Monahan snorted and gave his head a little shake. "Blue, let's you and me go see to General Grant."

The dog barked out a soft acknowledgement and shimmied under the fence rail.

Monahan chuckled. "Damned if I don't half think you understand every word that's said inside your earshot, you ol' fur ball."

Blue woofed happily, and Monahan turned his back on the crowd across the way, swung himself over the fence, and walked toward General Grant. "How you doin', big feller? Did that nasty ol' Alf hit you with a lucky shot? Pretty certain he didn't do much more 'n surprise you, ol' son."

He reached the horse, gave his forehead a good rub and then, with Blue standing out front and giving the General 'the eye,' Monahan went over the horse, inch by inch.

Up the street, Dev Baylor stood in an alley's shadows, angrily and rhythmically clenching and unclenching his fists as he watched his brother being marched into the jail across the road. The damn idiot! he thought. Couldn't even kill the old buzzard from thirty feet away! He'd known for years Alf was a bad shot but he'd rarely had a chance to see him demonstrate the fact so publicly.

There had been nothing he could do to help him out. Alf had chosen a most public place to gun down Monahan, and there was paper out on both brothers. Dev had been forced to watch from the shadows, and hold his fire even though Monahan would have been a fairly easy shot, standing right out in the open as he'd been.

Dev ground his teeth. *Even I could have picked you off, old man,* he thought. *Just the way you picked off our big brother. 'Cept he was a whole lot easier target, just sittin' across the table and mindin' his own business.*

The whole situation was just plain embarrassing, that's what it was. Alf had let Monahan take the chance to reload! That was inexcusable, to Dev's way of thinking. Of course, due to there being a kink in the road, he hadn't seen that Alf was bleeding until the deputy hauled him off. Just what had happened to bring that much blood was another thing entirely. *Be just like ol' Alf to go and shoot himself, now wouldn't it?* he thought, and growled under his breath.

But it wasn't the time to figure that out. It was time to figure a way to break Alf out of jail. Not that the concept had Dev exactly quaking in his boots. It was something he'd done countless times before. And one he would probably be called upon to do many times in the future.

He looked across the street toward the sheriff's office again. The place was bubbling with activity.

Well, for a little town like Iron Creek. He reached into his pocket, pulled out a ready-made, and lit it. The deputy emerged from the front door and assumed position to stand guard. The rifle was held across his chest, and his face appeared to be practicing a mean and menacing look. He wasn't very good at the last part.

Dev snorted out smoke, then moved back a little, but not so far that he couldn't see the sheriff's yawning doorway. If he held his head just right, he could make out the shadow falling across Alf's grimy trouser leg at the back of the building, behind a row of iron bars.

You never could do anything the easy way, could you, Alf? he thought, his head shaking slightly.

"Said it weren't nothin'," Monahan repeated for the third time, leaning in toward Sweeney. The crowd in the saloon was noisy and all out of proportion for barely past noon on a weekday.

He hadn't yet realized it had been his and Alf's little dog and pony show that had provided an excuse for the townsmen. "Just creased the hair over his croup is all." He lifted his mug and took another deep drink.

Sweeney nodded his head, indicating he'd understood, then answered. Monahan couldn't hear him, but he believed he'd said something like, "Good, good," so he nodded in reply and took another healthy bite of the sandwich the bartender had provided for them—thin-cut, cold, tender roast beef on thick, homemade sourdough bread still warm from the oven.

Out of what was quickly becoming habit, he tore off a corner and held it down to the dog. Two chews and a gulp, and then Blue was staring back up again, a fresh, pleading expression on his face.

"You sure are somethin' else, dog." A wave of sentiment rose up to burn at Monahan's eyes, and it was a good thing Sweeney tapped him on the shoulder just then, or he might have embarrassed himself.

Sweeney's mouth moved again, but Monahan still couldn't hear squat. He pointed to his ear and shook his head. Sweeney tried yelling louder, which had no effect at all, and then pointed toward the door.

Gravity, I'm givin' in, Monahan thought, sliding off his barstool. He tossed the last of the sandwich to the dog (much to its delight), grabbed his beer mug, and set off in the direction of Sweeney's pointing finger. Once outside, he leaned up against a porch post and waited.

Sweeney appeared shortly, followed by the blue merle dog. "Thanks for comin' out. Too noisy in there to converse." He jabbed his thumb back toward the saloon.

Monahan nodded. He lifted his beer a final time, drained it, and leaned back with the empty mug dangling from a thumb.

"What I was gonna tell you is that I'm goin' back to the hotel," Sweeney started in. "If you're right about Dev bein' around, I wanna make myself a hard target."

"As in tough to find?" Monahan twisted to the side, looking down toward the livery. Tommy had taken the horses inside. Good.

"Exactly." Sweeney turned his thumb back to point at himself. "If he's gonna kill us, I'm gonna make this target one he has to work for."

Monahan couldn't think of any argument to counter his theory, and told him so. Then he asked, "That lawman say anythin' about a reward?"

Sweeney nodded. "Said he'd talk about it once he got time to interview you. I guess that means he wants to ask you some questions." He sniffed and turned his head away, as if he was guarding himself from being overheard. "Busy little son of a gun, ain't he?"

"That he is." Monahan nodded. "Y'know, I'd swear there was somethin' I was achin' to tell you, 'cept I'll be damned if I can remember what it is."

Sweeny shrugged.

"Was it about the little gal, maybe?" Monahan tried.

"Julia? Nope. Don't think so. By the way—and I hate like sin to be givin' her credit for it—she was the one what sent Blue chargin' up the street after that gunman."

Monahan furrowed his brow. "How the hell did she do that? I mean, she ain't known that dog more 'n a couple o' days!"

Sweeney shrugged his shoulders. "Reckon it was long enough. She just got down on one knee and whispered somethin' to him, then pointed up the street to him, and bang! That hound was off and runnin'."

"Well, I'll be," Monahan muttered. Blue was still at their feet, sniffing at the boards in case he'd dropped any sandwich on the way out. Hell, Julia had probably whispered that Alf had a sandwich he wasn't sharing!

The dog gave up, and thumped down onto the boards with a low moan, reminding Monahan of the last shot Alf had gotten off. He looked up. "Hey, Butch, you check him over? I mean, Alf didn't get off a lucky shot, did he? Don't want nobody shootin' my dog full o' holes."

Sweeney smiled. "He's fine. Ain't got a scratch on him."

"You certain?"

"Go over him yourself. Ain't no skin off my nose. You checked Chili when you were 'cross the street, right?"

Monahan hadn't, but he said, "Looked fine," then added Sweeney's own, "Go over him yourself," and swung an arm toward the stable. There was no way Alf could have been lucky enough to wing both horses! he thought.

Was there?

Oh, now he was being a silly old man!

Before he had a chance to dig himself a hole any deeper, he said, "Believe I'll take in my mug, then go back to the hotel." He stood erect and held the mug out in front of him. "Mind?" he added when Sweeney didn't move fast enough to suit him.

"Sorry," Sweeney muttered, and stepped to the side.

Monahan swung in one side of the batwing doors, sat his mug on a chair rail, then turned and made his way on down to the hotel with Blue happily trailing at his heels.

Not being in any hurry, he did a bit of window-shopping on the way. Once he climbed up the stairs, fully expecting to find that Sweeney had beat him back and was snoring blissfully on the other bed, he and Blue found themselves alone. Blue didn't mind. He took possession of Sweeney's bed, dug himself a nest in the rumpled bedclothes, and settled in for the duration.

"He's gonna show up any second," Monahan warned as he pulled off his boots, then lay back on his own berth. All he heard out of the dog was a deep sigh. And then he didn't hear anything, because he was asleep.

Monahan dreamed deep, falling back, back in time, back to days long, long ago when he was young and so was the country.

He was sitting beside a campfire, and the night was damp, not crack-your-hide dry, like Arizona. It was a Missouri night, a Missouri night in the open. It was summer, but the evening hadn't brought much cool with it. There wasn't even a breeze to trick a body into thinking it had cooled off.

He looked across the fire and saw the picket line, with his old gelding Tony tied to it and drowsing.

On some level, he knew he was in his past, but it felt like . . . like right now. Somewhere deeper in the shadows, another horse stamped his hoof and snorted softly.

To his right, a voice asked, "You gonna argue me on this one, too, Dooley?"

The young man turned toward the voice, recognizing the speaker immediately. "You're Vince George, aren't you."

Vince gave him one of those looks, as if he'd gone crazy, but before either of them could say another word, Red Usher appeared, dropping into a sit next to Vince and catty-corner from Dooley around the fire. He looked angry and mean.

Real friendly, Dooley said, "Hey, Red."

"Real funny," came the reply. Red's face doubled up on the 'mean.'

For the first time, Dooley knew it was aimed at him and him alone. Sent a cold shiver right through him, it did.

Vince spoke again. "Well, Dooley? What's it gonna be?"

He didn't have the slightest idea what to say, and shortly, he had no chance. The only thing in the world he could see was the enormity of Vince's knuckles as they rapidly grew in their race toward his face.

For a while, things got murky. Somebody was hitting him, and every punch hurt like the devil. He heard the hollow sound of slapping leathers as his body was slung across Ol' Tony's saddle and headed out into the night.

He was hit again and again and again until his brain sloshed inside his skull, sloshed like a lone boiled egg in a big pickling jar. And then he opened his eyes just a crack. Sunlight near to blinded him. He passed out, convinced he was surely dying, traveling down the River Styx.

But he woke again—later in the day, or maybe the next, or the next. The light wasn't so bright. The ferryman bent over him touched his face, and changed into a woman—a beautiful woman. He began to weep. He recognized her as the woman he would one day marry, and he was happy. His horse was grazing nearby, he was shed of Monty's Raiders for good, and Kathleen would—

Monahan sat up in the bed, wide awake and straight and stiff as a frozen snake, blinking rapidly.

13

Julia sat in the alley behind the hotel, arms wrapped around her legs and face buried in her knees, thinking what to do next. Once she'd seen the sheriff coming down the walk, Alf wailing and holding his hand, and the dog springing up into Monahan's arms, she'd turned and scampered back into the alley behind the buildings. There was no way she'd let her uncle catch her unawares.

If the peckerwood was even in town.

And he wasn't even her uncle!

He'd taken her in when she was nine, her parents having gone to the Lord when the fever came through their corner of Texas. At first, she'd thought he was wonderful. He'd gotten her a horse of her very own, and taught her how to take care of it. She'd already known how to cook the few things he was interested in eating, and past that, he didn't much care what she did. Although she missed her parents greatly, she was grateful to him.

At first.

Homes with room and vittles for a child not their own were hard to come by, and she knew she was lucky he'd taken an interest in her. She was too young and too sheltered to think it odd that he'd passed over several boys in sore need of a parental figure and chosen her, a poor, plain, little child hiding under a considerable mop of red hair.

She was no good at anything that came in handy for him on the trail, and barely good for company. She was afraid to talk much when she was younger. Afraid of most everything, come to think of it. In fact, she was terrified of most everything the world had to offer, with the single, glowing exception of him.

After they'd settled in Iron Creek and she had started school and begun to make friends, God thrust the weight of the world on her. She was terrified when her first menses came. Miss Kellogg, the teacher, found her huddled and shivering in the back corner of the little schoolhouse's storage closet, and it had taken Julia a world of courage to tell even her, who had been nothing but kind. But Julia had managed to tell her, falteringly, about the unthinkable thing she had discovered in the outhouse.

Miss Kellogg let out a tiny, subdued laugh and hugged her shoulders tight. "It's nothing you did, Julia. Most girls look on it as a wonderful thing, a blessing. It's a signal from God that you are a woman."

Julia decided she didn't like God's messaging system and later on, she told him so in her prayers.

By that time, Miss Kellogg had explained the whole business to her, told her how to "fix herself up," and sent her on her way. Julia had also promised herself never to mention it to her uncle, who, she decided, wasn't privy to such information, being a man and all, and never having been married.

But late that night, he came into her room. "Julia? Julia, are you awake?"

She sat up in the darkness. "I am," she said groggily.

He cleared his throat as if gathering himself. "I, uh, talked to your Miss Kellogg this afternoon. She tells me . . . she says things are gonna be different for you from now on."

"Yes, sir," she had replied, glad for the darkness when she felt a hot flush rise up her neck.

"Shoulda known. Well, did know. I smelled it on you during dinner."

Softly, she whispered, "Sorry if you found it offensive." Then she offered a lame excuse. "I washed." Silently, she began to cry.

Thankfully, he left, but before he did, he paused in the doorway and made her promise to tell him when it was over.

She remembered agreeing, at the same time thinking how very strange it was that he'd want to know about such a personal thing.

Five days later, she found out.

Monahan had fallen back to sleep by the time Sweeney entered the hotel room. He had taken the time to have himself another sandwich and a tall beer, and was feeling unusually full. He sat down in the upholstered chair between the table and the window and stuck his long legs out into the room.

He looked over at Monahan. He sure was something!

"Is he your pa?" some of the townsmen had asked. Others had wanted to know if they were brothers or nephew and uncle. Sweeney knew it was only because they were both so tall and thin, and they traveled together, and that it seemed more important to a man to be able to say he took a drink with Dooley Monahan's son—Dooley having just put on the street show outside the hotel—than that he'd had a beer with Dooley Monahan's . . . what? He guessed he'd like to be remembered just as the man's friend than as anything else.

Sweeney lifted a foot and gave a playful nudge to the mattress. "C'mon, Blue," he whispered. "Get your fluffy old feathered backside outta my bed, or I'll lay down right on you."

The dog did no more than offer a low, rattling groan and allow himself a momentary shivery, shaky stretch of his limbs before falling back to sleep.

"Fine," Sweeney muttered. "I guess you're the mattress, then."

The dog made no reply.

Scraping himself up into a proper sit, Sweeney stood up. He pulled back the covers as well as he could, with Blue hogging them, and sat down on the bed. "God," he muttered to no one in particular as he lay back. If he was careful, he could lay down one side of the bed without disturbing the dog. That was a good thing, he reckoned. The dog had taken a true liking to Monahan. He'd best remember to keep his knobby knees and big feet to himself.

He lifted his hat, verified he had, indeed, taken off his spurs, then lowered it over his face like Dooley did when he was sleeping out on the trail before he allowed himself a deep sigh, and fell into a deep, if somewhat guarded, sleep.

By suppertime, Dev Baylor had given up guarding the jail, which remained congested with curiosity seekers and lawmen alike, and abandoned his alley for a perch at the Iron Creek Café, where he was digging his fork and knife into a thick, freshly-butchered steak. Well, according to the waiter. It couldn't have been proved by Dev, although considering all that had gone on in town, he wouldn't have put it past them to butcher every edible critter in outright, decadent celebration.

To tell the truth, he was more than a little jealous. To think that *Alf's* capture was the call for all the jubilation! It made his teeth hurt, that was what. If Alf had been handy, he would have backhanded him, just for trying to make himself look bigger. And don't forget failing to kill Monahan. That was the most stupid thing of all!

He sawed at his steak and poked another bloody bite into his mouth. It seemed he was chewing a lot more than normal, and he couldn't for the life of him find the salt. Salt would help. But he looked and looked and there was no—

A hand clasped his upper arm.

He twisted toward it.

"You be a stranger in these parts?" said the man who still had a hold on his shirtsleeve.

Once Dev's eyes followed the hand to the arm to the shoulder of the man, he made himself smile. "You shouldn't go 'round like that, grabbin' fellers out of the blue, Sheriff," he said, all teeth and charm. "And yeah, I rode into your fair city this afternoon." He was careful to make his time of entry fall after Alf's little "altercation" with Monahan. He leaned toward Sheriff Carmichael and propped an elbow on the table. He swept a hand toward the jostling, noisy crowd. "What the devil's got into these folks, or is Iron Creek just a naturally happy town?"

The sheriff let go of his arm. "You ever heard of the Baylor Boys?"

Dev introduced himself as Richard Blessing, a traveling wool merchant on his way to California to close a few new deals. He allowed that he'd never known anyone by that name. The sheriff filled him in on the recent doings in town. By which he was properly amazed, of course. So properly that before the sheriff moved on to quiz a lone man at a table in the back, he shook Dev's hand and welcomed him to town.

"Thank you, Sheriff," he said with a smile. "Glad to be here."

"Pleasure's mine," the sheriff replied.

For now, Dev was thinking. *But later tonight, the pleasure will be all mine. After all, even the sheriff has to go home sometime, doesn't he?*

Noontime had come and gone, and naptime along with it. Sweeney had risen on account of the dog's teeth being abruptly buried in his knee, and Monahan on account of Sweeney's yelps of pain.

"I don't know why you got to go provokin' that dog," Monahan said from beneath his hat.

"I ain't provokin' him!" whined Sweeney. "He bit *me,* not the other way 'round!" He separated the dog from his knee and yanked his pant leg up above the insult. It was bleeding, all right, but it might have been bleeding more or less, depending on your point of view. To Sweeney's mind, it would have been better if it hadn't bled and Blue hadn't broken his skin, so *less.* But if it was going to bleed at all, it should have been bleeding *more.* . . At least he would have looked more wounded if it had gushed a little!

But it didn't. It just kept slowly oozing. And hurting to beat the band.

"Real funny, Blue," he said, shooting the dog a sidelong glance. Blue just kept on with his lazy pant and Sweeney slowly shook his head with a muttered, "Real funny."

Monahan left Sweeney behind, nursing his knee, and tromped down the stairs with the dog. "You know, you'd better not bite him up too bad. He's your friend, too! Y'know, I been thinkin' 'bout Miss

Julia. Who was it sent you after that Baylor, anyhow? Was it her?"

The blue dog didn't answer.

They hit the main floor, and after giving a nod to the desk clerk, Monahan turned toward the back hall, pausing only to holler, "Which room?"

The clerk answered him right off, and Monahan went on down the hall to her room. He rapped on the door.

She answered it right off, but her eyes were tear-stained. Once she'd seen who it was, she turned her face away from him.

"You eat yet?"

She shook her head, but kept it turned away.

"Well, let's you and me go see if they have anything edible up to the café."

Nodding stiffly, she followed him from the room.

They were outside the front door before she broke down—out of the blue, it seemed to Monahan—and had to sit on the steps with her face in her hands. Blue, whimpering softly, gently nosed at the tears seeping through her fingers.

Monahan rubbed his neck, then sat down beside her, shaking his head. "All right, Miss Julia. You'd best be tellin' me what's botherin' you."

She did. It wasn't anything he wanted to hear—or even think about, for that matter—but once she opened up, getting her to stop was like trying to close the floodgates. She didn't want to go back home, and he could well see why. The fact was he'd like to get his hands around that uncle's neck for about five minutes, that was what.

Well, maybe not, especially when Julia described him as a big fellow—a mountain of a man—muscled up like a bull and twice as mean. Monahan wasn't young anymore, and doubted he'd survive an encounter. But Julia wasn't staying, not with a man like that. Hell, he had a hard time even thinking of him as a man!

He couldn't tell Sweeney. The cowboy was young enough to think he could take on the uncle. Well, maybe he could, but it wouldn't be easy.

Monahan didn't want the boy to end up running for the rest of his life, as he had. He was determined there wouldn't be another Dooley Monahan created that day!

"This 'uncle' of yours, whereabouts does he live? I mean, how likely is he to be in town?"

"He only lives about a mile up the creek," she replied between sniffs and snuffles. "I'm sorry. I never told anybody before."

His arm went around her and hugged her shoulders tight, which brought on a fresh onslaught of tears. "There, there," he soothed. As he rocked her, it occurred to him he might have been a good daddy, had he stayed put long enough to sink down stable roots, and had he taken up with a good woman.

He had, of course. He had taken up with Kathleen.

But he didn't remember that very often. He did remember having had a dream that made him nervous, but he couldn't for the life of him remember why.

"We'd best not go paradin' you out in the street,

then. What do you say you go back to your room, and I'll bring you a sandwich?"

Julia looked up through damp lashes. "And what about tomorrow?"

"We'll figure that out when we get there. But don't you fret none, we ain't gonna leave you nowhere near that nasty old skunk, not for peaches nor pearls." It was something he'd heard his mother say a thousand times, although he couldn't recall any more of it, just the saying. Repeating it made him feel warm inside.

"Now, go on back inside. Don't worry. I'll see to you." Monahan stood up, taking her with him. He watched her go back inside, and then he turned and trudged on up to the café, where he ordered a roast beef sandwich for himself, and another for her. He also bought two orders of home fries—one for him and one to go—and two slices of apple pie, only one wrapped up with a fork on top.

After checking to see that the horses were settled in all right, he took the food to her. As he watched her eat, he wondered if he shouldn't have brought her two sandwiches instead of just the one. She was halfway through it before he had the presence of mind to tell her about the potatoes. She wolfed them down before he thought to tell her about the fork wrapped up with the pie.

When he left her, she was stuffed and happy, nearly purring like a baby kitten. He paused at the door to say, "Reckon Butch or I'll stop by with some dinner for you around seven. Think you can hold out till then?"

Smiling, she nodded. "Mr. Monahan? They used to have some real good rhubarb pie at the café. If you wouldn't mind, could you—"

"Sure," he said with a grin. "If they got any, it's yours. And Mr. Monahan was my daddy. You call me Dooley." Softly, he closed the door between them.

By the time he reached the lobby, Sweeny was limping down the stairs. He raised a hand. "You goin' to Sheriff Carmichael's office, Dooley?"

"Why? Is he lookin' for me?"

Butch stepped down to the lobby floor. "Seems to me he was lookin' for you. I mean, you were involved in the arrest of Alf Baylor this mornin'. Or have I got the wrong Dooley Monahan?" He cocked his brow.

"Why you askin'? You found you got some time to kill?"

"Thought I might walk up there with you, iffen you don't mind. I'd like to have a look at this killer who's been doggin' us all over the territory."

Monahan walked toward the door. "No skin off my hide."

Sweeney scurried to catch up, which he did only after following the old cowboy's spur-jangling steps halfway to the café.

14

By the time suppertime rolled around, Monahan and Sweeney had been at Carmichael's mercy for several hours. The sheriff's office—also the jail and the courthouse—was cramped and only half-heartedly tended to.

Two cells sat side by side not ten feet from the back wall, and less than five feet from the sheriff's desk. On the opposite wall stood a spare chair and the requisite row of filing cabinets—topped by a teetering stack of unfiled paperwork and a jumbled pile of hardware so mixed Monahan couldn't tell what it was . . .or what it used to be. Two stacks of old newspapers swayed on the floor at the end of the file cabinets, and a door behind the desk led, according to the crooked sign, to the courthouse.

He'd got a good, close-up look at Alf for the first time, and allowed that he'd never seen him before, only heard of his handiwork, and showed the tattered voucher for his brother. Pulling his wallet out again, he handed over the precious clipping to Sweeney with a low, "Don't you lose that, hear?"

Sweeney filed it away in his pocket without looking at it.

Alf didn't seem like such a bloodthirsty killer when he was behind bars. He was so thin and lanky he fairly rattled in his clothes, although the age and condition of his frayed and grimy trousers and shirt indicated his physical condition was nothing new.

His visage revealed nothing more. His dull eyes were cloudy, which might explain his poor marksmanship. Or he could very simply be a bad shot.

Monahan didn't much care. He plain took a dislike to the man right off the bat, would have disliked him even if he hadn't been in Alf's sights earlier in the day. It was just the general principle of the thing.

As for his opinion of Sheriff Carmichael, well, that hadn't changed much since the night out at Blue's place. He still found the sheriff too sold on himself to be of any interest, let alone even a feigned friendship.

Sweeney was of a similar opinion. At least, he was no more polite than he had to be, and spent most of the interview slumped in the spare chair, staring at the floor or out at the street.

When the sheriff finally sent them on their way, Monahan was sure of two things. First, Alf would be free of Carmichael's custody within twenty-four hours. He could tell by Alf's confident manner and the state of the jail itself. Even if Dev Baylor turned out to be a seventy-year-old fat widower with rheumy joints and cataracts covering his eyes like peony petals, he could break Alf out of jail between drags on his smoke and never lose a flake of ash.

Unless he was a jackass as dumb as Alf.

Monahan didn't think that was possible. God could play nasty, which was true enough, but He wasn't outright cruel.

Second, Carmichael didn't seem to give a whit about securing his prisoner. The deputy who had been on guard at the door when they arrived had long since gone off duty, and it didn't look much like the sheriff was expecting anybody to take his place. In fact, when Carmichael followed them out, he made a show of locking the jailhouse door behind him, as if that was that.

Monahan was pretty certain a kid could have picked that door lock open with a half-sharp stick. He and Sweeney wandered up the street a bit to let the Arizona air blow the jail stench from their clothes, and then they turned around and walked back down the street to the café.

"Here or the saloon?" Sweeney asked.

"Here, I reckon. Promised the girl I'd bring her some café supper."

Sweeney nodded, and Monahan opened the door and stepped inside.

"Whoa! Ain't seen you fellas for a few minutes!" Sheriff Milton J. Carmichael laughed and stepped back, narrowly avoiding a collision with Monahan. "Crowd got thin in here all of a sudden. Hope it wasn't me what caused it." He gave a wave to the waiter at the front counter.

"Wasn't you, Milt," said the waiter, looking up from his newspaper. "Crowd thins out right about six on weekdays." He jabbed his thumb toward the clock on the back wall. The black, curlicued hands read six-twenty.

Sweeney gave a tip to the brim of his hat. "Be seein' you, Sheriff."

"Yeah, later," Monahan echoed, and they moved toward the rear of the establishment. He slid into the first empty chair they came to.

Sweeney seated himself across the table and picked up a menu. "I hear right? You takin' supper back for that girl?"

Monahan nodded. "'Less you'd rather let her starve."

"I'd ruther she took her meals at her own place."

Monahan raised a brow. "Ain't like you're payin' for 'em."

Sweeney let out a heavy sigh and put down his menu. "This ain't got nothin' to do with money. It's got to do with—"

"Can I take your order, gents?" The waiter stood next to their table, pencil poised over his pad of paper.

Sweeney ordered first, and Monahan ordered the fried chicken dinner, plus one to go. When they had the table to themselves again, Monahan said, "Eat up. You can tell me what you know about Julia and I'll explain what I know when we get back to the hotel."

* * *

While they were leaving the café, Dev Baylor was quietly letting himself into the jail. The front door proved no problem, and, as he had guessed, there was no official presence on the other side. Nobody but his stupid, addlepated, lousy shot of a brother, who stood up in the cell and smiled at the sight of him.

Alf started to say something, but Dev shushed him before he had his mouth all the way open. Alf had a tendency to shout when he was excited, the last thing Dev needed at the moment. He growled, "Don't say nothin' 'less you know where the key is." Alf cocked his head to one side, looked at Dev like he was a loon, and pointed to the wall next to the desk, from which depended a large iron key ring. Dev snatched it off the wall and began to sort through the keys, saying softly, "Any minute. Any minute and we'll have you outta here, Alf."

Monahan and Sweeney exited the café, well satisfied, and bearing a paper-wrapped dinner for Julia. Sweeney stopped for a moment outside on the boardwalk.

Curious, Monahan stopped too, following Sweeney's line of vision. He found himself staring straight up the street at the jailhouse. He couldn't see too clearly, but it looked to him like there was movement around the front door. "What'd you see?"

Sweeney shook his head. "Dunno. Coulda sworn the front door closed. I mean, it was wide open."

"Maybe it was the sheriff. Was he goin' back to the office? Did he say anythin' to you?"

"Fat chance. Of him goin' back to work or tellin' me about it, I mean."

"You thinkin' what I'm thinkin'?"

"Thinkin' you're probably wantin' to get Julia's supper to her 'fore she perishes or it goes cold or both, aren't you?" Sweeney offered, his voice wavering slightly.

"Yeah," muttered Monahan. "Yeah, that's the ticket." Turning, he hurried back down the boardwalk. Sweeney ran after him.

They dropped Julia's supper, complete with rhubarb pie and a tall glass of buttermilk, off at her door and went on upstairs. Sweeney went straight to the chair by the window, sat down, and stuck out his legs. "All right. What the hell's goin' on?"

Monahan scratched at his head. *Where to start?*

"C'mon, Dooley!" Sweeney insisted. "What's the deal with the gal, and with that deal up to the sheriff's office, and—"

"One damn thing at a time." Monahan sat down on the side of his bed and began to pull off his spurs. "First, Miss Julia." He stopped and stared down at the floor, unsure of how to tell the kid about such an awful thing.

Finally, in response to the third prodding, he cleared his throat and started talking. "About . . . about Miss Julia. She don't wanna go home. Fact is, she ain't got no home to go to, no people, either. Her uncle ain't really her uncle at all. He's a no-account that took her in after her folks died of the smallpox—she was eight, then—and moved her out here. He waited till he thought she got old enough—you know, started with her monthlies—and then he set in to rapin' her every chance he got."

Monahan's head shook with saying it out, and with the weight of knowing it. Once again, he was internally urged to go beat the hell out of Julia's 'uncle,' just *because.*

"Jesus," muttered Sweeney. By the look of him, the information had hit him hard. "That's why she said . . . I mean, that's why she talked so tough when we found her. You know, all that stuff about making a livin' on her back just to get away and well, you know. I didn't think she knew what she was talkin' about. But, Jesus."

"Since she was just turned eleven," added Monahan. "And she's thirteen now. Two years is a big chunk of a little kid's life." He dropped the final spur on the floor.

"Of anybody's. So we're takin' her along, then."

"Can't rightly leave her here."

"Nope. We'll have to get her a horse."

Monahan nodded. "I know. Reckon we can get one from Tommy, over at the livery."

"Who?"

The old cowboy smiled, despite everything. "Tommy Hawk. The Indian kid they got workin' over at the stables."

"Tommy Hawk?" asked Sweeney incredulously. "*Tommy Hawk*? You gotta be kiddin' me!"

Chuckling, Dooley shook his head.

"Well, hell!" Sweeney thumbed back his hat. "Maybe he should just up and go with us, too!"

"Mayhap he should," Monahan agreed. "He'll have to get a move on if he wants to leave with us, though."

Butch's brow furrowed.

"That thing up to the sheriff's office. I'm willin' to bet we was witness to a jailbreak."

Sweeney's head dropped forward to hang limply from his shoulders. "Aw, damn."

"Anybody ever say you got a way with words, boy?"

Sweeney snorted.

Just before dawn the two men and the young girl finally set out for the livery. Sweeney saddled the horses while Monahan looked over the rest of the stock and made a mental list of those he found unacceptable and those with promise. Tommy showed up about the time the first fingers of morning light appeared in the east, and Monahan quickly made a good deal on a bay gelding and some used tack.

Julia had been hoping for a wilder-colored, flashier horse, but accepted the bay gratefully. When Tommy admitted he didn't know the horse's name, she christened it Parnell, for reasons known only to her.

To Monahan's mind, it didn't much matter what name you gave a horse, so long as the horse knew it and it wasn't silly. Of course, he had ridden a washed out palomino gelding called Blondie for a while. It wasn't the best name, but then, it wasn't his horse. It was only a loaner after his old horse, Chesapeake, got gored by a Mexican fighting bull and died over in Alamogordo. He'd been against bull fighting before that—he thought it was pointless and not a sport at all—but afterward, he retracted his former opinion. Those bulls were mean through and through and deserved whatever life— or death—handed them.

At any rate, they rode out of town just past five-thirty, before hardly anyone else was up. Keeping to his word, Monahan asked the stable boy if he'd care to accompany them, but Tommy, who apparently didn't care about his joke of a name, declined.

"All right, then." Monahan threw a leg over General Grant. "You change your mind, you can track us."

"Understand." Tommy nodded as he stepped away from the horse. "Good luck to you. To all of you."

"Thank you, Tommy." Monahan reined out into the street to join Sweeney and Julia. "Let's go," he said softly.

They headed on down the street.

Shortly after eight, they stopped for breakfast, and Monahan announced over his coffee mug where they were going. Sweeney and Julia were rapt, for he'd given them no clue earlier. They'd been drifting generally southward with no destination either one of them could think of.

"Got a friend down here, lives on the Old Mormon Trail." Monahan said, out of the blue. "Got a ranch right smack-dab in the middle o' nowhere."

Sweeney frowned. "Mormons in Arizona?"

"Yeah. A battalion of Mormon volunteers marched through here to fight the Mexicans about twenty-five years ago. I figure we can bide there for a spell. At least, until the heat overtakin' Julia dies down."

"Takin' me?" Julia sat up ramrod straight, her spine stiff with umbrage. "You didn't 'take' me. Nobody takes me!"

Sweeney mumbled something just under Monahan's hearing range, and then all hell broke loose. Monahan ducked under Julia's plate, which came sailing through the air without warning and then dove behind a prickly pear. The shouts got louder as Julia screeched something wretched about Sweency's mother.

Sweeney yelled, "Why you so damned touchy? Ouch! That hurt!"

"I wouldn't be so touchy if you could keep your dirty mind outta the gutter!"

"The gutter? What the hell you talkin' about? All I did was make a remark, one you weren't supposed to be hearin'!"

"You badger's butt!"

"Oh, try to make it my fault now! And you set yourself up for it! Ain't my fault if you—"

The fight continued while Monahan—along with the dog—carefully climbed to his feet and stuck his head around the cactus. At least they were out of things to throw. "Hold it!" he yelled, waving his arms. "Just hold it!"

They stopped stock still, and stared at him. Well, glared, more like.

"Damn it, Butch. You made some sorta crack, didn't you?"

Sweeney had the grace to look a little embarrassed, and so Monahan was a little softer on him than he would have been otherwise. He shook his head sadly. "There ain't none so unintentionally cruel as the very young. Now Butch, you keep your smart remarks to yourself. And the same goes for you, Miss Julia." He kept an eye on them while he stepped out from behind the cactus and into the clearing and when he saw Julia start to open her mouth—with the probable intention of using it like a Gatling gun—he said, "I mean it. *Both* of you, Julia."

She closed her mouth with a click, but her eyes still beamed daggers—at both men. She was a pretty little thing but she had one ugly temper.

If she gave him much more trouble, Monahan was likely to dump her on the side of the trail. He was a loner by nature, and already had one extra too many—that being Sweeney—without adding Little Miss Loudmouth to the mix. He was trying to simplify, but God and all His angels—or maybe it was the devil and all his demons—kept doing everything in their power to complicate things.

"All right, then," he said after silence took over the camp and the birds in the surrounding scrub began to softly call and twitter again. "Gather up your stuff. We're pullin' out."

15

Come mid-afternoon, they had turned toward the east when they hit the first signs of the Old Mormon Trail. It was marked on both sides by broken glass that sparkled for miles before and behind them; by abandoned Conestoga wagons with the weathered remains of broken axles plunging upward through wagon beds; by big, heavy objects like pianos or chifforobes discarded after being hauled for miles; and by graves marked with everything from granite slabs to wooden crosses tied together with rotting cloth to simple cairns of rocks. And except for the low hills that marked the distant horizons, there was nothing around but desert.

Sweeney and Julia gawked at first, then became jaded to the sights as the afternoon wore on and the temperature rose. Neither was accustomed to the heat on the flats, and several times Monahan seriously considered calling a halt until the evening.

But that all changed when he saw the first signs of Hoskins' farm. He spied cattle here and there, scattered in the distance ahead. They roamed aimlessly or rooted through the low scrub, looking for anything they might have missed earlier.

As they drew nearer, more and more stray memories floated through his mind like so many wandering balloons. Some floated within his reach, like the face of Buckshot Bob Hoskins' daughter, Meggie, and her little pup, Daisy-June; the inside of the Hoskins' home, the warm kitchen in particular, and the roast beef Buckshot Bob's wife Mae had served on his last visit; and the stock pond Buckshot Bob was just beginning to dig out back behind the barns.

It wasn't much longer before he saw the house and the barns dimly outlined in the distance. He felt his heart flood with joy that he remembered them. Without realizing it, he nudged General Grant into a trot.

The trio gained the Hoskins spread within a half hour. They rode into the yard and dismounted as the house door opened and people poured out.

Monahan recognized Mae and Buckshot Bob right away. He didn't recognize Meggie—who, at fifteen, was almost grown—or her younger brother Robbie, although he was the spitting image of his father. Their dog, Daisy-June, having long left puppyhood behind, followed in their wake, wagging her little stub of a tail behind her.

"Oh, Dooley! Is it you?" Mae cried as she threw

her arms around him. "It's been over eight years, hasn't it, Bob?"

"Nine, mayhap ten!" Bob's wide grin was framed by a close-cropped goatee and graying mustaches. He kept slapping Monahan on the back, barking out a big belly laugh, and then slapping him again.

As for Monahan, he just laughed and laughed.

Buckshot Bob Hoskins had met up with Monahan long ago, back when he was trying to retrieve his memories of Iowa and his folks, Missouri and Monty's Raiders, and Kathleen.

After two long nights on the front porch, too many cigarettes, and countless pots of coffee, Buckshot Bob and Monahan had relived their experiences together through the years up to just prior to the Civil War. Sweeney had sat with them and listened.

The two old friends sat on the porch steps, the yard filled with crushed out and discarded smokes before them and a half-gone pitcher of lemonade between them. Sweeney sat behind so as not to intrude, the slow rhythmic meter of his rocking reminding Monahan of home and Iowa, of his ma rocking softly while she sewed and mended in the main room when he was just a little tyke and had been put down for a nap. The sound soothed him as he listened to the tale of his wandering during the years before the war.

He remembered most of it with Buckshot Bob there to provoke his mind, but part of it sounded like something out of a storybook—outlandish tales some writer had made up, featuring a hero—or maybe a villain—who happened to carry the name of Dooley Monahan. He was torn about that part.

He leaned back, resting his spine against the center step, and lit a fresh smoke. "My goodness," he said as he exhaled. "That's quite a story, there, Bob. I greatly appreciate you takin' the time to remember it, and to say it all out for me."

Bob poured them each a fresh glass of lemonade, then turned and offered the pitcher to Sweeney, who shook his head. "Had enough, thanks."

Bob put the pitcher back down and pulled his fixings pouch from his pocket.

He yanked it open, then looked up. "Dooley, I swan, that's three times you've rode in here and three times I've said it out for you. You ought to write it down or somethin'. I mean . . . I might get killed before you ride through again!"

Monahan smiled. "Ain't dead yet, are you?"

Buckshot Bob Hoskins threw his hands in the air, snapping, "That's what you said last time!"

Monahan caught the fixings bag in midair before it had the chance to pick up any dust from the ground and handed it back. "Mayhap that's why you're still kickin', Bob. Ever think o' that?"

Behind him, Sweeney laughed softly.

Beside, Bob furrowed his brow.

Sweeney had listened to everything Buckshot Bob had told Monahan for three nights, and he had to admit that the old cowboy had surely had one hell of a tangled life. He'd sure been banged up a lot, too. Been thumped upside the head more often than Hector had pups! Any other fellow would've been dead, but Monahan? No way! It had made him a little scrambled in his brain, but he was still around.

Now, that was the sign of one tough customer!

Of course, the story Bob had told didn't really match up, Sweeney thought. More like, the story was broken into three segments—one long stretch of time and two short ones. The long one lasted from Dooley's time with Monty's Raiders back to, well, Iowa and his childhood. The next one, shorter than the first, was about Kathleen and his wild times in the South. And the third was later still, up around the end of the Civil War. He imagined Monahan's whole life as a great big hunk of Swiss cheese, all full of holes filled with nothing but mystery, and none of them connected. Not that he could figure, anyhow.

If he'd had access to paper and pen, he would have tried to chart it out, to figure the big empty places still remaining and the ones that had been filled in by Bob. He figured there were big, deep holes that would surprise the puddin' out of Monahan himself, things buried so deep he had forgotten that he'd forgotten!

Sweeney hadn't had a chance to talk about it. Bob and Mae had put him up in Robbie's room like he was some kind of kid, and Monahan was sleeping in the barn, by his own choice.

He hadn't had a chance to talk to Julia, either. She was bunking in with Meggie, and the girls were having a high time of it, whispering and giggling, and doing all kinds of, well, *girl* stuff. He had no time for any of it, and they in turn had no time for him whatsoever. Even the Blue dog wasn't giving him the time of day, preferring to follow Hoskins' dog, Daisy-June, around like she was the beginning and end-all of the world.

Only his horse, Chili, seemed to have the slightest interest in him, and that was only around feeding time.

But nothing could disinterest him in the story he'd been hearing out on the front porch, and nothing could pull him from Monahan's side. Not even the threat of the Baylor boys, who might be coming from the north at any minute. Not even that story about "Man Eater" Monahan and the business with the alligator. Sweeney had latched on to the old cowboy, for good or ill, and once he got his boots slid into the stirrups, he stayed around for the whole ride.

He rolled onto his side. Robbie was asleep on the other bed, and he watched the boy's chest slowly rise and fall a couple of times before rolling all the way over to his back. He stared at the ceiling and wondered what the Baylor boys were doing. Had they set out in the right direction once they got clear of Iron Creek? Had they made it out of Iron Creek in the first place?

He made a face at the darkness. That was a stupid question. Milton J. Carmichael couldn't keep a weak dog on a strong chain, let alone Alf Baylor in jail!

Sweeney snorted at the moon, which he could see through the window. It hung in the sky, bright and high and almost full, making promises only the moon can make, and then promptly ignoring the consequences of its empty guarantees. The moon was nothing but a snake-oil salesman, he thought. Prettier than most, but just as untrustworthy.

"Moon's nice tonight." Alf stood about ten feet out from the campfire, staring upward. A half-smoked cigarette hung limply from his fingers.

His brother sat about the same distance from him, shaking his head. Since they'd ridden out of Iron City Alf had carried on about the moon or the grass or the trees or the cactus. Not once had he so much as noticed that Dev had broken him out of jail again. He shook his head again, mumbling, "You'd think he'd take note o' something like that. You'd think he'd at least say thanks or something."

You'd think . . . well, you'd think a lot of things, but where Alf was concerned? You'd be wrong every time.

Dev sighed. "You're gonna burn your fingers."

Quickly, Alf looked down at his hand. The smoke was, indeed, burning very close to his fingertips, and he threw it down and stomped the life out of it.

"It's out," Dev said, when Alf kept on stomping.

Alf ignored him.

"Alf! You already got it!"

"What?" Alf said, giving a final stamp of his foot.

Dev slowly shook his head. "Never mind. Better get back by the fire."

"Sure," Alf replied absently. He made his way back to the fire and slumped down next to his bedroll. "I ain't sure we're goin' the right way," he said, out of the blue.

Actually, Dev wasn't certain either, but he played along. "Then, just where do you think we oughta be goin'?"

Alf didn't hesitate. "North."

Dev scratched at his chin. "Why north?"

Alf shrugged. "The moon told me."

Well, that was a new one. Clouds had talked to him before. Trees, sagebrush, the occasional saguaro cactus, titmice, badgers, pronghorn, even the wind—they all talked to Alf at one time or another. But never the moon.

Dev, torn between amusement and wanting to thump his brother with an axe handle, asked, "Why's the moon talkin' to you all of a sudden? I mean, why ain't it talkin' to the president or the queen or somebody?"

"Dunno. Mayhap they ain't awake." Alf spread out his blanket. "We got any biscuits left?"

"Pan by the fire."

Alf helped himself. He popped one in his mouth, whole, then managed to say around it, "Any coffee?"

"By the fire."

Alf poured himself a cup and Dev, hidden by

shadows, shook his head again, thinking they'd been dead wrong to bust Alf out of that asylum. At least he hadn't sleep-talked any of that crazy English stuff—roos and wallabies, whatever they were—while they were on the trail. Seemed to Dev, Alf was always trying to get himself killed, or worse, get him killed.

One day, he was bound to succeed.

Dev let out a heavy sigh and considered Alf's recommended direction. North was exactly where he figured Dooley Monahan wasn't headed, but he decided to keep it to himself for a bit. "I'll keep that in mind, Alf. I mean, what the moon has to say. But I wanna keep on headin' west for another day or so. Just to make sure."

Alf, who was already half asleep, muttered, "Just to make sure," and turned over, putting his back to Dev before his breathing deepened. Sleep settled over him like a mantle.

16

The next day was a Sunday, so Monahan was a little surprised when Buckshot Bob came stomping into the barn at six in the morning, serious as a heart attack, and began feeding and grooming the the six big bays stalled alongside the old cowboy's sleeping place. Being understandably curious, he stretched his legs and arms, and sat up.

"Whatcha doin' there, Buckshot Bob?" he asked softly, so as not to startle either the man or the horses.

Bob didn't startle easily. Without missing a brushstroke, he said, "Now Dooley, what's it look like I'm up to?" He chortled softly under his breath.

Monahan stood up. "Well, it appears to me like you're tryin' to brush all the bay off that gelding. What you expectin' to find underneath?"

Buckshot Bob's chortle turned into a guffaw. "You're a real card, Dooley. If you gotta know, today's a workday around here, just like every other Friday, Sunday, and Wednesday."

Monahan's face bunched up. He hadn't noticed Bob giving the horses any special grooming on Friday. But then, he'd gone to bed late Thursday night and had let himself sleep in for a bit in the morning. Hell, it had been past nine when he woke. He looked closely at the bays. Come to think of it, these weren't even the same horses!

Buckshot Bob finished with the first horse, and began to work on the second.

"I don't mean to be buttin' in, but you're sure doin' a bum job of it if you're planning to take 'em out for a ride."

Bob turned around and laughed right out loud. "Dooley, you really *was* down for the count on Friday mornin'! And here I was thinkin' you was fakin' it."

Monahan opened up his mouth, then closed it again. Finally, he said, "Now, you really got me confuddled! What the hell you up to, Bob?"

Currycomb in one hand, body brush in the other, Bob paused and turned toward him. "Thought it was obvious, Dooley. I'm gettin' these six ready for a quick switch out for when the stage comes in."

Monahan let out a big chest full of air with an audible sigh. "Well, damn! Now that crappy groomin' job you're doin' makes sense!" He found himself some brushes and went to work on the third horse, a leggy bay mare.

The two men, working in tandem, had all the horses groomed and turned out in a matter of minutes. Buckshot Bob had a look at his watch. One grizzled eyebrow shot up in question. "I think we about got time for a cuppa coffee before the stage comes roarin' in here."

Dooley nodded in response.

When they gained the house, Mae was already pouring them steaming cups of coffee. Buckshot Bob grinned at her when she shoved a mug into his hands. After taking a sip, he asked, "You spied us from the window, didn't you?"

A quick nod and the hint of a smile indicated yes, she'd been spying on him, and yes, that's why she had the coffee ready, and that he'd best drink it down if he expected to be ready when the stage pulled in.

People, Monahan mused, were the same wherever you went. Married folks, anyway. And then it came to him, he and Kathy. Had they communicated in this silent sort of married people's Morse code? It occurred to him they must have done just that, if he so easily recognized it in others.

He smiled a little and tested his coffee. It was hot, but not too hot to drink. He watched Mae poke bacon inside a fresh-baked biscuit and hand it to young Robbie on his way out the door. "You makin' those for any who as ask?"

"Oh, not for just anyone." She grinned, poked a couple of strips into another biscuit, and handed it to him. "Only for folks I love."

"Thankee, ma'am." He took a big bite.

The biscuit was barely swallowed when he heard a commotion out front.

Bob grabbed his arm. "That's for us." He headed

out the back door again, with Monahan dogging his tracks to keep up.

And speaking of dogs, he hadn't seen Blue all morning. Now, Blue usually came down to the barn with Buckshot Bob in the mornings, to lick Dooley awake. Or sort through his pockets, more like. He'd made the mistake of nodding off with a couple of Mae's good sugar cookies in his shirt pocket one night, and that was what had awakened him the next morning—Blue's big old nose and hot, snuffling breath, spreading his pocket wide to get at those cookies!

"Ease up, there, Dooley!" Buckshot Bob called from across the paddock. "They gotta take time to use the outhouse and eat a bite of breakfast afore they take off again."

Relieved at the news, Monahan slowed down. A little. Reaching the barn, he helped Buckshot Bob harness the six bays. It wasn't until he had the last of his three horses strapped into its harness that he said anything about the dog.

"Oh, he's around," said Buckshot Bob. "I mean, where's he gonna go?"

"Ain't like him, that's all," Monahan grumbled. "Usually, I have to shove him outta my way every two minutes until I give him his breakfast."

Bob laughed. "In case you ain't noticed, he's a lot more interested in our Daisy-June than in anythin' else, lately. A bitch in heat'll distract even the keenest cow dog, y'know."

Monahan thumbed the strap through its buckle and pulled it tight, muttering, "Not this one, it don't." He moved to the head of the lead horse and walked it outside. Just as he turned to take the horses toward the road and the front of the house, he heard something new. A shout! The shout of a kid in distress.

He turned toward the noise and found himself facing the outbuildings, just as another cry sounded. Without thinking, he dropped the reins of the horse and sprinted toward the sound, calling, "Hold on, keep hollerin'! I'm comin', I'm comin'!"

He skidded to a halt before the first shed. The kid hadn't called out again, and Monahan pictured him inside one of the outbuildings, hanging by his fingertips—or toes—from a rafter over a pack of snarling wolves. He threw open the door and was greeted by a sea of saddles and other tack hanging from ropes depending from the ceiling. "Kid!" he cried. "Kid! You in here?"

The voice sounded again, but it was weaker than before. More strangled, he thought. It came from outside, and far away.

He ran outside, slammed the door behind him, and raced around to the back of the shed. There, he found himself facing the stock pond. Alone and at the bottom of a shallow rise, it sat against clay colored banks, its shallow water still and muddy.

He scanned the banks, but could see nothing until his eyes came to rest on a clump of boulders and weeds on the far edge of the water. There, he picked out the shape of a dog, muddy and bedraggled. Softly, he said, "Blue?" even though he didn't recognize him, and knew the dog couldn't hear him. No sign of a human.

Suddenly, the dog tucked its head and with a mighty heave, shook itself free of the mud and water. Then it turned. It seemed to be paying a great deal of attention to something on the ground.

Monahan turned to his left, which looked to be the shortest way around the pond and broke into a jog just as Bob burst from between the two sheds ahead of him, shouting, "Dooley! Dooley, you hear me?"

"Here! Behind you!" then pointed across the pond. "There! On the far bank!"

Buckshot Bob took off, running toward the dog, and Monahan—who suddenly realized how out of breath he was—slid down and sat right on the ground. He squinted and watched, while across the way, Bob closed in on the dog and whatever it was he was guarding.

"Oh, God!" Bob shouted when he gained the dog's position. "Robbie, Robbie!" He dropped to his knees, then rose up again, the boy's limp body dangling in his arms.

Butch Sweeney peeked out front and saw the stage parked there, and the men hurriedly unhitching the spent team. He hadn't been prepared for it, but he found it exciting just the same. Had Monahan suspected? He couldn't imagine the old man had, or he would have said something.

He stepped into the kitchen with a grin on

his face, ready to greet the new day and the new visitors.

He found four strangers seated around the table along with Julia and Meggie, and Mae trying to keep up with the demand for flapjacks. Bob, Monahan, and Robbie were nowhere in sight, so he nonchalantly pulled out a chair and sat himself down. "I'll take a stack o' them flapjacks if you don't mind, Miss Mae."

"Certainly, Butch!" she replied. "Let me introduce our stagecoach passengers to you." She pointed first to a somber fellow in a back-East suit. "This is Dr. Forbes." Dr. Forbes nodded, and she moved to the next fellow. "And next to him is Billy Burness. Across from them are sitting Mrs. Matthews and Miss Coltrane." Mae turned to the stove and flipped the flapjacks in their skillet.

"How do, folks?" Sweeney asked, all the while giving Miss Coltrane the eye. Danged if she wasn't as pretty as a sunset on the prairie! He suddenly wished he'd bothered to put on clean clothes before he came sashaying into the kitchen.

Miss Coltrane started to open her mouth, but Mrs. Matthews, a paunchy, weather-beaten old crone with a thick mustache, beat her to it. "We do quite well, thank you, young man. And what was your name again?"

He swallowed nervously. "I'm Butch Sweeney, Mrs. Matthews, ma'am."

"Mrs. Matthews?!" she blurted, scratching at the wart on her nose. "No, my dear, I'm Miss Coltrane!" Suddenly, she burst out in a rough guffaw that seemed to go on and on, whereas Butch suddenly wanted to be out in the hayloft where he could quietly put a pistol to his head. "Sorry, ma'am, I didn't mean to—"

Her big, rough hand came to rest, hard, on his back, and knocked the air out of him. "Don't think twice about it, Butch. Why, she's as flattered as I am!"

The young woman next to her didn't look the least bit flattered. In fact, she looked as if she'd like to borrow that head-shooting pistol from Butch and then turn it on Miss Coltrane!

In the end he was saved by Dr. Forbes, who sensed his distress. "Now, Miss Coltrane, let the poor boy eat his breakfast!" He said it with enough doctoral harrumphs of authority that she did, indeed, desist.

Safe for the moment, Butch accepted a stack of flapjacks slathered with butter, and helped himself to the syrup. Giving a whispered "Sorry!" to the pretty Mrs. Matthews before he dug in, he managed to wolf down more than half the stack before Mae suddenly froze in her tracks. With a horrific expression on her face, she stared out the window over the sink.

"Mae?" he said softly, and then again, "Mae?" His tone quieted the travelers.

She didn't turn toward him. Still staring, her mouth opened, and her voice trembled. "Robbie!"

Sweeney burst out of the kitchen, running full tilt toward the line of small outbuildings to the northeast. He couldn't see Robbie—or anyone else—but he knew the outbuildings formed a sort of crooked little maze that screened the house from the stock pond.

It wasn't until he was most of the way to the first building that he heard Monahan's shout over the sound of his own footsteps and his own panting breath. "Upside down, Bob! Upside down! You gotta drain the water from his lungs!"

He knew then what had happened, and despite his own hollow pants, forced himself into a harder run.

Buckshot Bob had finally got the boy upside down by the time Monahan had reached his side, but he still wasn't doing it right. The kid was dying before his eyes, and he couldn't stand for that! He fairly tore the boy from his father's arms and held him upside down, jouncing him up and down, up and down with hard jerks until the child finally expelled a good amount of muddy fluid with a spasmodic shudder and a strangled cough.

Monahan next laid him on the ground, face-first, and began to pump the rest of the water out of him. When Buckshot Bob figured out what he was doing, Monahan moved aside and let him take over. It was better for the boy to come back to consciousness and find his daddy was saving him, he reckoned. Better his daddy than some beat up old saddle tramp who was only there a few days.

Butch came skidding up beside him, breathless and muttering, "Is he okay? Is he okay?"

The boy was stirring, and Monahan nodded.

"He's fine. Gonna be fine and dandy." He put a hand on Buckshot Bob's shoulder and added, "That's enough, Bob. You pump at him anymore, you're gonna make him spit up his lungs."

Smiling like a madman, Bob turned the boy faceup, pulled him up, and crushed him to his chest. "Robbie, my Robbie." He wept.

Robbie's arms came up to circle his pa's neck and he began to weep, too.

"Let's get him back up to the house," Monahan said.

Buckshot Bob got to his feet, carrying the boy. They started toward the house before Monahan remembered the dog.

"Take him on back," Dooley said to Butch. "I'll take care of the horses." *And the dog,* he thought. As the others walked back to the house, he cast his gaze about for Blue, and found him not far from where he'd last seen him—standing over the place where he'd dragged the unconscious boy, his coat still dripping with muddy water.

"Damned if you ain't somethin' else, dog," he said quietly, shaking his head. For a moment, he wondered if it was some sort of shift in the eternal equilibrium of things. The dog had lost one boy scarcely older that Robbie, and he had just insured that Robbie kept on breathing—quite literally—for some time to come.

He shook his head again and felt a chill shudder through him. Surely the Good Lord would strike him dead for even thinking . . .

But the Lord didn't strike him, and he pushed

the thought—the whole business—from his mind, squatted down on his haunches, and held out his hand, repeating, "You're somethin' else, Blue."

Wagging its hindquarters, the dog came over to him, sat down, and held forth its wet paw.

"What? You wanna shake my hand?"

The dog waved its paw in the air, and Monahan took it and gave it a firm, pumping shake before he stood up again. "You better come on, Blue. I gotta get them horses, or else find 'em if they run off! And you, you old blue goose, we gotta dig you out from all that mud you're dryin' under." He started toward the backs of the outbuildings with the dog, rear end wiggling, at his heels.

17

"Because, in my 'sperience, most medical men are the honest sort," Monahan said.

It was the next afternoon, and he and Sweeney and young Julia and Blue were on the road again, traveling west, backtracking over the Mormon Trail. They had set out at six in the morning, and Monahan was just getting around to telling the others what had possessed him to leave Mae and Bob's so early in the morning, especially when they were so grateful about the rescue of their boy they probably would have been happy to let them move in, permanent-like. As it was, a weeping Mae had stuffed a gunnysack full of food for the trail, and it clunked against Julia's leg once for every strike of her horse's left front foot.

"Doesn't mean *he* was," Butch said doggedly. He hadn't let up once he started in.

"Don't mean as how he wasn't, either," Monahan answered, probably extending Butch's question and answer session for another half hour. But he was almost past caring.

"Oh, stop it, you two!" Julia growled. "Honest to Pete!" She turned toward Monahan. "All he asked was why we cut out like that. Without talkin' it over, I mean. I mean, he means. He meant. Oh, cripes! Now you got me all confused, too!"

"Sorry, Miss Julia," Monahan said with a tip of his hat. And for the instant, he truly meant it.

"Then, can we stop and have lunch *now*?" she asked.

"If we're votin', put me down for her side," Sweeney jumped in. "I'm hungry!"

"That stuff Mae packed up for us looks too good to put off eatin' any longer!" Julia had herself set on it.

"All right, all right," Monahan said in self-defense, reining General Grant over to one side of the trail. The ground was littered with too much broken glass to veer all the way off, he figured.

Those Mormons had sure been bottle slingers! he thought as he dismounted. When the sun was right, its light glittered off two endless lines of broken bottles—baby bottles, jars of fruit or vegetables, patent medicine, with an occasional broken mirror or lantern shade thrown in for variety—that bracketed the trail the Mormon wagons had worn into the land. There was enough glittering glass that if he could paint something on it to hold the light for a few extra hours, a man could travel in light all the way to California, even after sundown! That was sure one humdinger of an idea, wasn't it?

Smiling to himself, he scratched General Grant's forehead.

That wouldn't work. It had to be oil lamps! If he could just set down a lit oil lamp every ten feet or so . . .

"Wake up!" Julia at him.

He blinked. Apparently he'd been daydreaming. Julia and Butch had dismounted and were staring at him with the most incredulous looks on their faces.

Monahan cleared his throat and scratched the back of his neck. "Sorry."

It was enough. Sweeney still stared at him, but Julia held out a sack, its mouth open. "Ham, fried chicken, or boiled eggs. You choose."

"Beg pardon?"

"Which do you want? We've got ham, fried chicken, and boiled eggs . . . and bread to make sandwiches." She was looking at him like he was a ninny.

Well, he supposed he was. "Fried chicken, if you please.

"Best water the horses, boy," he instructed, to give the young cowboy something to keep him from thinking any questions going on in his head. "Dog's bound to be thirsty, too."

Sweeney let out a bland, "Right," without looking at him. As he retrieved the canteens he looked back several times to see how Julia was coming along with the vittles bag. When he returned with the water, Monahan held out the General's empty nose bag and Blue's bowl and Butch filled both.

It turned out he wasn't the one Monahan needed to worry about.

After she'd handed Sweeney a thick ham sandwich, given a couple of pieces of fried hen to Monahan, and pulled a couple of thick pieces of ham off the bone for herself Julia sat on the ground and said, "So, start from the beginnin', Dooley."

She munched on her ham and stared at him like she thought if she stared long enough, he would eventually tell her what she wanted to hear.

She was right.

He pulled up some ground and sat down across from her, barely aware Sweeney had sat down and was listening intently. "All right. The reason we left first thing this mornin' was that I was afraid if we didn't, the reason for leavin' would get lost in the shuffle."

"I'm lost right now," said Julia.

"Don't blame you, missy. Let me say out more of it, and mayhap you can put the pieces together better 'n me. I'm a little confuddled on the details."

She narrowed her brows, but stayed quiet.

"Reckon Butch has already told you about Buckshot Bob bein' my livin' memory for a few years of my life." He took a bite of chicken.

She nodded.

He chewed for a bit, then swallowed. "I want you should keep listenin' and he should keep on tellin', 'cause if anythin' should happen to ol' Buckshot Bob, you'll be the ones I'm lookin' up every decade or so." He stared at Julia. "Got that?"

"Yes, sir."

He looked toward Sweeney.

The young cowboy looked up from his sandwich. "Got it."

Monahan nodded, snorted out air, and took another bite of chicken. It was dang tasty, if you asked him.

"All right. Well, now we got that settled . . . yesterday morning, when we had us that hurrah about young Robbie and the stock pond and ol' Blue—"

The dog barked at the mention of his name, and Monahan paused to smile and ruffle the speckled hair between Blue's ears.

He continued. "Anyway, while the doc was seein' to Robbie, Butch and the driver was out on the front porch, talkin' 'bout what was goin' on out West. Driver happened to mention a little place— wide spot on the trail, more like—called Heber's Kiss. Said he'd stopped there about a week, maybe a week and a half ago. Am I right, Butch?"

Sweeney, having a mouthful of ham sandwich, nodded his head enthusiastically.

"Anyhow, don't nothin' much go on out there. According to the stage driver's story, the old man who owned the saloon passed on. It was natural-like, no bullets or Apache involved, but before he went, he give over his share in the Lucky Strike Bar to a feller just passin' through town. His name was Vince George. And I recalled that I knowed a Vince George from way back. He was ridin' with Monty's Raiders when I joined up. He was the first one who beat my brains into a pulp." Monahan took another bite of chicken and said, "I owe him."

Julia and Sweeney had stopped eating, and were staring at each other. He looked more than a little perturbed, and she appeared confused.

Monahan squeezed his lips shut. He'd been expecting more from them. Anything at all would have been nice! Finally, he said, "What?!"

With a frown on his face, Sweeney asked, "Is that why you brung her along? Revenge? When she could have stayed back at Buckshot Bob's and got the benefit of some book learnin'?"

Monahan had brought her along because . . . well, because she was there. And, much as he hated to admit it, he was used to her. But he didn't say that. Instead, he snapped, "You wanna be the one to take her back?"

Sweeney started to say something he was most likely going to regret, but Julia beat him to it. "I don't care whether he wants to or not. I'm stayin' with you and Blue. So there. I feel like I gotta get my revenge on somebody, and it don't much matter who. This Vince George is as good a candidate as anybody."

While Sweeney's mouth hung open at her clipped words, she turned to him. "And don't you go questionin' Dooley Monahan! This is his trip, and I'm along for the ride just like you are."

Sweeney closed his mouth with a click.

"So, how you gonna recognize him after all these years?" she asked, twisting back toward Monahan. "By my reckonin' it's been twenty or so years since you seen him."

"Oh, I'll know him," Dooley said with assurance. "You will, too. He's got a long scar upside his face."

He drew an imaginary line with his finger from his cheek, up through his eye, through his eyebrow, and past his hairline. "He got cut bad in a knife fight, and once you seen it, you won't forget it. Got a way about him, too. Acts like a scofflaw."

She snorted. "Never met a feller who didn't."

"Well, you met me!" Sweeney stopped his canteen halfway up to his mouth. "I ain't no outlaw."

"I said, 'acts like,' not that you *were* one," she insisted.

"All right, children," Monahan said, hoping to belittle them into silence. "Enough."

Interestingly, he got the loudest yelp of protest from Sweeney. "Don't go callin' me that!" he cried, hopping to his feet. "Just 'cause I'm younger than you don't mean I'm some child. Hell, everybody's younger than you!"

Too late, he realized his insult and cringed, fearing the worst.

But Monahan just laughed until his sides hurt. "Boy howdy, Butch, you have surely got some bark on you!"

That night, they found a small area where Monahan felt it was safe to lead the horses off the road a ways, and they made camp. Sweeney told Julia the story of Monahan's life—he was up to the part with the alligator—and she listened while making supper. It was a makeshift stew with chunks of leftover ham and chicken and vegetables Mae had included in the bag.

As for Monahan, he lay on his bedroll, hands clasped behind his head, drifting in and out of sleep. He thought he was too excited about his impending meeting with Vince George to relax, but found excitement had been replaced by a calm inner surety. Things were finally going the way they were supposed to, and he was finally feeling . . . justified. Whether it was right or not, it was justified, by God!

Three days away from Monahan's position, the Baylor boys had stopped for the day, too. Dev washed his dirty clothes in the nearby creek and was setting the coffeepot on a flat rock near the fire when Alf suddenly exploded. "Gawdammit!"

Dev heaved a sigh before he glanced over.

Alf sat across from him, his right hand cradling his left, while he quietly swore a blue streak into the night.

Softly, Dev asked, "Hurt yourself, there, Alf?"

Alf stared out at the ground before him, scowling. "Damn knife. Playin' mumble peg."

Dev shook his head almost imperceptibly. "Lemme see your hand."

His brother pulled the hand closer in to his chest. "No."

Dev shrugged his shoulders. "Okay, fine. If you don't care if you get blood poisonin', I guess I don't neither." He went back to staring at the coffeepot.

Alf had been asking to get knocked upside the head for the last three nights. He'd been talking in his sleep—that weird sort of jabber, on and on . . . and two of those nights he'd wakened Dev in the middle of the night with tirades on everything from the lousy job the blacksmith three towns back had done, to why he was certain if a man got on a boat in California and sailed straight west he'd land in London, to how cheddar cheese got to be yellow when it was made from white milk, just like Swiss. The sweat of mice was his answer, to which Dev could think of absolutely nothing in the way of a counter.

At any rate, he had been too tired to put up much of a fight, although he finally told Alf, "When we get to the coast, you can get on a ship and sail west. Just make sure to ask what happened to Asia and Europe once you get to London.

As he watched his brother cradling his hand, Dev hoped Alf had finally done something with fatal consequences to himself, if only so he'd shut the hell up.

After a few minutes of silence, Alf said, "Dev? Would you look at it now?"

Dev sighed, then held out his hand. "Give it here."

Alf did, and Dev turned it over, searching through the grime. He found one small wound—a little blood blister which looked to have been caused by a too-close association with the dull edge of Alf's pocketknife. He let go of the hand. "You'll live," he said, grudgingly.

"Ain't gonna git poisoned blood?" Alf asked.

"No. You clean them squirrels you shot this afternoon?"

There was a long pause before Alf said, "No. Sorry."

"Well, sorry don't get us fed. Best get 'em cleaned, and now."

After another long pause, he mumbled, "I meant I was sorry 'cause I ain't got 'em."

Dev narrowed his eyes. "What'd you do? Lose 'em along the trail someplace? You beat everything, you know that, Alfonse? Just everything! What you propose we have for our dinner now?"

Alf looked down and shrugged. Dev knew he was suitably cowed. Best to call a halt before he got his back up. "All right. I reckon I can just make extra biscuits."

"We got enough honey?"

Dev shook his head and growled under his breath. His brother Alf beat all!

Later, while Alf was scraping at the bottom of the honey jar, Dev checked his laundry drying on the nearby bushes and announced, "Come mornin', we're going south."

Alf looked up. "Why come?"

"Thought you'd be happy. You're the one who wanted so bad to stop goin' west."

"I wanted to go north, not south!"

Dev nodded. "So you did, so you did. But I don't think Monahan went that way. My money's on the south. Maybe the south of Arizona, not California."

"Aw, damn!" Alf said with a scowl. "That's a whole territory we gotta backtrack!"

"Not the way I got it figured. You just calm yourself, Alf, and lemme take care of it." The truth was he wasn't certain where to head, but he knew it wasn't to the north, and it sure wasn't toward the west. At least not any farther than they'd already traveled. He figured Dooley Monahan was close by, holed up in some little smidge of a town where there were hardly any people. That fit southern Arizona the best. Well, about all of Arizona if you wanted to get right down to it, but since they were closer to the southern part, he was sticking to his story.

Besides, he'd like to get the killing of Monahan over and done with while he still had clean clothes.

"You sure?"

"Sure as anythin'. Go ahead and eat that last biscuit, Alf. I ain't hungry anymore." Actually, Alf had just polished off the last of the honey, and Dev had the capacity to eat only so many dry biscuits.

"Why, thanks, Dev!" Alf scooped it up.

When the hoot owls had come out to serenade and the bats had swarmed out of their caves to catch flying insects on the wing, Alf, who was supposedly asleep, suddenly sat up. "You reckon Jason left us anythin'? Like, in his will?"

"Jason? He probably didn't have no will."

"You can't be sure though, can you?"

Dev turned over to face him. "I can't be sure about anythin', but you knew him as well as I did. And he wasn't the sort to go makin' out a will."

"But—"

"Just go to sleep, Alf."

18

Morning found Monahan, Sweeney, and Julia still on the Old Mormon Trail, slowly taking them west toward California. Monahan mused as he rode. He hoped the kids would keep repeating his life story, or at least the chunk Buckshot Bob held for him. It was real exciting, once he'd divorced himself from it and made it seem like someone else's life.

Once they got to the Colorado River, Monahan had it in his mind they'd turn south and follow its banks past Yuma, to where Heber's Kiss was supposed to be. He'd never been there, but he'd heard a few hands speak of it over the years. It was supposed to be a pretty dismal place, all told, with a combination store saloon, practically no populace, and no law to speak of.

Just the sort of place Vince George would end up leading him to, he thought. Some no-account, sun-bleached corner of hell.

But it was just as well that the outlaw hadn't

chosen a more populated spot, with more possibilities for witnesses. Fighting it out to the end might as well happen in Heber's Kiss, where there would be few people to laugh at Monahan if he failed, and no one to lock him up if he came out the winner . . . especially since he didn't plan to give the other man a fair chance. No fairer than he'd already received at Vince George's hands, anyway. He had Sweeney and the dog, but didn't suppose the two of them together could make up for a sidekick chosen from any one of Monty's Raiders, especially Red Usher.

As he plodded along, Monahan could hear the outlaw's silly, girlish titter and remembered the rifle butt cracking his skull for the third time. It was a highly unpleasant sound, that titter—forever after associated with crippling pain—and it marked the beginning of Monahan's unraveling patchwork of a life.

Although Red hadn't struck the first blow or the hardest—those had been dealt by Vince—he had struck the last, and it was the one that had sent the young Dooley tumbling down the lifelong maze he had come to know—and forget, and remember, and forget again—as his existence on earth. A life with no past, no future, only a present; a life without a woman or children or grandchildren; a life without stability, without a place to call home, with no history, good or ill, and a life forever on the scout. He realized for the first time, it was what those idiot boys had clubbed him toward and what they had made him into.

He was going to have his vengeance, by God. He was going to make Vince sorry he'd ever *heard* of Dooley Monahan.

And so, he found himself smiling as he called a temporary halt. The horses needed rest and water, and he decided he'd like to sit on something that wasn't moving. He dismounted, watered the General and Blue, then sat down in the center of that wide, rutted excuse for a road and had himself a long drink of cool water. Combined with the certainty of his plan and the big blue dog climbing into his lap, it was the best water he'd tasted since Hector was a pup.

Julia sat down in the middle of the road, too, but it was getting old. She wondered what on earth Monahan was smiling about? She shot Sweeney a questioning look, but his only response was to wiggle his eyebrows at her. She decided she would never, not so long as she lived, understand the male of the species. If she asked a boy under the age of twelve a question, he'd say something mean or hit her and run away. Anyone over that age would pretend she was joking or he was joking or somebody, somewhere, was joking. Mostly she figured to never expect a straight answer at all.

Blue whined, and Monahan held the bowl up for him, never once adjusting the smile on his face. Julia watched, remembering the dog being in town a couple of times in the past. She remembered Sheriff Carmichael back in Iron Creek had hated him. Her uncle, along with most of the shopkeepers in town, hadn't liked the dog much either.

She wondered why. He seemed awful sweet, all curled up on Monahan's lap, or at least as much of him as would fit. His nose was pointed straight up in the air so Monahan could keep scratching his throat up and down, up and down. Blue made funny little chirps that started out high-pitched, then wound down maybe three octaves and ended in exceedingly self-satisfied, happy, low groans. She thought of them as "yummy" sounds.

Sweeney had watered his horse and was sitting with Monahan and Julia, but kept quiet, not paying much attention to either. He was getting tired of being Monahan's toady, tired of doing everything Monahan's way. He had wanted to ride with the famous Dooley Monahan because he'd thought the old cowboy would have some magical information to share, some sort of mystique that would rub off on him. So far, the only thing that had rubbed off was dog hair.

Well, there was the Vince George character to consider. 'Course, he dated from way back in Dooley's life. He was likely a half-dead old cripple, plagued by rheumatism, arthritis, and a lifelong case of worms! And the scabies! And those dementia trembler things, from years of living inside a whiskey bottle.

The longer Sweeney thought on it, the worse candidate for a gunfight Vince George became. In fact, it didn't take long for him to reduce the outlaw to an incoherent, syphilitic, pustule-covered, moronic invalid who no longer knew which end of a gun the bullet came out.

But, then again . . .

Sweeney shook his head and mumbled, "Don't think about it. Thinking only brings trouble." A glance at Monahan showed he was on his feet and getting ready to mount up. Julia was just getting to her feet, so Sweeney did, too. He decided not to say anything, not yet. He'd ride to Heber's Kiss and take a look at the Vince George fellow, and when he turned out to be a silly old man and nothing more than a monster under the bed built solely from Monahan's faulty memory, Sweeney would tip his hat, say good-bye, and go on alone.

That was fair, wasn't it?

He'd wanted some Dooley Monahan stories, and thought he had most of the tale. There was no more Dooley Monahan could teach or tell him.

Julia said something to him, he ignored her, deciding he no longer had to be nice. Once they got to Heber's Kiss, he'd cut them both loose, anyway.

Silently, he tightened his horse's girth strap. The road ahead looked just like the road behind— deserted and desolate, a land only the devil could love.

Two days later, they reached the Colorado River and turned south, following along its eastern bank. They stopped a few hours in Yuma, which wasn't long enough for Sweeney, but far too long a stay for Monahan, considering the territorial prison was there. Julia seemed happy to take in the sights, such as they were, and to find a store that sold lemon drops.

She bought a huge bag of them—it filled up half of one of her saddlebags—and spent the whole of that day sucking away at the candy. As they left town, she offered them to Monahan and Sweeney. The young cowboy took her up on it and helped himself to a handful, the old man turned her down, though he pointed out that Blue might like one, just for the sugar in it. And danged if she didn't unwrap one and toss it to him. He crunched it up then and there, swallowed it down, and begged her for another!

Monahan had never heard of a dog liking lemons—not fresh ones or lemonade or lemon candy or even lemon pie—and it sorely confused him. Since that state of mind was nothing new for him, neither of his companions paid it much heed. He had been teasing Julia about the candy, but maybe he'd been right without knowing it. Maybe dogs did like lemons in any form.

That would sure be a new one—him being right, by accident. Only a few days ago, he couldn't have been correct on purpose for love nor money.

And frankly, his old head was too full of Heber's Kiss and Vince George to dwell on much of anything else. He wondered how the years had treated Vince. Badly, he hoped. It'd be a lot easier for him to kill a man who only had one arm or one leg.

He'd never hoped for anybody to be blind in both eyes with such committed vigor.

* * *

They made camp along the banks of the river before the sun set. They hadn't seen a soul since they left Yuma, although Julia had seen something in the distance that might have been a building. It was hard to tell, what with the desert heat playing games with their eyes and all. But still, she had heeded Monahan's warnings. "Watch for Apache signs," he had said. "And keep your eyes and ears open, both of you."

Of course, Sweeney hadn't heeded him. He hadn't been even slightly interesting let alone entertaining since that business with Robbie and the dog back at Mae and Bob's.

Julia reached over and put her hand on Blue's back. He was stretched out, flat as a frog, between her and Monahan in the gloom. He turned his head toward her and threw her his old Blue dog smile. At least, she was pretty certain it was a smile. She was convinced that if Blue could laugh, he'd be laughing to beat the band all day long. That was what kind of traveling companion *he* was!

He was a sight better than the two men, of late. Monahan had been pretty much silent for the whole day. He hadn't flinched when they rode past the prison in Yuma, although he'd kept his head low . . . and he hadn't argued with her when she asked to stop for candy. Actually, it was kind of a shame he hadn't, because she'd had her reasons already figured out in her head and ready for spewing why she should be allowed to do anything she dang well pleased. Practically the only thing he'd said all day was to warn them about Apache, and she hadn't seen one sign of them, not one!

It sort of ruined a person's faith in their Beware the Heathen Horde fantasy. She decided she'd never believe another dime novel again. Why, for the whole time she'd been in the Arizona Territory, she'd never seen an Indian of any sort! Not an Apache, not a Yuma, not a Navajo, not any of them. Well, except maybe for that boy who worked at the Iron Creek livery. Tommy something or other.

Monahan tapped her on the arm. "Biscuits?" He was putting clumps of dough into a skillet for baking.

She nodded enthusiastically. Although Mae's food had been good, Julia enjoyed his just as much, if the truth be told, and his sourdough biscuits best of all.

Next to her, he set the lid on the biscuit's skillet, then pulled out a large pot and began pulling the last of the remaining vegetables from Mae's sack of victuals.

"Stew?" she asked.

Monahan nodded. "Yeah."

Hoping to get a conversation—*any* conversation—started, she asked, "What kind?"

"Vegetable, unless you got some desert quail or pork chops hid in your saddlebags."

She shrugged. "'Fraid not."

He grinned. "Didn't think so."

She waited a couple of minutes, then said, "Don't you wanna have a conversation?"

He gave her a funny look, like she was crazy.

"Oh, never mind!" She flopped down flat on the ground next to the dog. At least, he was glad to see her, and wiggled his hind end in welcome.

She put her arm around him and softly said, "Won't they talk to you, neither?"

In reply, he slung his muzzle toward her and licked her across the nose.

She sputtered, then giggled. "Guess that means yes."

"What're you two talkin' about?" Monahan's voice surprised her. She'd thought he wasn't interested.

She rolled onto her side. "We were just sayin' as how you 'n' Butch are keepin' your own company of late, and got no time for girls or dogs."

"That's not true, is it, Butch?"

Sweeney looked up, startled by the mention of his name. "Huh?"

Monahan scratched his ear, then looked down at Julia. "Well, mayhap it is."

While she smiled up at him Sweeney said, "What, Dooley?"

Monahan gave Julia a wink, covered his mouth to hide a chuckle, then said, "Sorry, boy. It was nothin'."

Unable to keep the tickle out of her voice, Julia said softly, "Dooley, you're a bad man. Very bad."

Monahan sat back and dangled his wrists over

his knees. "Yes, ma'am." He nodded his head in agreement. "I sure enough am."

She allowed herself a soft laugh, and then followed his gaze off into the distance. "What you see out there? Apache?"

He shook his head. "Nope. Nothin' like."

"Then what?"

"Nothin' at all. Just an old man's past, lookin' toward his future."

Julia was confused and said so.

Monahan tried to put her mind at ease. "Honey, my head's so fuzzy and disjointed . . . If you're smart, you won't listen to a dang thing I say."

"Okay." She rested her head in her hands. Maybe he was right. Maybe he was all fuzz-brained. Maybe they'd finally get down to Heber's Kiss and that Vince feller would kill him, and that would be the end of it. But that made her sad, about as sad as anything she could think of. The old cowboy had saved her—from the desert, and then from her previous caretaker—and she figured she kind of owed him.

Julia stretched out and heaved a sigh.

Beside her, Monahan continued staring blankly out over the desert. There was nothing to see but distant hills picking up the last weak rays of the setting sun and the first feeble rays of the crescent moon just beginning to rise. He wondered about old Vince and Heber's Kiss. Monahan shook his head. He didn't know the name Heber except from the Book of Mormon somebody had thrust on him in prison—that was a part of his life he'd like to forget, permanently!—but he couldn't think why anyone would name a whole town after the man or his kiss in particular. Danged if he could even remember if Heber had kissed anybody.

19

Not far from where Monahan and his companions sat near their pot of simmering stew, Vincent George sat alone in the main room of his new bar. Well, new to him, anyway. There were no customers. There were never any customers. Heber's Kiss was an Arizona town with two boots dangling over the edge of a grave.

Sean Jacoby, former owner of Jacoby's Saloon, had sworn to him the saloon was a cash cow. When Vince pointed out he hadn't seen a customer since he rode into "town" the day before, Jacoby had insisted the owlhoot had just come on an off day. Customers were thick as thieves in Heber's Kiss, Jacoby swore. Folks in dire need of drink rode in day and night. The only place of business that could supply their demand and quench their thirst was his saloon!

Well, Vince had taken his word—like a blamed idiot—and he'd been sitting there day and night since Jacoby died, but he hadn't seen one lousy soul, thirsty or otherwise. He wished he'd plugged Jacoby instead of letting him die naturally. For sure, he wished he hadn't witnessed that paper for him, which had been Jacoby's will, such as it was, naming Vince the sole beneficiary. Of course there was no lawyer in town to untangle the mess. Not that Vince had ever had much faith in the law.

The whole deal confused him so badly he'd hung around for a while, trying to get it straight in his head . . . and to see if anybody showed up.

Nobody had. And so Vince George had decided to take his leave of Heber's Kiss, Arizona Territory, in general, and Jacoby's Saloon in particular. He'd spent one day rummaging through Jacoby's victuals and another trying to scare up some game.

Jacoby had owned a donkey or a burro or something, and he'd figured to take that along, too. He might get ten bucks for it in a town like Tucson, if he ended up going that way. On the other hand, he could always turn it loose, or butcher it if worse came to worse.

George poured himself a drink. That was one thing there hadn't been a shortage of in Heber's Kiss—liquor. For a man who'd claimed to be doing such a stellar business, old Jacoby certainly had a monstrous backlog of stock. There were cases of it, and not just the bad stuff, either!

At that moment, Vince decided he was riding out in the morning and *definitely* taking the mule, if only to haul its weight in booze. He poured out another drink, thinking of the man-high piles of cases in the back room, and tossed it back.

* * *

A few miles north, Julia and Sweeney had finally gone to sleep, but Monahan sat up and smoked for a time, thinking his next actions would shape the whole of his future. Surely, he had come to similar junctures before, but he couldn't remember them. The ten years Buckshot Bob Hoskins had kept for him were already slipping away. He could feel the tides that ebbed and flowed in his mind sweeping them from the trembling sands of his memory.

He had known Bob from . . . prison, that was it. But which one? And why had he been in prison, anyway? He took a deep drag on his smoke. Damned if he could remember!

Monahan took another deep drag and concentrated on prison. He managed to dredge up a tiny snatch of a mental picture. He'd sat at night beside a feeble fire, manacles on his wrists, wishing he had some food or at least a smoke. Other men were there—live men, dead men, sick men, injured men.

Injured men . . . was it wartime? He concentrated harder on the mental picture, trying to see his sleeves to find a trace of a uniform, blue or gray, but couldn't find one. He could see only muddy rags like those worn by the few men standing in the murky, misty background.

He took a last drag on his smoke and stubbed it out on a rock beside him. Stretching out, he decided to join Sweeney and Julia in comfortable slumber. He lay down in his spot beside the fire with the nagging half memory of those poor men in the mist, swathed in rags, and so lost.

Morning broke, and Monahan was up with the sun. By the time Julia and Sweeney woke, he had finished giving General Grant the grooming of a lifetime. The horse had fallen asleep twice, and threatened to doze off again. Stroking the General's low-hanging neck, he ruffled the precisely combed mane with his fingers.

"When do we leave?" asked a soft, female voice from behind him.

He turned toward the source. She was familiar, safe—a slip of a little, redheaded girl, riding the cusp of womanhood. He squinted. Instead of asking for her name, he said, "What's for breakfast?"

"I was about to ask you the same," she replied.

"Somebody say breakfast?" asked a sleepy voice from across the camp. A young man sat up, scratching his neck and yawning.

The girl scrunched up her face. "Who'd want to waste good vittles by lettin' you stuff your face with 'em, Butch?"

Monahan frowned. *Who the hell are these folks?* The boy was fully grown, but young enough to be his, he supposed, and the girl . . . well, he must have wed himself a fine young woman to have sired such a beauty with her. He was a lucky man!

He glanced over at the dog, still lying where it had been when he woke. It still stared at him curiously, occasionally cocking its head to the left or to the right, eyeing him with something akin to suspicion.

"And what's the trouble with you?" he asked the dog. It didn't even blink.

"You feed him any breakfast yet?" the girl asked.

"No, don't think so," Monahan replied, frowning again. He couldn't remember waking up. He ran his hand through the horse's mane again, realizing he could remember the horse's name, and that it was his. He'd won it in a poker game. He couldn't recall the monikers of either the man or the gal, but they both seemed familiar to him, as did the dog.

The girl stuck her arm in a big flour sack beside his bedroll and began to dig. Assuming she had located the grub, he finished up with the General, then sat down in what he took to be his place. If it wasn't the damnedest thing, not being able to remember! He would've said something to somebody in the hopes that they could sort it out for him, but despite the feeling that his companions were familiar and could be trusted, there was still a niggling doubt at the back of his mind. He'd let the day play out and see what happened.

He leaned back, pulled the brim of his hat low to shield his eyes from the sun, and dozed off to the sounds of the girl making coffee.

Something was wrong with Monahan. Julia was certain of it. From the looks of things, he had gotten up a long time before her and Sweeney, but hadn't roused them to get a start on this supposedly important day. He'd wolfed down the breakfast she'd made before he hopped up and tacked her horse for her, something he never did! And the topper was that once they were mounted up, he had just sat there on General Grant, looking at her and Butch like they were supposed to lead the way.

Something was wrong when Dooley Monahan didn't take charge right off the bat. Sweeney had noticed something too, so at least she wasn't going crazy. Julia had caught his eye after they rode out of camp, and he looked as confused as she felt, but did no more than shrug by way of an answer. She had guessed, and rightly so, that she'd get no answers from him. Not at that time, anyway.

Sweeney gave a quick glance around, wondering how much longer they would continue riding aimlessly. He shook his head. They'd been moving since early morning, traveling for all the world as if they had nowhere to go and no business to see to. Monahan rode that old bay horse like some kind of saddle tramp, a man with no purpose and no goal. They couldn't be more than a half hour from their goal, perhaps just minutes.

Sweeney mumbled, "You'd think he'd at least show some enthusiasm! Or nervousness."

But Monahan plodded along like there was nothing on his mind, like he hadn't put Julia in danger just by bringing her along, and like there was nothing ahead of any particular import he had to attend to. It was a downright puzzle, that's what it was!

Sweeney would have called a halt to everything and asked him outright, except . . . except, well, it was Dooley Monahan. Sweeney had too much respect for his elders to call the old cowboy on his behavior. Well, not his elders so much, but Monahan, anyway. With a sigh, Sweeney continued riding.

The vegetation was weird. They'd pass clumps of trees, then ride through desert for a while, then come to a big grove of trees, and all with the river rushing along not fifteen feet from his right ear. He tried to figure out how close they were to Mexico, but had no frame of reference upon which to draw. He figured they were pretty well near the border country, since Monahan had told them to watch for Apaches. They raided farther north, of course, but he hadn't even seen *old* signs, let alone new, and that told him he and his companions were pretty safe from redskins.

Still, he kept his right hand near the butt of his gun.

Roughly fifteen minutes later, Sweeney involuntarily reined in Chili, stood in his stirrups, and pointed to the east. "Dooley!"

Julia reined in right away, but Monahan kept on riding until Sweeney hollered a second time.

Monahan reined his horse and turned around in his saddle. "You say somethin', son?"

Sweeney was so taken by the salutation that he reined up short, but he managed to stutter,

"Th-them buildings over there. Is that Heber's Kiss?"

In the far distance, the roofs of two buildings peeked through the rocks. After taking a long look, Monahan turned back to Sweeney. "Heber's Kiss?" He cocked a brow as if he'd never heard of the town before.

Julia broke in with the question Sweeney had been putting off. "Dooley, are you broke in the head or somethin'?"

Monahan tilted his head a little, "Why? Do I act like it?"

"You do," Julia said right out and with no hint of a smile. "You been actin' funny since this mornin'."

Monahan crossed his wrists over his saddle horn and leaned toward her. "Do tell."

Julia tucked her chin. "Well, you know! Stuff! You been actin' like you got . . . Well, I dunno! But your head ain't screwed on right!"

"Since this mornin'?"

Sweeney couldn't stand it any longer. "Since this mornin', Dooley," he repeated firmly. He wasn't going to let Monahan weasel his way out. As Sweeney figured it, he and Julia had risked life and limb, and at the least, were owed an explanation. He realized all of a sudden, Monahan hadn't called either of them by name since the night before. Hell, the old cowboy hadn't even used the *dog's* name!

The young cowboy lost his patience. "Dooley, just what in the name of ever'thing holy is goin' on with you?"

Monahan surprised everyone by calmly drawing his gun.

Sweeney heard an audible hiss as Julia abruptly took in air. "W-what are you g-gonna d-d-do?" he asked haltingly.

"Just who the hell are you, boy?"

Sweeney's brows shot up. "It's me, Dooley! Butch. Butch Sweeney!"

"And her?" Monahan indicated Julia with the nose of his gun.

"Ju—"

"Julia Cooperman," she snapped, slapping her crossed arms over her chest. "As if you didn't know!" When all he did was look annoyed, she jabbed a finger toward Blue and added, "You could at least say good mornin' to your own dog."

"But you called him a scruffy monster!" Julia said again, full of righteous indignation. They had just ridden into the town, but it was barely a wide spot in the road, conveniently equipped with a dusty old saloon, a falling-in-on-itself livery, and one other building, which she took for an outhouse. Blue tagged along happily, his tongue lolling, but she saw no signs of people until they rounded the saloon, to what she guessed was the front. It had a big sign, although she couldn't make out the letters on the weathered boards, and a burro tethered to the remnants of a hitching rail. The burro was halfway packed.

She looked over at Sweeney, who shrugged.

"This must be the place, I reckon. You got any more o' them lemon drops?"

"'Course I do, but now ain't the time to—"

"Shut up, the both of you!" Monahan growled as they stopped between the two ramshackle buildings. "Get down."

He eased himself off his horse and down to the ground. He led the General forward. "Well, c'mon," he said over his shoulder.

Sweeney dismounted and ran forward to catch him by the shoulder. "You're *not* takin' her in there!" he insisted.

Julia could tell he was plenty riled up, and made a mental note of it.

Monahan whirled about and brushed Sweeney's hand aside. He kept his tone low. "I'm takin' her, dammit! For sure, he saw us ridin' up. If we leave her outside, he's bound to figure somethin's afoot."

"Oh." The angry look left Sweeney's face. "She just better not got hurt, Dooley. I mean it."

Curtly, Monahan nodded and continued forward, leading General Grant. Julia, feeling safe as a baby, hopped down off her horse and followed. Sweeney brought up the rear, leading their horses.

They tied the horses at the broken rail and entered the saloon. It was deserted. Sweeney looked around. "Maybe he's closed."

Somebody in the back room dropped a case of something that broke like wood and shattered like glass and set the air practically throbbing with the scent of good bourbon whiskey.

"Or maybe he's not." Sweeney sniffed the air and licked his lips.

"If he'd bust just one little vial of eau de cologne, it'd smell like that French sportin' house up in"—Monahan hesitated, screwing up his face—"somewhere . . . I forget." He pulled out a ragged-looking chair at the only usable table in the place, and waved Julia into it. He sat down next to her, facing the bar, and Sweeney pulled out the chair next to him.

Blue walked farther into the shotgun-shaped building and took up a position at the far end of the bar, out of everybody's sight excepting Julia's. She thought it was odd, and was about to remark on it when the man came out of the backroom, scrubbing the backs of his hands with a bar rag.

He was a hard man to look at, Julia thought.

His hair was a white shock, and the scar ran up his cheek and across his eye, just as Monahan had described it. He was on the thin side, and appeared to have been brought up on hard living. His face was haggard and nasty, lined with age. He was death incarnate, and would think no more about ending their lives than another man might feel about swatting a fly.

For the first time since they'd set out for Heber's Kiss, Monahan's quest for revenge became horribly real to her.

The man smiled, but spoke with a voice that cut the air like a blade. "So there's folks around here after all. I'd about give up. Hope y'all have got a powerful thirst." He hesitated, taking note of the trio's silence, then leaned on the bar. He gave no sign of recognizing Monahan. though. "So, what can I get you?"

The old cowboy spoke up clear and clean. "We'd like a couple shots of that good bourbon I'm scentin', with beer chasers. And somethin' plain, with no hooch in it, for the missy, here." He angled a look at Julia for her preference.

She could only bring herself to shrug and say, "Surprise me."

She heard Monahan say, "You heard the lady," then listened while their host walked out of the room and into the storage area.

"It's Vince, all right," Monahan said softly.

Julia looked up from the table's scarred surface. "He scares the pee waddin' outta me!" came her whispered words. "I mean, I know you told us, but seein' him is somethin' else." She flicked a glance across the table at Sweeney.

His face echoed her unspoken fears. "He's obviously loadin' the good stuff onto the burro outside. He's plannin' on movin' out. I say we let him."

Monahan told it straight. "You ain't got a choice, boy."

Vince George emerged from the back room carrying two bottles under one arm and three glasses clipped between the fingers of the other.

Julia jumped a little at his return, but managed to keep from yipping with fear. She could never remember being so frightened of anyone in her life, not even the night her so-called "uncle" had stolen her innocence. She had no doubt the bar owner would kill her for no reason. Uncle Kirby might very well have killed her eventually, but at least he would have had a reason. He would have had to get something out of the deal—decent horse, or better yet, another girl.

The thought did little to comfort her.

She stared at the table while George poured bourbon into shot glasses and slid them in front of the men. Beside her, Monahan dug in his pocket while Sweeney slouched nervously on his other side, ticking the edge of his left cuff with his right thumbnail.

A minute later, the barman shoved a full glass—and a dusty old bottle, marked SULLIVAN'S SARSAPARILLA—toward Julia, then accepted coins from Monahan. "That's for the whole bottle o' sasperilla. You fellers change your mind about wantin' more bourbon, I'll leave it on the bar."

For a moment, Julia heard another sound in the bar, something besides the scraping of the bottle off the table and the footsteps of George walking back behind the bar. She could barely hear the soft and menacing *I-mean-business* growl.

The rumble calmed her at first, but then gave her something new to worry about. If this Vince person would kill her for the sport of it, what compunctions would he have about killing Blue? None, that's what!

Silently, she began to cry.

Monahan elbowed her in the ribs and whispered, "Not the time for it, yet."

20

The time came sooner than anyone expected.

The door to the back room burst open with a bang, and they all jumped at the noise. Blue, too. He leaped up on the top of a broken table pushed against the end of the bar, and flattened himself below the height of the bar top. Only his hackles, raised high like angry shoulder wisps, gave his position away.

Vince George didn't notice the dog as he strode behind the bar, holding a shotgun across his chest, and barked, "Ain't I seen you before, mister?"

Sweeney piped up right off. "No sir, I don't think I ever had the pleasure."

"Not you, idiot!" George swung the shotgun, its muzzle aimed straight at Monahan. "You, old buzzard. Who are you? Iffen you gimme a summer name, I'll know it!"

Monahan, who should have been scared out of his skin, leaned back in his chair and smiled real friendly. "Didn't think a normal person could recollect clear back to the old Monty's Raiders days. Congratulations."

Vince cocked his head, surprised, but still determined.

Down at the end of the bar, Blue silently raised himself up and put one paw on the scarred bar's surface.

Monahan noticed him, and did everything he could to not call attention by looking at him. He smiled wider. "I'm curious. Who'd you think I was?"

"Still don't rightly know. Fella I thought you was, well, he's long dead."

Silently, Blue brought his other front foot up onto the bar top.

"Well, some folks figger as how I'm long dead, even whilst they're talkin' to my face. A body's mind plays 'em funny, sometimes." Monahan gave a shrug as if he hadn't a care in the world and tossed back the rest of his bourbon.

Vince George gave a wag of his gun's barrel. Make that *barrels*. It was a double-barreled shotgun he was holding on them.

Weakly, Julia wondered just how far the kill zone would extend. *Probably just far enough to send me to Jesus,* she thought.

"Believe I'll take me another shot o' that bourbon." Monahan rose to create a huge vacuum in the space he'd been sitting. Julia, who had been leaning toward him without realizing it, had to grab the table's edge to keep from being sucked into the empty space his absence created.

"Hold it right there," Vince barked. The cock of the gun underlined his words. "Either you say who the hell you are, mister, or I'm gonna give you a mouthful of—"

Blue leaped down the bar.

Vince swung the barrel toward the movement.

At the same moment, the old cowboy shoved Julia's chair over sideways, leaped over her sprawled body, and grabbed the shotgun's swinging barrel, yanking it upward and shouting, "Leave go, you murderous ruffian!"

Vince's face opened wide with sudden recognition. "Dooley?"

The gun went off, the dog's open mouth latched onto the bar owner's arm, and Monahan yanked the shotgun out of Vince's hands.

Blue changed his angle of attack, clamping down on the side of Vince's face, and the old owlhoot fell backward, cracking his head hard on the floor. Sweeney shouted bloody murder and Julia scrambled helplessly in an effort to regain her footing.

Monahan set the spent shotgun on the bar and poured himself another shot of bourbon. Three fingers, this time.

Julia grasped her chair and dragged it upright, then hauled herself up by its seat. "What happened?" she asked weakly.

She looked around and saw Sweeney on the floor, Monahan lifting a glass to his lips, and nothing else. No sign of the dog, or of Vince. "I wish I was a man."

Monahan frowned. "Whatever for?"

She sighed and slumped back into her chair. "So's I could have me a drink."

"Don't see any reason why you can't." He poured out a second drink while he flicked a glance over at Sweeney. "You all right, boy?"

"Hell, no, I'm not," Sweeney said directly into the saw-dusted floor. "I'm goddamn shot! I'm dyin'!"

"Aw, crap," Dooley replied. He set Julia's bourbon on the table, and took two long steps over to where the young cowboy lay. Taking hold of Sweeney's shoulder, he rolled him onto his back. "If you're dyin', it ain't from them little drill holes that buckshot put in you." He raised his hand and picked out a single piece of buckshot from the man's forehead. "See that? There's your slug of death."

Sweeney made a halfhearted grab for it, but Monahan held it up for Julia. "Here. You keep that for him."

Numbly, she took it. Things were moving too fast for her. Monahan turned his attention back up toward the bar. "Blue?" he called softly.

She heard the click of nails on the plank floor as the dog rounded the end of the bar and came toward her. She held down her hands. "Hello, baby. Are you all right?"

Wagging his rump, Blue leaned into her hug. There was blood on his mouth and down one side of his muzzle, but that was all she could find. Still clinging to the dog, she looked up at Monahan. "I don't think he's hurt, but there's so much blood."

Monahan nodded curtly. "Vince's."

"Is he . . . ?"

"Banged his head, I reckon. Leastwise, there ain't no more bubbles in his blood. Boy, are you gonna figure out you ain't dyin' and come help me?"

Sweeney slowly pulled himself into a sit. He wiped at his forehead with the back of his sleeve.

Julia said, "Lemme look at that for you."

He shook his head, scattering the last few droplets of blood. "Wanna have me a look at Dooley's old friend, Vince." Slowly, he got to his feet.

"Don't believe he's dead?" Monahan asked from behind the bar.

"Just wanna double check, that's all." Sweeney went to the bar and looked over and down. "Sure looks dead."

Monahan appeared to study on the statement, then said, "Don't he just."

Vince George was dead, indeed, but Monahan didn't feel like burying him. Part of him figured the old owlhoot just plain wasn't worth it, and the other part of him was too bone tired. He settled for dragging the body out to the street.

Sweeney helped him with the body, and then they unloaded the hooch from the burro and shut him in the corral for the time being. They unhitched their three horses and settled them in the barn where they discovered Vince's horse. He was an old bangtail gelding, a solid blue roan, and hungry looking. Sweeney grained him good and set out hay and fresh, clear water for the horses and the burro.

Blue kept an eye on them, as if monitoring the proceedings.

After they'd taken care of the horses, Monahan took pity on Sweeney. "All right. Back to the saloon, again."

They started across the road, and Sweeney, who hadn't said much in the last hour or so, asked, "What the hell just happened?"

Monahan slid him a glance, like he was looking at an idiot. "We just took care of the stock, Butch."

Sweeney grumbled, "I'm talking about the whole thing, Dooley."

They gained the other side of the street and the saloon. Flies were already crawling over the dead man's face and were thick on the bloody head. Sweeney looked away and stepped through the batwing doors. He went to his chair, sat down, and faced Monahan. "Dooley? You gonna tell me, or what?"

"Don't know exactly what it is you want me to tell you, son."

Sweeney raised his voice in frustration. "What just happened, and why, and how come we're any of us still alive?"

Julia, still sitting where they'd left her, put her hands over her ears and squeezed her eyes closed.

* * *

Monahan lay his head down on the floor—well, leastwise on his saddle, which was serving as a pillow, as usual—and closed his eyes. They had done what they had come to do, and he couldn't make it more simple that that. He was still alive and Vince George was out front, drawing flies, and that was nothing more than a whim of fate. One of the fates had chosen to smile upon Monahan for a change.

It was not often fate shrugged off a whim in his direction, especially in his favor, and he intended to sit back and enjoy it while he could. He had explained it to Sweeney the best and only way he knew how, and the boy had accepted it. The girl had been easier. He didn't have to tell her anything. She had just closed her eyes in that *woman* way—he didn't know how else to describe it—and it was understood, just like that.

On the other hand, Sweeney had seemed to accept it, but he was still sitting up at a table, nursing a bourbon and contemplating the night sky through the open doors.

Oh well, Dooley thought. *Whether he can fathom it or not, it's done. And I'm goin' to sleep.* He settled himself more comfortably on the floor, wondering that he'd remembered a big chunk of his past—a miracle in its own right—and had scored a victory over a demon from it.

He gave his head a little shake, snorted out air, and pulled his hat down over his eyes. It was May the second, a day to remember, all right.

* * *

Dev and Alf Baylor rode into Yuma, stopping just long enough to pick up word about travelers fitting the descriptions of Monahan and his friends, right down to the dog, and to spot an old "friend" in the prison yard.

Alf was about to call out and raise his arm in greeting—and alert everyone in the surrounding area that they were on the owlhoot trail—but Dev stopped him just in time.

Alf never made things any easier.

He was running true to form an hour later when they ran across a fellow's campsite between the side of the road—which had petered out into a trail by then—and the river. He was a big fellow, cooking his beans and didn't seem happy to see them.

Alf rode right over and slid down off his horse. "Howdy!" he said, holding out his hand.

Dev cringed, remembering advice he'd heard from someone, somewhere. *Never, never offer your hand to a stranger, for reasons too obvious to go into.*

Luckily, the stranger ignored Alf's offer. "If you boys're plannin' to rob me, you're gonna be plumb disappointed."

"No, sir," Dev answered right off. Unlike his brother, he had wisely stayed mounted. "Didn't even plan to stop. Sorry to bother you. C'mon, Alf."

Alf simply sank down onto his heels and asked, "You run across an old geezer name o' Monahan? He's ridin' with a young feller and a gal—she's just a kid—and some kinda dog? Got word they were headed down this way." Having finished his speech, he smiled in self-congratulation.

The man looked up. "Your friend call you Alf? That your name?"

Alf nodded.

"Well, it's like this, Alf. They're headed down to a little wide spot in the road called Heber's Kiss. Probably there already. You find 'em before me, you can do whatever you want with 'em, but leave the girl be. She's mine."

The chilling tone sent ice shooting down Dev's spine and clear to the bottom of his boots . . . but was completely lost on Alf.

Dev wondered what on earth the girl was to the man—kin or hired help? He was pretty intense for her to be just hired help, though. She wasn't somebody just doing his dishes or sweeping his floors. Mayhap she was a runaway. "We'll leave the gal be, mister. Got no quarrel with her."

The big man nodded. "Name's Smithers. Kirby Smithers."

Dev nodded in acknowledgement. "We're the Baylors. I'm Dev. This is—"

"Alf!" he cried, jumping to his feet.

"And Alf," Dev repeated, shaking his head slowly.

Kirby Smithers hiked a brow, but said nothing.

He had been grossly misnamed, Dev thought, with uncharacteristic sympathy. What kind of parents would give the moniker of traveling notions salesman to a rough fellow better suited to busting broncs or wrestling steers than to promenading a poodle in the park somewhere?

"C'mon, Alf," he said. "Let's leave Mr. Smithers alone."

"But, Dev—"

"Now, Alf."

Reluctantly, Alf remounted and tipped his hat to Smithers, who did little more than scowl.

"Thank you kindly," Dev said. "We'll heed your advice about the girl."

"You'd better," growled Smithers, turning his attention back to his cook fire.

"Dev?" Alf asked in a strained voice when they were a decent way off from Smithers' camp. "How come we couldn't eat? He was makin' stew!"

"'Cause he didn't ask us, that's why. And we can make our own damn stew," Dev said, still puzzling over why Smithers was trailing that girl child.

"But have we got any meat? I can shoot some, I think. Can you shoot a fish? Or mayhap we could have frog stew. I hear 'em croakin' out there!"

Dev closed his eyes for a moment. "There's ham in my saddlebags. Just shut the hell up and keep ridin'. I mean it!"

21

The next morning Monahan woke early as usual, and tended the horses while Julia and Sweeney were still asleep. Everything was fine outside, except for the burro. He'd apparently taken exception to the horses, and had climbed up on top of the straw mound to sleep. How he'd gotten up there, Monahan couldn't figure, but he sure had a dickens of a time talking him down.

By the time he'd finished feeding and watering, Blue was carrying on something awful to rush him along. The dog wanted breakfast right that minute, and Monahan couldn't say as how he blamed him. The day before had been long and he figured they all were past peckish.

He walked past the corpse out front, just beginning to bloat, and went inside with Blue tagging his heels. Sweeney was awake and sitting up in a chair, but Julia was nowhere in sight. Monahan's face wrinkled. "Where's—"

"She found the kitchen. Says it ain't nothin' to brag on, but it'll do," Sweeney broke in.

At the sound of a bang, they turned toward the back room. A muffled female curse followed, and they turned back toward each other again.

Monahan asked, "You reckon she found a pump back there, too?"

"Must've. She said as how she's makin' coffee."

It was good news to his ears, because it meant he was off the hook for making breakfast. He collapsed into a chair, rolled a smoke, lit it, and leaned back. It was a good morning for reflection.

"I was born and raised up on my family's farm in Iowa," he began, addressing no one in particular. "They were the Monahans, David and Janine, and they came from Pennsylvania. When I was about twenty, I rode south, toward the Missouri border, to pick up a new milk cow for my ma, except I got waylaid by bad company . . . ."

He rambled on through the years, about Monty's Raiders and Kathy and the chain gang and all the rest that he remembered—or at least, from what Buckshot Bob had told him. Sweeney had the good sense to keep his mouth shut and let the old man talk himself out, talk it dry and to the bone, and say it all while he remembered it as clear as he was ever going to.

He ended with the burro up on the big pile of straw outside, and the body swelling up in front of the saloon, and then he knit his fingers together behind his head. "And that's the end of the story."

"Not yet, it ain't," said a cocky young female,

who'd entered the main room of the saloon along with the tantalizing scent of fried ham. She rounded the end of the bar, a plate in each hand, and slid them onto the table. "There you go. Fried ham out of a can and some good canned tomatoes I found in the back. Not much to choose from, but then, I figure beggars can't be choosers. I'll get the coffee."

The men didn't waste any time. They dug right in, and boy, it was good! In fact, Monahan didn't miss having potatoes or toast one bit. Julia brought out the coffee and her own plate and joined them for the rest of the meal.

Monahan was feeling so chipper he thought he might give old Vince a semblance of a burial today. After all, nothing else was apt to pull his attention away from it. He verbalized the notion to the other two.

"It's about time," Julia said flatly.

"Be glad to lend you a hand, Dooley."

Monahan ignored Julia, but said, "I'd be right appreciative there, Butch. After we let breakfast settle a mite?"

"Sounds good to me." Sweeney pushed away his empty plate, polished off his cup of coffee, and leaned back in his chair with his arms crossed over his belly. "I could use a nap."

"Quit statin' the obvious." Julia was clearing the table, and snatched up Sweeney's plate and mug. "You're practically facedown in your coffee, you slug."

"Stop it." Monahan said, hands raised, before they could start in. "Just hold on."

Julia, hands full of dirty dishes, walked back around the bar and threw Sweeney a dirty look before she disappeared into the back room.

Monahan and Sweeney were out front, digging the grave, when Julia heard a shot. Alarmed, she started to run out the front of the saloon but was stopped by the old cowboy's warning shout.

On the ground by the half-dug grave, Sweeney was bleeding. He tried to roll closer to Monahan, who'd managed to roll close to the saloon steps, and was tucked under the narrow lip of the walk.

A second shot missed Sweeney by a foot, but cut a groove into the dirt near his head. He held mostly still after that, but managed to get his gun drawn. He held it low, hugged next to his body.

Julia ran for Monahan's rifle, which he'd left in the saloon with his saddlebags. She wrestled it free, and quickly locked the building's back door. Back up to the front, she cocked the rifle and stood at the ready.

And then, nothing happened.

She waited a tense five minutes before she whispered, "Where are they, Dooley?"

A hand slowly rose up from below, at the edge of the walk. It pointed behind her and behind the saloon, then sank back down.

She furrowed her brow. After another quick look around, she softly called the dog. "Blue?"

There was an understated noise, something like a mumbled bark, before the dog entered the saloon by slinking under the batwing doors, setting one of them slightly swinging. Before she knew it, he was pushing his head into her hands. It was hard to take it and hold the rifle at the same time, but she managed. She dropped her head down toward his and whispered, "Who's out there, Blue? Who's shootin' at us?"

Blue licked her face, but didn't answer her.

She heard a noise from the back of the building. Blue did, too, because he started to growl, low and menacing. The noise was coming from the door she'd just locked. Somebody was trying to break in!

Quickly, she shifted herself and the dog. She leaned back against the front wall and rested the rifle on her knees. She had a straight shot down the back hall to the rear door. Whether he broke the latch or busted in the lone window in the storage room off to the right and crawled in that way, whoever it was would have to walk up that short little hall, and she was convinced he wouldn't live to get to the end of it.

She might have been only thirteen, but she was bound and determined to be a hundred years' worth of trouble to anyone who tried to mess with her. Or Dooley, or Butch, or Blue.

From outside, she heard Monahan loudly whisper, "Julia! Julie girl!" and turned toward the sound. There was nothing but wall behind her. To peek under the doors, she'd have to scoot over seven, maybe eight feet, but didn't want to take her eyes off that back hall.

So she sat where she was, eyes pinned to the rear of the building, and hissed, *"What?"*

"Julia! Whatever you do, don't—"

Bang! The door burst in. Julia steadied her aim and squeezed the trigger. But the form kept coming at her, and she had to repeat the process.

Blue leaped up and raced toward the crumpled form halfway down the back hall, barking and snarling.

From out front, came Dooley's whispered, "What the hell's happenin' in there?"

"Got 'im!" she almost shouted.

"Got who?"

"Dunno. One of 'em, anyway." She started to stand, but Dooley's voice stopped her.

"Don't move!" came the whispered call, more along the order of a croak.

Julia slumped back to her former position, got the rifle settled on her knees again, then called the dog. He came and she pulled him close, even though he had a bloody front from nosing the corpse. "This time you stay here no matter what," she said, soft and low.

"I love you, you big dope," she whispered, one arm around the dog and the other steadying the rifle. "Don't you go runnin' between me and that hall. I'm dangerous!"

According to Monahan's figuring, the remaining Baylor boy was still around the side of the building, biding his time. He could be six inches from the front or six inches from the back, or anywhere in between. And on either side of the building! But wherever he was, Monahan hoped the petty outlaw had heard Julia say she'd killed his brother.

Sweeney was still lying near the grave; leastwise, the beginnings of it. But he was all right, thank God. He had signaled Monahan with his eyes just before that Baylor had taken his last shot.

"Pssst!"

Monahan looked toward the source of the sound.

Sweeney whispered, "He's walked around the back o' the saloon. Tell Julia."

"You coulda told her yourself!"

Butch scowled. "You're closer."

"Aw, criminy!" Dooley turned toward the saloon, raised his head, and called out to the girl, again. "Julia! He's comin' your way."

She didn't answer.

He was about to call to her again when the rifle barked, followed shortly by a pistol shot, followed immediately by another blast from the rifle, and then . . . nothing.

Monahan started to sit straight up, banged his forehead on the walk's overhang, readjusted, then sat up all the way. "Julia!" he called, rubbing his head. He wondered which astrology sign covered the head, because he was surely bound and determined to bang his up. Wasn't there a woman up in . . . somewhere, he forgot where . . . who'd drawn up his chart one time? Hadn't she said . . . He pulled himself back to the present. "Julie, honey, you hear me?"

Preceded by a soft whoosh of parting air, an

arrow dug into the dirt not a foot and a half from him. He jumped to the side, but his panic wasn't long-lived. It turned into downright terror when he realized the arrow piercing the dirt too near him was Apache in origin, just like the next that came whizzing in and sank effortlessly into the hard, clay soil next to it.

Inside, Julia sat in the same place. Wide-eyed, her expression momentarily frozen with shock, her fingers were laced through the thick coat on the dog's neck and locked into place. Blue had attempted to cross the room after the second rifle shot, but her hand had stilled him.

Down the hall lay the Baylors, sprawled over each other in a dark, back-lit heap. The second one had come in quick, but she'd been ready. He had fired, but he hadn't hit anything except for an old slate, hung up when the saloon had pretended to offer food.

Her second shot had been the lucky one. Well, lucky for her. She supposed it depended on which end of the lead she was on. She'd been on the fortunate side.

But he wasn't dead yet. One leg, bent at the knee, kept thumping against the wall. She wasn't going to go check him, and she couldn't unlock her fingers from the dog's coat so that he could go, which he was getting pretty insistent about.

She finally found her voice, and over the dog's fussing, she called, "I'm all right. But he's not dead! What do I do?"

Monahan didn't whisper any longer. "Just keep

shootin' till he stops doin' whatever it is that's got you worried."

"C-can you do it?" For the first time, terror began to seep into her voice. She hadn't realized how very frightened she was, and the realization only served to frighten her even more.

Monahan didn't answer her. His attention was drawn elsewhere. "Can you move?" he hissed at Sweeney, who had eyes for nothing but the twin arrows.

"Th-think so," Sweeney stammered. "I mean, don't we gotta?"

"Start crawlin' up toward the steps."

The young cowboy made slow progress, and when he reached the two steps up to the board-walk, he took them on his belly. It wasn't that he was a coward: he just didn't like to take unnecessary chances. At least, that's what he kept telling himself.

He felt something kick him in the heel as he dragged himself the last few inches through the bar's door. Once he was through and clear, he turned over, ready to holler at Monahan for kicking a wounded man. But no one was there. Nothing, but for an arrow, sprouting from the side of the thick heel of his left boot.

Momentarily forgetting himself, he shouted, "Katie, bar the door!" and made another scramble into the saloon. It moved him back another five feet and out of the line of fire from the back hall—down which, a transfixed Julia seemed to be staring. Only the dog initiated any movement. Blue was trying to get away, to move ahead of her and get after something down the hall, but her thin fingers appeared to be threaded through the coat on his neck and locked tight.

From outside, he heard Monahan's age-rasped voice call, "Butch!"

"Come on ahead!" Sweeney shouted without thinking, then quickly regrouped and dragged himself a few feet farther inside.

It was just in time. Monahan came hurling through those batwing doors like he'd been shot from a cannon's mouth. Several arrows came right along with him, landing in the floor, the swinging doors, into a stray case of whiskey sitting out on the porch, which exploded on the impact, and the wall just above Sweeney's lowered head. But not into Monahan.

The thought flitted through Sweeney's brain that Monahan was too old and corded up, too twisted and petrified, for an arrow to penetrate.

"Where?" Monahan stood just inside the front door.

Julia said, "B-b-back hall."

He nodded and motioned Sweeney to the far wall. Though the young cowboy paid him no mind, Monahan went toward the bodies. He bent over them for what seemed like hours, during which time Sweeney was roused from his torpor by another arrow that missed his shoulder by inches and sent him scrambling for the far side of the building.

The old cowboy turned toward Julia. "It's all right, honey. It was just a muscle twitchin'. They're both dead as a couple o' fence posts." He turned to Sweeney. "Get over here, boy, and lemme dig that lead outta you."

Julia began to cry.

22

"You ain't got the time," Sweeney protested as another arrow flew under the batwings and sank into the raw plank floor . . . right where Butch had been.

Monahan cocked his head to look at the arrow. "Mebbe not. And you, missy—" he turned to Julia, who looked relieved about the men in the back hall and very close to releasing her hand and letting Blue free—"keep ahold of that dog. Don't wanna take a chance with him and those Apache. Not yet, anyhow."

He hunkered down close to the floor. "Slide me the rifle, girl." Two more arrows came sailing through the doors and sank into the back wall. Julia swallowed hard before she sent the Winchester skittering in Monahan's direction. Before it had the time to reach him, she closed her eyes and was hugging Blue's neck with both arms, her trembling face half buried in his fur.

Dooley picked up the rifle and opened the

chambers with one smooth movement. Just as he'd thought, she was nearly out of ammo, and he hollered at Sweeney to scoot him over a box of cartridges. A moment later, he felt the box slide into his leg, and proceeded to scoop out enough cartridges to reload. He cracked the rifle closed and stuffed the box into his vest pocket. Slick as a minnow in shallow water, he scooted over the arrows stuck in the grimy wooden floor like pins in a pincushion and stopped on the far side of the small front window, peering out quickly through the dust-spotted and cobwebbed glass just long enough to assess the situation out front.

An arrow shattered one of the glass panes overhead.

That brave was closer than he'd looked!

Sweeney, who'd been watching, yelled, "How many of 'em are there?"

"Three that I could see," Monahan replied, rising carefully to his knees. "Means at least six." His back was pressed to the outside wall, the rifle's sights to his eye. "You find a minute, you slide that spare pistol over to Julia. Load it first." He flicked a glance her way. He could tell she wasn't listening. Too scared, most like. "Shout at her to make sure she's listenin'," he hollered.

With that, he moved the few inches to swing the rifle's muzzle through the last remaining window pane and fired twice—once to send them skittering and once at a specific target. The slug traveled better than he'd hoped—it must be something in the stars, he thought in passing—and the brave on whom he drew a bead gave out a yelp and dropped down behind the dusty water trough across the way.

"There's one," he muttered to himself as he quickly took aim on what he thought was a second brave's shoulder sticking out from the side of a big boulder.

He missed, but he'd been right about the target. The naked shoulder pulled back even as the slug sang off the rock in front of it.

Sweeney slid the spare pistol skittering across the floor toward Julia, and let out a little sigh of relief when she actually noticed and picked it up. She pointed it toward the back hall before he had a chance to tell her to do it. The dog was fussing, but her fingers were locked tight in his fur and held him still. Physically, anyhow.

He heard the rifle discharge two times, then a third, and looked toward Monahan in time to see his controlled slide toward the floor.

"You all right?" Sweeney shouted.

"Ain't deaf," the old man muttered. "Got one of 'em, by the way. Don't know how many friends he's got, though."

Another arrow whipped through the window above Monahan's head and buried itself in the wall halfway between him and Sweeney.

The young cowboy gulped. The old cowboy didn't even flinch. The only sound, for the moment, was the arrhythmic thump and thud of Blue's elbows against the floor. And breathing. Sweeney could hear the girl breathing in small, controlled gasps and pants.

And then he realized it wasn't the girl at all. It was him.

He slapped a hand over his mouth and nose. *Just calm the hell down,* he told himself when he realized his teeth were chattering. *They're gonna kill you, you damn fool, and you don't wanna die with your teeth clatterin' like Mex castanets, do you?* "Hell, I don't wanna die no way, no how!" he whispered. Softly, he thought.

But Monahan still crouching beneath the front windowpane, half turned toward him and said, "Then get up here!"

Before he knew what he was doing, Sweeney wriggled his way up toward the front of the building and lit beneath the other side of the window with his pistol at the ready.

Monahan muttered, "Good. Now get over by the door."

"What?"

"Get over by the door. On your belly, boy!"

Sweeney figured it out, and got himself over beside the batwing doors—but still behind the wall—then inched over until he could see. What he saw was a brave, crouched and hustling from behind one cactus to the next sage, not forty feet from where he lay. He aimed and fired.

He missed.

But he fired a second time and had the satisfaction of seeing the brave pitch forward. It wasn't until then that he noticed Vince's body still sprawled beside the hole they'd been digging for him. Arrows rose from his back and side like so many porcupine quills.

Sweeney wondered if the Apache had really missed that many times, or if they were just using the corpse for target practice. He was so fixed on the question the next blast from Monahan's long gun scared him, and he jumped. Not quite certain what happened next, all he knew was that he was suddenly on Julia's side of the door, and an arrow stuck weakly in the top of his shoulder. It hurt, but he didn't make a sound when Julia reached over and yanked it out.

"Don't worry," she murmured. "The arrowhead was only partway in." Not once did he see her look at him. Her vision was riveted straight down the hallway ahead of her, past the bodies, and to the open desert beyond the rear of the building. Her right hand held the pistol so tightly her fingers and knuckles were white. Her left was still woven through the fur on Blue's ruff. She had him gripped so tightly he whimpered softly and rolled his blue eyes back toward Sweeney. "Let him go," he heard himself say.

"No. Dooley said not to." Her voice sounded odd, small, not like Julia at all.

Sweeney put his gun down long enough to grab her hand and try to unlock her fingers, but it seemed they were made of iron. Just as cold, too, even though it had to be a hundred degrees, even in the shade. "I said, let go!" he hissed at her.

After a moment, her fingers joints began to unlock with soft, barely audible clicks.

* * *

Although they never could agree on the exact sequence of events of the next few minutes, they at least agreed on most of what happened. Julia claimed the first thing was the Indian's face peeking around the side of the back door's frame. Sweeney was certain the dog snarled and vaulted forward first. They both agreed Julia fired her pistol—two handed—and that she missed. Monahan had no opinion because he was busy at the window, taking an arrow to the side of his neck.

He made no sound when it sliced a deep groove just below his right ear, but he toppled to the side with a thud that rattled the dusty floorboards and turned Sweeney's attention away from the back door, around the opening of which the dog's hind end disappeared.

Julia watched. She knew the signs of a dog in hot pursuit of its quarry, all right, and she sure wouldn't want to be that brave when Blue came close enough to sink fangs into flesh. As Sweeney rolled across the floor fast enough to evade three arrows that came swiftly under the door, tracking his path, she heard Blue barking outside the bar, heard the barks go around the building, and heard someone shouting in guttural tones. In Apache.

She didn't remember moving, but found herself peeking out underneath the batwing doors and seeing something that shocked her. An Apache brave was standing in the middle of the street out front, not ten feet from the grave. His arms were flung wide, his bow slung around one elbow, and he actually looked . . . frightened?

Blue, ears flattened and neck ruff standing on end, his head down, and his posture that of a wolf about to pounce, held that Apache exactly where he stood by barking, growling, and lunging forward at the brave's smallest movement.

Slowly, she brought up her pistol.

She centered the sights on the brave's chest.

Her finger began to tighten on the trigger.

"Don't do it."`

She looked across the room at Sweeney. He had wrapped Monahan's neck with his bandanna, and propped him up so he could see out the window.

Shaking his head, Sweeney repeated, "Don't do it, Miss Julia. Please."

Slowly, she let her finger slide from the trigger and rest against the guard. She pulled the gun back inside.

A scraping sound drew her attention across the room again. Monahan heaved himself up a little higher. In a loud voice, just as guttural and foreign as the brave, he spouted off a string of mumbo jumbo that seemed to surprise the brave out front as much as it did her. And Sweeney, too, by the looks of him.

The Apache, whose eyes never left the dog's, said something softly, just loud enough for her to hear. Monahan answered something right off, and then hollered the first thing that made any sense to her. "Blue! C'mon in here, boy!"

* * *

Julia watched while close to a dozen Indians left. They came out of the brush slowly, one by one, creeping off to disappear down the edge of the dry riverbank where she assumed they had left their ponies.

Blue did, indeed, return from the street to the saloon, but not all the way inside. He mounted the steps and sat on the porch, his back to Julia and the doors, and watched the Apache leave. Every once in a while she gave his backside a scratch, and each time he responded with a little wiggle of his tailless rear. But he never turned his head, never took his eyes off those Indians.

Why the fight had come to such a sudden and unexpected halt was a mystery to her, and she planned to press Monahan on the subject.

After the Apache were gone.

Once they were alone again.

23

An hour later, Monahan and Sweeney had finished putting the late Vince George—plucked of twenty-nine Apache arrows, which they left in a pile on the porch—underground at exactly eight feet from the overhang. He was correctly positioned to be the recipient of any manure deposited by the first horse tethered to the rail. They did not mark the grave, since it was out in what was supposed to be the middle of the street, and also because Monahan claimed he'd be damned if he'd go overboard by marking it for everyone and his brother to see.

Vince George's old blue roan lay halfway between the barn and the corral, the victim of a stray slug.

Monahan, Sweeney, and Julia gathered their gear, mounted their horses and set out to the west. Monahan, his neck packed with bourbon-soaked cotton covered by two bandannas, sat General Grant, leading the way; a bandaged but cheerful

Sweeney followed on Chili, leading the Baylor boys, each strapped to his horse; Julia, numb from it all, rode the horse she called Parnell, leading the burro, whom she had christened Goat, on account of he was up on the straw mound again when she went to get him ready to travel.

It was Monahan's plan to drop the Baylors off in Yuma. There would surely be some reward money in it for Julia, and she would have need for money in the years to come. He wouldn't go to the law himself. He was convinced they would recognize him and arrest him without delay for some unknown crime he couldn't remember committing in the times between memories. He'd be dad-gummed if he'd let somebody lock him up—or worse!—for something he didn't remember doing. Buckshot Bob had already told him he couldn't be locked up for anything he'd done as part of Monty's Raiders so long in the past. He'd never done anything so terrible back in those days that the law hadn't sooner or later reached its limit.

He could be grateful for that part.

Sweeney was primed to take Julia—along with the Baylors—to the marshal's office and collect the money, while Monahan would take the burro and Blue and wait for them outside town. He could have cashed in his voucher from all those years ago, too, if he'd only remembered it was in his wallet.

When they were closer to the river and could see the green of its banks full of trees, a shot suddenly sounded, and Sweeney toppled from his saddle.

Monahan cried out, "Off your horse! Now!"

Julia obeyed practically before the words left him. She and Parnell and the burro and the Baylors were off the road and down in the sage and scrub on the northern side.

With Sweeney hobbling under his arm, Monahan headed to the south side. Blue followed, low to the ground, with the end of Chili's rein in his mouth.

"Good boy," Sweeney said, once the old cowboy had put him down in the weeds. He'd been hit, all right, but in the same shoulder where Dev Baylor had plugged him, and the slug had passed clean through. He took the rein from Blue and scratched him between the ears. "You wouldn't happen to know who's shootin' at us, would ya?"

Blue didn't answer, but Monahan, up ahead in the weeds, said, "It's sure the day for it, ain't it? You reckon those Apache have a half brother up the road with a rifle? I'm only gonna let you get away with limpin' like you did, one time."

Sweeney had the sense to look embarrassed. "You got no idea at all?"

"Not buyin' the stray half-breed idea, are you?" Monahan shrugged. "Not the first cluc."

"Makes two of us. 'Less somebody painted a sign on us that says 'Hit me and win a pie'."

The old cowboy snickered, then said, "Hope that girl is okay."

"Reckon she is," Sweeney replied. "Reckon that one could walk through a fire fight with ten pounds of dynamite strapped to her and not suffer in the slightest part."

"She's a tough little bird, all right," Monahan

allowed, and smiled to himself. He turned toward the opposite side of the road, and called, "Give us a peep to let us know you're safe!"

Once she'd let out the requested peep, Julia rolled herself up into a ball and snuggled down into the weeds. She quickly learned that was a mistake—a gray wolf or a coyote had spent time in the very spot she'd picked to lay low, and he'd left her a gift.

She felt . . . and smelled . . . it as it slowly soaked its way into the seat of her britches. She made a face, then rolled off to one side.

She didn't want to look, but couldn't help it. On the ground, where the seat of her britches had been, were the smashed and flattened canine turds, and the patch on her back pocket had left a partial reversed imprint: Levi Strau—.

At least it wasn't *her* name in the wolf scat.

Suddenly, she realized hoofbeats approached. Not galloping hooves, but slow, walking ones, more cautious than in a hurry. She almost sat up before she caught herself and instead, ventured a whispered, "Dooley?"

There was no answer, save for the quick scuffle and skid of hooves, and the *click* of a gun cocking.

That, and the realization that she had no pistol.

Half a second later, the hoofbeats stopped and a shadow loomed directly over her. Automatically, she thought, *It must be noon.*

"Well, you little she-cat," said a gruff voice that was far too familiar, far too unwelcome, and far too near.

She swallowed hard, and nearly choked when she could find no spittle.

"Stand up, so's I can shoot you." He sounded too pleased to be breathing.

She would have shot him without compunction if she'd only had a gun. Or better yet, Monahan's rifle. But she didn't. All she had was a butt-smashed pile of wolf scat with somebody's name pressed into it backwards.

"C'mon, Ju-Ju," he said, in that coaxing tone she had grown to loathe and fear through those countless assaults on her young and frail body. "C'mon and let your Uncle Kirby shoot you."

She was almost halfway to her feet, falling into the old habit of "do what he wants and he'll just go away" when a shot cut the bright stillness of the day, cut it into scarlet ribbons that were falling all around her.

But they weren't ribbons. They were the long stems of the tall spring grass that came with the rains, and they were scarlet with blood, warm and drenching, red as red could be.

Slowly, she rose up the rest of the way, through the scarlet weeds until her head rose into the clear light and she saw him.

Or what was left of him . . . sitting on his horse with a hole blown clean through his chest.

Monahan stood on the trail, ten feet behind him, holding the rifle. "Your so-called uncle, I take it."

She nodded. "Kirby Smithers, in the flesh. Or out of it, I guess. You blew a hole clean through him."

The old cowboy pursed his lips. "Well, the rifle did, not me."

"It's a hole and it's clean through him, just the same."

Blue came from behind Monahan and crossed to her, baring his teeth and growling softly when he circled Smithers. Even the dog knew he was no good. Even Blue was smarter than she had been when she went with him eagerly, when she trusted him.

She felt her mouth open. "Is Butch . . . ?"

"He'll be fine. Appears that he's a hard feller to shoot square in the middle. People keep just skinnin' the edges." Monahan walked forward and held a hand down to her. "C'mon, now. We gotta get to Yuma before those Baylors o' yours start stinkin' any more than they did when they rode in."

But she shook her head. "I gotta round up the horses. They're probably ten miles away by—"

She felt something push against her leg and looked down to see Blue through the bloody weeds. He had one of Parnell's reins and the lead rope to the burro in his mouth, and he was wagging his hind quarters like a dog possessed.

Monahan guessed what she was seeing by the look on her face. "A little herdin' does him a worlda good, don't it?"

She took the rein and the lead rope, wiping Blue's spittle away on her bloody shirt, and moved toward the trail which had once borne the gaudy title of Heber's Kiss Highway.

Blue had already rounded up Chili, the Baylors' horses, and General Grant, who had wandered

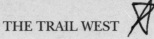

about a half mile south of the road and were darn near invisible, since they were standing in thick scrub and grazing with their heads down in the grass.

She watched while Monahan fixed up Sweeney. She figured he must have a curse on his left side, except the latest bullet had hit his upper arm instead of his shoulder. It had gone through clean and the wound didn't need sewing, but still, it had to hurt something fierce.

They tied Smithers—deader than a bent spoon but still stubbornly slumped over—into his saddle. She swore she could see right through him where the slug had passed through the cage of his rib bones and burst out his front. She was a little surprised the sight didn't make her throw up.

As they started toward Yuma again, she remembered to ask Monahan just where he got off speaking Apache. He had the nerve to say he didn't know what she was talking about, claiming he'd never heard it let alone spoken it.

Sweeney spoke up. "Oh, quit horsin' her, Dooley! We both heard you talkin' Apache like you was one o' them!

"I don't know what the heck's got you two so addled!" Monahan replied, all of a sudden a little cranky.

Julia looked at Sweeney and Sweeney looked at Julia, silently agreeing it wasn't the time to be pressing the old cowboy. It must be one of his "forgetful things."

Behind them trailed a string of bodies, a cranky burro, and the blue dog.

* * *

Statement of *Miss Julia Cooperman*
As Given at *Yuma Prison Marshal's Office*
Received by *Marshal Sam Peck*
This *May 3*, Year of Our Lord *1873*

*My name is Julia Cooperman, age thirteen,
formerly of Iron Creek, Arizona Territory. My
friends and I were passing through a town south
of here called Heber's Kiss when we were beset by
outlaws, who we later learned were the infamous
Baylor brothers, Alf and Dev.*

*They cornered us in the old saloon, which was
deserted aside from us, and where we had taken
shelter the night before.*

*They shot my friend, Butch Sweeney, twice in
the shoulder, and left him lying in the street. I was
pinned down inside the building.*

*The back door opened and Alf Baylor burst in.
He carried a pistol and was swinging it around
like he wanted to shoot at somebody, so I shot at
him. Well, he shot first, but missed me. I didn't
miss him.*

*Mr. Sweeney called to me from outside to watch
out, as Dev was going around the back. He came
in, all right, firing his gun. I shot back. My slug
struck him and he fell to the floor. I called to Mr.
Sweeney, who came in to see that I was safe. He
checked the men to see if they were dead. They were.*

*The other body belongs to my guardian, Mr.
Kirby Smithers, also of Iron Creek. He was shot in*

the back by one of those Baylors, I don't know
which one because he was in the stable and I
couldn't see him.

I hereby swear this is my true statement, and I
witness it by signing here, below.

(Signed) Julia Cooperman
(Date) May 3, 1873

After Julia made her statement and signed it—
while she nervously crossed the fingers of her left
hand in her pocket—the marshal filed it away in
his office.

He took a brief statement from Sweeney about
the Apache attack, but the young cowboy had to
leave him hanging at the end, for obvious reasons.

"I don't get it. I mean, unless you could talk to
'em or do somethin' to spook 'em off . . ." The
marshal shook his head slowly.

Julia saw their whole story going up in a puff of
smoke with each head shake, before she blurted,
"We had that dog with us, Butch. Some kind of
fuzzy little shepherd dog with no tail. He had blue
eyes. Don't they call 'em . . . whatcha call . . . spirit
dogs or somethin'? The Indians, I mean?"

The Marshal leaned forward on his elbows.
"Ghost dogs! I ain't never seen one myself, but I
hear tell they can have a powerful effect on the
heathen."

"That must o' been what done it," Sweeney
agreed enthusiastically. "When they saw that dog,
they just filed right back from wherever it was

they come from. Too bad about that dog," he added sorrowfully and dropped his head. "He run off after those Indians. That was the last we seen of him."

There was a little more small talk, but the marshal bought their story and bought it whole. "I'll get one copy of your statement sent to the bank up in Prescott tomorrow," Marshal Peck told Julia. "You'll have yours and your voucher to show when you get to a bank."

Sweeney asked why she couldn't get her money right then. The Marshal explained that the bank in Yuma didn't have the funds to cover what they owed her. Sweeney started to take exception, but Julia stopped him. She was afraid he was pushing it.

Besides, she didn't want to irritate the marshal. She was grateful to get those corpses off her hands and not get charged with murder in the process. Getting shed of Uncle Kirby's body was just icing on the cake, so far as she was concerned.

She only wanted to get out of town, collect Monahan, and get moving east. She missed the dog, and wanted to put as much distance between herself and all that death as she possibly could.

24

Julia and Sweeney rode out of Yuma at last, leading only the burro, Goat. Half an hour later, they joined Monahan. The afternoon was nearly gone, but they kept on moving until they ran out of daylight and the old cowboy called a halt.

They camped by the river's bank. Monahan made a fire near some scattered boulders about fifteen feet from the water's edge, and threw together the fixings for a good beef stew made with the vittles he had bought in town. Sweeney took some more of the pain medicine the doc in town had given him for his arm and shoulder after he dug out the last of the slugs, and Julia snuggled down with her old Navajo blanket and waited for her supper. The evening air was crisp, and she was glad for the blanket's comfort.

"I been thinkin'," she said into the silence.

Monahan looked up and nodded approvingly. "Ever'body oughta think. Good for the soul. What's got the bee in your bonnet?"

She tightened the blanket around her neck. "What hasn't?"

Monahan cocked his head. "You're thinkin' that you seen enough bad things in the past couple o' days to last you more 'n a lifetime."

Surprised, she nodded. "How'd you know that?"

"Reckon we all feel about the same way. A little bit of dyin' an' bodies shootin' at you with arrows or iron goes a long way with most folks."

She let out a sigh. "Yeah. Reckon it does."

"Even when it comes for some trashy pond scum like it come for the Baylors. And Vince."

"And Uncle Kirby?"

"Your uncle, too." Monahan poured them both a cup of coffee, and after he handed hers over, he sniffed the air, then made a face. "Blue take a crap close to camp?"

Julia felt herself flush. "It's me, not Blue."

Monahan's head cocked again.

"I sat in some wolf scat earlier. Back when Kirby put us all in the weeds."

"You wanna get yourself cleaned up?"

She slowly got to her feet and scowled at him. "If you're tryin' to hint, you ain't doin' a very good job of bein' roundabout."

The old cowboy smiled. "Got just enough time before dinner. Get outta here and take that wolf stink with you. It's upsettin' the dog."

Blue, stretched out on the other side of the fire, yawned.

Julia said, "Yeah, I can see that he's all outta shape about it." She pulled her spare britches out of her saddle bags, found the yellowed sliver of soap she'd stolen from the saloon's makeshift kitchen, and made her way down to the riverbank. Having already calculated the way to be naked for the least amount of time, she left the clean britches and her boots up on a flat boulder and waded out before she squatted into the water and began to scrub the seat of her pants.

She heard Sweeney's voice, and quickly glanced at the fire. The smell of the stew had roused him at last, and he was sitting up with his eyes open, and holding his plate out toward Monahan. She snorted under her breath and shook her head. *That darn Butch,* she was thinking. *He can always force himself to eat, can't he?*

By the time she'd scrubbed the britches clean, dried off, changed clothes, and made her way back over to the fire, Sweeney was scraping his plate clean. She laid her pants out flat over a rock as she said, "Guess I got back just in time to get my measly bite of stew."

Sweeney raised a brow. "Measly? Since when did you ever take a measly bite of anything?"

"Since I made your acquaintance and started havin' to share grub with you," she said without a second's hesitation. She peered into the pot and made a face. "See there? It's practically gone already, and I ain't yet et a bite of it!"

"Hold it!" Monahan thundered, his hand in the air. "I swear, if words were clubs, you two would be black and blue! Here." He held her plate—full and still steaming—out toward her. "Oh," she said, and accepted it numbly. "Guess I yelled without thinkin'. Sorry, Butch."

"That's more like it, girl!" Sweeney said.

Monahan promptly threw a spoonful of hot beef gravy in his direction.

The next day found the trio back on the Old Mormon Trail, again heading east toward Phoenix, and more important, back toward Buckshot Bob and Mae Hoskins's ranch and stage stop. They couldn't get there fast enough to suit Monahan, although Sweeney, who was still healing from his shoulder wounds, would have been content to throw down temporary roots anywhere along the trail and just sleep for a few days. And eat, too, of course.

As for young Julia, she went along with mixed feelings. She missed the safety and comfort of the Hoskins' home and the friendship of their daughter, Meggie. She had never had a real buddy before, but despite their short acquaintance and the slight difference in their ages, she and Meggie had become great friends.

But what would she do without Monahan to protect her?

As for Sweeney, she'd miss him more than she'd ever admit, but it was the old cowboy and the dog who tugged hardest at her heartstrings. Not that she'd say as much to him. She'd already told Blue—who miraculously managed to keep up with them, despite the heat—trotting at a steady pace in one of the horse's shadow, and she figured that was enough.

It took them several days on the sparkling-sided trail to reach the Hoskins ranch, and once there, they received the warmest of welcomes. It was like they were genuine conquering heroes, Julia would later say. It seemed no one who had met Dooley Monahan escaped his presence without becoming a fan, and while she wasn't right, she was close to it.

"I appreciate it, Bob," Monahan said. The two men were sitting out on the front porch, smoking, and everyone else had gone off to bed. "Poor little thing ain't got nobody or no place to belong."

"The gals have taken a real strong likin' to each other," Buckshot Bob said, nodding. "It's as good for Meggie as it is for Julia."

The old cowboy took a drag on his smoke. "'Bout what I thought . . . Now, don't forget about them reward vouchers. That's her money for her life."

Buckshot Bob nodded thoughtfully, then flicked his ash. "It's a lot, all right."

Beside Monahan, Blue stretched and yawned, then flipped over onto his back and groaned happily. It was the end of a long, hot journey, and he was grateful for a night with good food and fresh water. He sensed that Monahan was relieved, too. He'd felt the old cowboy truly relax for the first time, and it was good.

Blue stretched again, lifting his front paws to rake at invisible ladder rungs and relaxing his mouth so that his lips fell open, leaving him with a big, toothy, upside down doggy grin.

It was *all* good.

Julia woke to the sounds of shuffling boots on wooden floors and of men tramping through the house. Yawning, she got up and wandered out to the kitchen, letting Meggie sleep while she could.

Julia found a stack of hotcakes on the table, along with a bowl half filled with fresh whipped cream and a pitcher of blueberry syrup. There was oatmeal on the stove, too, but not one living soul in evidence.

She started calling for people as she walked through the house, but didn't find anyone until she was clear outside—Monahan and Sweeney were out front, General Grant and Chili were tacked up and ready to go, and Bob and Mae were bidding them farewell.

"You're leavin, and you weren't even gonna wake me up?" Julia asked from the front porch.

Monahan let the cinch strap drop, then pulled the stirrup free from the saddle horn and let it swing down into place. He turned toward her and said grandly, "Well, good mornin' to you, Miss Julia!"

"Don't try to make me feel guilty just 'cause I didn't say good mornin!" she huffed.

"Now, honey . . ."

"You were gonna just leave me, without so much as a by-your-leave!" She felt the tears welling and felt the thickness in her throat, both as surprising as they were sudden. "Please, don't . . . you can't . . ." She began to cry, and clutched the post and rail to hold herself erect.

Monahan tossed his reins to Sweeney, then stepped toward her. "Now, honey," he said as he took her in his arms. "Don't go and make a thing of it."

She let go of the porch rail, relying on him to hold her up, and cried into his shoulder.

"I just convinced myself it'd be easier if we . . . Well, if we was already gone when you got up."

She shook her head *no* and sobbed harder.

"I don't know what to say to you, Julia honey. Just didn't figure you'd take it this hard. Now, me and Butch ain't goin' to Europe or nothin'. We'll see you again."

She lifted her head and looked up into his rheumy old eyes and whispered, "I wish you were my pa." She ducked back down again.

She felt him kiss the top of her head, then release her, and she fell into a sit on the porch step. She heard him say, "All right then, Bob. Take care o' those kids, Mae."

His saddle leather creaked. "Good-bye, Julia. Take 'er easy."

Sweeney said something similar in farewell, although she couldn't have told you what it was to save her life. She felt warm fur brush against her arm as Blue came over to say good-bye, too. His tongue wiped the tears from her nose and chin, and he whined softly.

"Oh, good-bye, Blue dog." She wept as she buried her face in his ruff. "Travel safe." She opened her eyes, and found him looking back at her, his eyes filled with love. "Travel safe, Blue."

25

In five days, the men had got as far as Phoenix. Just what Monahan had intended to do. Sweeney had no clue regarding a plan. Every time he had broached the subject, Monahan had managed to turn the conversation on its head and thoroughly distract him.

The old cowboy had parked them in a hotel far from anything interesting, and Sweeney was bored silly. He had never before been to a town the size of Phoenix, and despite the nagging ache in his wounded shoulder, he'd been looking forward to spending some time in the big city.

But all Monahan did was complain . . . about how expensive everything was . . . and Apaches . . . and how far they had to go yet, which was still a mystery to Sweeney.

He'd only been out of the hotel twice, to check the horses. He'd taken his time on both occasions, walking down the street several blocks in every direction, north, south, east, and west. He'd seen houses—big houses, little houses, shanties and lean-tos barely cobbled together, nice houses where families lived, and fancy houses. He'd been tempted to go into one of the latter, just to see what it was like—well, and test their wares, he had to admit—but he was too poor to walk through their front gates, let alone ask a lady upstairs to pleasure him. He was broke.

He wondered if Monahan had any cash on him. He'd spent more time with the bodies than Sweeney had. Maybe the dead men had been carrying a roll. He hoped it had been the Baylors' cash. Somehow, he didn't want to be living on money that should have gone to Julia, which her uncle's surely should have.

Fresh from his latest fruitless visit around the town, Sweeney walked into the hotel lobby, only to meet Monahan, who had just come downstairs.

Sweeney had done little more than open his mouth when the old cowboy grinned wide, threw his arm around Sweeney's shoulders, and said, "Let's get us some dinner, boy!"

Sweeney was too hungry to do anything but accept.

They went into the hotel's dining room and were seated. The serving girl handed them menus and left them to consider the choices.

When the serving girl returned, Sweeney said, "I'll have the special with extra potatoes, and a beer."

Dooley ordered, then lit the smoke he'd been

fiddling with. It was a ready-made. He favored them when he could get them, but he could only find them in big towns.

Phoenix qualified, he guessed. W*hy, there must be better than a thousand people here!*

There was a big cotton gin and a medium-sized ice-house, and a fellow raised Appaloosa horses on the edge of town. A public schoolhouse was planned, and work was already being done on the courthouse, since the capitol was switched between Phoenix and Prescott every five minutes. The Capitol on Wheels, people called it.

Monahan just called it foolish. But all in all, he liked the city. The folks were friendly but they didn't overwhelm a fellow, dogs were welcome most everywhere, and Mexicans could go about anywhere in town and not get sniffed at nor get a rock upside the head, like they got in many towns.

There was also the big First Territorial Bank of Arizona, where he planned to go in the morning to finally cash in his voucher. He supposed it was still good, anyway, even though he'd been carrying it for a few years. He'd found it again while they were still camped outside of town. He also discovered something was missing, some piece of paper or other, but he couldn't remember what exactly. He'd been puzzling over it all day, in fact, and had remembered at long last—not what it was, of course, but the fact that it had existed. He'd been planning to ask Sweeney about it at dinner.

Their dinners arrived at that moment. As they began eating, Monahan asked, "Butch? Do you remember as how I had a slip of paper, somethin' or other, in my wallet? Do you remember? Did I ask you or the girl to carry it for me, maybe?"

Butch roused out of his stupor. "You mean, like a newspaper article or somethin'?"

The mists cleared for Monahan. "Yeah. A newspaper clippin'." He could almost see it . . . .

Sweeney reached for his wallet and pulled it from his pocket. He rummaged around for a moment before he took the paper out between two fingers. "Like this? About Alaska?" He held it out.

Monahan took it from him. "Yeah, about Alaska." He let the words soak into his brain. "About how a body can strike gold up in Alaska." He rubbed at his chin, then took hold of it like he was going to pinch it off. He announced, "Screw that ranch."

Butch looked at him like he'd gone crazy.

Monahan frowned. "Why the hell should I go to work on some lousy cow spread for ten bucks a month when I can go to Alaska and get myself rich? You go up there and work if you're so dang set on it!"

"Fine. I'm goin' with you!" Sweeney roared all of a sudden.

The old cowboy almost physically jumped back. "Go with me? You crazy?"

"Why should I get my legs or ribs busted up by some crazy cow when I could be taggin' after you, makin' my million? If I hadn't given you that clippin' you woulda forgot all about it!"

He had a point. Monahan had hold of his old chin again, rubbing and squeezing it. He didn't want to let Sweeney know how mad he was, or how close he was to just killing him. Well, not killing him all the way to death, but something awful close to it! "Jus' who the hell do you think you are to muscle in on another man's dream?"

Sweeney didn't say anything for a long minute, and Monahan thought he'd pretty well got him buffaloed, figuratively speaking, anyway. But the young cowboy leaned his chair back against the wall, pillowed the back of his head in his hands, and said like he had never insulted anybody in his whole live-long life, "I ain't musclin' in on nothin', Dooley. Sounds like a good plan, that's all. Why, the fact is, I'm fair keen on the idea."

All the air went out of the old cowboy like he was a big balloon somebody had just stabbed a hat pin into. He leaned his elbows on the table with his head in his hands.

A few seconds of silence later, he heard Sweeney say, "Dooley? Dooley, are you all right?"

Monahan looked up suddenly and snarled. "No, goddamn it, I'm not alright! Just who in tarnation do you think you are, stealin' everybody's dreams and makin' them your own? You think I'd just roll over and let you do it, 'cause you been of some sorta help these last weeks? You think I'd just hand over everything I been wishin' for, just like that?"

Butch blinked, but said nothing.

Monahan stood up and huffed, "I didn't think so!"

And then, before he had a chance to do any more thinking on the matter, he marched out of the dining room, hoping Sweeney heard his footsteps, loud and never faltering. And he hoped they scared the hell out of him.

It wasn't until three hours later—he hoped Sweeney had thought he'd spent them in a bar, but which he really spent alone in the boarding stable, talking to General Grant—that he came halfway to his senses. He didn't own Alaska. He didn't even own a parcel of land up there. He had never been to the place and had no say in who went where. Who did he think he was? God Almighty?

He suddenly felt very small, so small that he nearly got shorter.

"Gotta do it, General. Gotta back down and let the boy go where he wants. Gotta let him be his own man. After all, he might've seen that clippin' anywhere. He might've talked to a feller on the street or in a bar. Anybody might've told him about Alaska. He's not got nothin' against me, and it ain't all on me."

"You in here all alone, waxin' poetic over Alaska? Still?" asked a voice from the doorway.

It came so unexpectedly that Monahan started, but he managed to catch himself on the side of the stall. His eyes narrowed to see through the gloom. He made out a spare man—not tall, but not somebody you'd call short, either—dressed in cowboy gear, and leaning in the shadowed doorway. *Dark hair,* he thought. *Clean shaven.*

He didn't have the first clue to the man's identity. The man didn't seem to be having the same trouble with him, though. He finished rolling his smoke, saying, "Been a while. How you been keepin'?"

"Tolerable," replied Monahan, his guard still up. "And you?"

The man flicked a match into flame and lit his smoke. "'Bout the same. Still got bunions. Still on the scout."

Oddly, that sounded a little familiar, but out of long-standing habit, Monahan didn't relax one iota. Behind the cover of the stall's walls, he let his hand drop to dangle stiffly near his Colt. And then, without warning, a word sprang from his lips. "Miller."

The man smiled. "I was thinkin' you had another of those 'clobbered' times o' yours. It's good that you remembered my name, Dooley. I feel better about you, now."

Monahan didn't know how to respond, so he just said, "Good for you." He still couldn't place the fellow, still couldn't consciously fit him into any background or with any group of people.

The man shook his head and sighed. "Think, Dooley. Think the spring roundup in Fort Carroll, Wyoming. About six, eight years back?" The man stared at him, looking for some sign of recognition. Apparently, he didn't see one, because next he said, "Don't you remember? Scalper Johnson was up there with us, and the Kid, and Darby. You spent the summer carvin' skunks outta pine knots when we wasn't workin', and the Kid spent 'bout all his time tryin' to figure out how to sell 'em? Aw, c'mon, Dooley! Say you remember just a little?"

The man's tone had become pleading, but Dooley kept his hand by his gun, and said, "I may know your name, but that's all I know. Not your face, not any of those other names you said. I'm an old man, and I got enough ghosts already. Leave me be."

Miller, who appeared to be about forty, maybe forty-five, shook his head sadly. "Well, all right. I'll let you get on with it. But I'm stayin' at the Adams, and if you remember anything, gimme a shout, okay? Room two-oh-seven."

Monahan nodded.

"Don't forget?" said Miller.

"I won't." The old cowboy might have forgotten where the hell he was five or six years ago, but he wouldn't forget this little encounter if he had anything to do with it. It might take him a while, but . . . "Luden," he said suddenly. "Luden's Mill."

A grin bloomed across Miller's face. "That's right, Dooley! The L slash M. Colonel Harry Luden's spread! Knew you'd remember, iffen I gave you enough time."

Monahan felt his fingers twitch and his hand rise away from his gun. "Colonel Luden wasn't there, he'd been called up." He remembered something about the Ludens. They hadn't owned the spread that long, and he'd been told that after Vicksburg, the colonel had been called back into service by the North. He had been gone before Monahan showed up, and he left before the colonel returned. Two

THE TRAIL WEST 259

years had been spent on the Luden spread, two years filled with ravening Indians and cougars and unrest, and . . . "Did I serve?"

"In what?" Miller asked. "The war?"

Monahan nodded.

"Sure you did. Least, you said so."

"For the North?"

Miller's brows went up warily at the question. But he nodded and said, "Yup."

All of a sudden, the rest came flooding in. Monahan slapped the side of his head, spooking General Grant. "Now I remember. George Miller, right?"

Miller's smile grew into a grin that exposed the hole left by a missing incisor on the bottom and a gold crown on top. He tossed his cigarette butt to the street outside, and came forward to greet Monahan with both arms out.

They embraced over the stall's rail, and the old cowboy was suddenly exceedingly grateful he hadn't shot Miller on first sight. He'd been sorely tempted. He'd admit that, if only to himself.

George Miller was some years younger than Dooley Monahan. At five-foot-ten, he was taller than average, and his dark brown hair had only just begun to gray. When Monahan had known him up in Wyoming, it hadn't yet begun to turn, and he remembered being mad at George then for not aging like he had. He'd felt old age slowly covering him all over like candle wax. But his anger had disappeared in no time once he got to know George.

And just like then, he felt all his initial uneasiness melt away as the two men began to rehash old times and tell each other over and over again just how plain *good* it was to set an eye on the other.

He returned to the hotel alone, but in much better spirits than he had left it. In fact, he didn't even remember the argument about Alaska until he'd been tiptoeing around Sweeney's sleeping form for about five minutes.

Even then, he held no hard feelings. Why, if he hadn't argued over Alaska he never would have stormed out of the hotel, never would have gone to the livery, and never would have run in to George! He reckoned he owed Sweeney a word or two of gratitude. But later. He was plumb worn out.

He climbed into bed with the dog right behind him, got his feet angled over the end of the mattress like he wanted, and fell asleep thinking happy thoughts.

26

Out at the Hoskins' station it was coming noon, and all three kids, Julia included, were in the kitchen, sitting down at the big worktable. They weren't complete, though. Somebody was still missing.

Buckshot Bob had been gone since the morning after Monahan and Sweeney had left. Mae hadn't explained his absence in any detail, and seemed just as puzzled as the kids, although she tried to put up a good, solid front, saying he'd had to go into Phoenix to pick up a piece of harness.

But Julia had seen the lie right from the beginning. Why had he traveled clear into Phoenix when stages went there, then came back out, regular as clockwork? One of the drivers could have picked up a piece of harness as easily as he, and he wouldn't have had to lose days and days of work time.

So where on earth had he gone?

Julia could buy the Phoenix part, because they had all seen him ride off in that direction. Of course, he could have changed his heading once he got clear of them, but Phoenix was as good as anyplace else. For a start.

But what had tempted him away? For all she'd seen of him, he was content to be out on the station with his family. He was proud of his livestock, his wife and kids, and the home they'd built on the Old Mormon Trail. He seemed content. He actually seemed happy!

She had a lot to think about as she ate her lunch.

Sweeney woke before Monahan. In fact, he had shaved, changed his underwear, and got clear ready for the new day before the old cowboy showed the first signs of rousing with a twitch of his stockinged foot.

"Well, good mornin', sunshine," Sweeney said.

Monahan growled softly, then cracked open one eye. "What the hell time is it? And who you callin' sunshine?"

Sweeney snorted out a laugh. "It's nine-thirty. And it don't mean nothin'. It's just somethin' my mama used to say, bless her heart."

Monahan sat up and began searching for his boots. He found them, and put the first one on. "Well, it wasn't somethin' she'd have called me." He thumped his heel on the floor, seating the boot on his foot, then picked up the other. He let the second one swing between his fingers. "Nine-thirty, you say?"

"Yeah. Why? You got a pressin' appointment or somethin'?"

Monahan chuckled. "Not so's you'd notice. But I've gotta get to the bank, and then I'm meetin' somebody for lunch."

Sweeney felt his face screw up. "You're meetin' somebody for lunch?"

Monahan ceased dangling the boot, and stomped it onto his foot. "I can eat, can't I?"

Sweeney shrugged. "Didn't know you knew anybody in Phoenix to eat with. Wanna have some breakfast with me?"

"Wouldn't mind," said Monahan, taking to his feet. He headed toward the door. "It's George Miller I'm havin' lunch with. Used to work with him up in Wyoming." When Sweeney raised a brow, he added, "Ran into him last night, down to the livery."

Monahan stepped through the doorway and into the hall, with Blue trying to fit through at the same time. Sweeney followed, shaking his head at the dog. It seemed strange to him Monahan should remember Miller all on his own and right out of the blue. He'd never done that since Sweeney had been with him. Well, except for Buckshot Bob Hoskins and Vince George, anyway. Those two he'd remembered just fine.

Sweeney just didn't know how the old cowboy kept things straight! It was a mystery to him.

He went on down to a nearest cantina, trailing in Monahan's—well, actually the dog's—wake and had himself a nice big breakfast of scrambled eggs and warm tortillas and cactus jelly.

Once Monahan had paid for the meal and they had wandered outside, he excused himself to go to the bank.

"You got your voucher on you?" Sweeney asked, hoping Monahan hadn't misplaced the paper and then forgotten.

Dooley grinned. "Why you bein' so worrisome, boy?"

Sweeney didn't hesitate. "Because you're actin' funny! Because you're a different person from one minute to the next!"

Monahan responded by laughing and digging into his pocket. He pulled out a wad of bills, which he placed in Sweeney's reluctant hands. "That there's 'bout half o' what I took off them Baylor boys. That should ease your mind, son."

The gesture was so unexpected that before Sweeney thought what to say, the old cowboy had disappeared down the sidewalk, headed for the bank.

He walked a good half mile before he came to the bank. It was the biggest he'd seen in a while and located in what he guessed was called the business district. Once again, he felt his pocket. The wallet was still there. He paused before he went through the door to check once again. The voucher was still there. He read it.

PAY TO THE ORDER OF *Dooley Monahan*
THE SUM OF *$500.00 Gold* FOR *Reward
for Baylor, Jason: Wanted for various crimes,
Territorial and Federal.*

It was dated September 4, 1869, in Twin Pines, South Dakota, and signed by Marshal Tobin. Monahan remembered him. He could almost picture him . . . if he closed his eyes.

But the important thing was that he was at a good-sized bank, he had his voucher, and he was going to cash it, by God. He opened the door and walked inside.

The guard eyed him, but apparently didn't see much of a threat. At least, after half a minute he went back to his newspaper. Monahan walked on up to a teller—there were four—and slid his voucher under the partition. "Like to cash this in," he said casually.

The clerk, young and clean shaven, smiled and said, "Yes sir," then looked at the paper. His brows rose up until Monahan could have sworn they were going to meet his hairline!

He said, "You all right there, boy?"

The teller gulped and said, "Y-yes. Did you know that this paper is three years old, sir?"

Monahan narrowed his brows. "I do. Why? Ain't it no good anymore?"

"Oh! Yes, sir. It certainly is good!" The clerk was clearly flustered. "It's just that, well, there were three Baylor brothers to begin with, right?"

Now, Dooley was the confused party. "Yeah . . ?"

"Well, I just had reason to check back through some old posters, and three years back, the reward was the same for all three Baylors. They were all the same amount, I mean."

"Yeah?"

"This Marshal Tobin," the clerk said. "He's somewhere up in South Dakota. Is that a pretty small town? Somewhere that's kinda outta the circle?"

"Huh?"

"Oh, you know. Someplace that isn't exactly up to date on the news. A place that doesn't have a telegraph or anything."

"Well, I'd guess you'd say that Twin Pines is pretty outta the way," Monahan allowed. As he recalled, it wasn't even on the stage line.

The teller nodded as if he'd known it all long. "Just what I figured," he said smugly. "Now, accordin' to what I read, those boys were worth a different amount right after August the thirty-first."

"What's that mean to me?" Monahan was bored. He wanted his money, and was quickly running out of patience.

The teller smiled, wide and toothy, if not terribly white. "'Bout a thousand dollars, I'd say. Hang on a minute."

Monahan waited while the clerk disappeared into the manager's office, then came out and went into the vault. He came out carrying a sack, which was heavy by the way he handled it. Monahan knew what it was right off.

"Gold," said the clerk with a look of satisfaction. He opened the sack and began to count it out, measuring a small portion on a little scale he brought up from under the desk for just that reason.

Monahan felt like jumping out in the middle of the big room, grabbing a pillar post, and dancing a jig right around it, just out of joy. But he kept his features calm and said, "What reason you say you had to be lookin' through the old posters? Seems like a pretty strong coincidence to me."

The clerk looked up from his scales. "Funny, ain't it? Fact is, these skunky Baylors are all gone, officially, as of today. It's not often I get to cross off a whole family of bank robbin' killers in one day, and for so much money!" His eyes went back down to his scales. "Boy howdy! I'll bet this sets a record for the most monies ever paid in one day! Bet it comes close, anyway."

The corner of Monahan's mouth ticked up. "Oh, I doubt that."

The clerk stacked the gold—mostly in coins, with nuggets and a little bottle of dust—in front of Monahan. "There's one thousand, six hundred and twenty-five dollars, sir." He pushed a piece of paper through the opening at the bottom of the partition. "If you'd sign that receipt for me, please?"

Monahan took the proffered pen from his hand and signed. And then, he initialed another paper that said the reason for the bank having paid out the extra money over that for which the voucher was made. "Don't know how you fellers keep all this straight. Can you gimme an envelope for the nuggets?"

"Certainly!"

While the boy was digging for an envelope, Monahan asked, "You say you cashed out all the Baylors this very day?"

"That I did."

"Who cashed in the other ones?"

"A feller." The clerk slid out an envelope. "There you are."

"Did he have a young gal with him, 'bout thirteen?"

The clerk pursed his lips. "No. No, I believe he was all alone."

"How long ago did he leave?"

"Ten minutes, maybe," said the clerk, who was looking more and more suspicious. "Hey, why are you asking?"

"You'd best be worried about yourself, son. I figure you just paid the wrong person a whole lot of money." Monahan snatched up his gold, stuffed his pockets, and hurried back to the main entrance, where he stopped by the security guard. "'Bout ten minutes ago, you see a feller leave here?"

The guard looked at him funny. "Folks leave here all the time, buddy. In fact, just as many as come in."

"This one was carrying 'bout thirty-two hundred and fifty," Monahan said.

"Oh, *that* one!" A look of realization crossed the guard's face, and he smiled. "The feller hummin' and dancin'. Sure, I recall him, all right. He was shakin' hands with ever'body who crossed his path, celebratin' his good fortune. Accidentally run himself into the Baylor boys, he said, and come out on top!"

There were a lot of things Monahan wanted to say right then, but he didn't have time. He just asked, "Where'd he go?"

The clerk pointed up the street. "Said he was goin' to Driscoll's Bar, and that he was buyin'."

Sweeney sat in Driscoll's Bar, thinking over the past few days and what had happened to him—and the others—and what, if anything, it had done for him in a positive way. He couldn't say any of it had adversely affected him. He'd survived it all, hadn't he? Of course, he'd been shot at a lot—his shoulder was witness to that!—but nobody had drilled his ticker. He guessed he'd been pretty dadgum lucky, all things considered.

He guessed he couldn't be mad at Dooley Monahan for carrying him—hadn't he practically pleaded with the old cowboy to take him along?—or at Julia Cooperman. She was pretty much innocent, although part of him wanted to blame her. She was a handy scapegoat.

But what was she the scapegoat for?

Danged if he knew. He ordered another beer and settled back to stew in his own juices a little longer.

27

Monahan walked quietly into Driscoll's, sidled up to the bar, and ordered a beer. Before the bartender slid it down in front of him, he saw Buckshot Bob at the other end, joking with two cowboys he took to be town dudes dressed up for the day.

Monahan took a sip of his beer and stared toward Bob, waiting to be recognized. It didn't take long. Fear washed over the man's face, answering Monahan's question before it was asked. He quickly tamped it down and flashed a big, innocent smile.

Smiling back, Monahan raised his glass and made a mock toast in the air. Bob started over toward him, carrying his own beer. His pockets bulged with the gold coins he was carrying.

But they aren't his, Dooley thought. *They belong to Julia.* Buckshot Bob had no call to be in a saloon, even if it was a nice one, spending her money on men she didn't know. He had given his word that he'd bring her along to claim her reward. That part of his promise he'd broken for certain, and it sure looked like he was going to break his word straight down the line.

But Monahan couldn't prove Bob was planning on stealing all of Julia's money, not unless he got a confession out of him. He seriously doubted Bob was stupid enough to just give him one.

Monahan was torn. Buckshot Bob was his memory. He had nearly ten years of Monahan's life, condensed into bite-sized chunks he could reel out like so much fish line any time it was asked for, and the old cowboy surely did appreciate it. But he didn't appreciate it so much from a fellow who was stealing Miss Julia's money, stealing money from a thirteen-year-old kid when it was all she had in the world. Sure, he was giving her lodging, but to Monahan's mind, that was just something you *did*, wasn't it?

"Well, howdy, Dooley! What brings you to Driscoll's?" Bob asked, his face as innocent as a baby's.

Monahan wanted to slug him, but held himself in check. "Followed you in." He took a drink of his beer. "I was just up at the bank."

There was a slight tic in Bob's smile, but not one anyone could have sworn meant anything. It might have been the effects of a bad bite of hardboiled egg. "The bank?" he said, just a little thinner than normal.

That, too, Monahan could chalk up to a bad choice in the culinary department. "Where you come by all that gold you was payin' the bartender with, Bob?"

Casually, with his back to the bar, Bob leaned his elbow on the bar and hooked his boot heel on the rail. "Oh, I had 'er saved up for a rainy day. Don't get myself into town much as I'd like. Ready for another beer?"

"I'm fine." Monahan just asked Bob, right out, "You come in to cash Julia's vouchers?"

Bob showed only a hint of hesitation, then said, "I surely did. Got it right here." He slapped his pockets. "That's a helluva lotta money, Dooley." He lowered his tone. "They give it to me all in gold!"

Monahan nodded. He leaned back against the bar, too, casually aping Bob's position. All he had to do at this juncture was figure out how to get word to Sweeney, three-quarters of a mile away through the confusing city, to get down there on the double and babysit Buckshot Bob.

Monahan needn't have worried, for Sweeney was just up the street, wandering along with the dog lazily following in great loops and circles. He stopped in front of the milliner's shop, staring through the window at the cockeyed things women put on their heads, moving on only when the saleswomen tried to sell him one through the glass.

He and the dog ambled on down the street, stopping to help a woman burdened with packages walk from one side of the street to the other and load them into her buggy. The dog wandered off during the loading to chase some goats in a weedy lot up the street, and that was when Monahan saw him. He'd just turned to look out the window, and there he was!

"Just a minute, Bob," Monahan said, shoving his

beer mug at him. "I'll be jiggered if that ain't my Blue! Hold on there a second." He slipped through the swinging doors as quick as you please, and shouted the dog's name. Before he knew it, the dog had crossed the street at a mad gallop and was jumping up and down beside him, his whole body doing a double-time wag.

That caught Sweeney's attention, all right. He helped the lady up into her buggy, doffed his hat, and joined Monahan and Blue at a jog. He skidded to a stop in front of Driscoll's.

Monahan said, "Boy howdy, Butch! What brings you out this way?"

Sweeney explained that he hadn't had anything else to do, and he and Blue had just started window shopping. "And we ended up here," he finished with a shrug.

"Well, we got us a little problem . . ."

Just then, the door swung open and Buckshot Bob stepped out onto the walk.

While Sweeney tried to wipe the surprised look off his face, Monahan explained that he'd just run into Bob, and Bob invited them both in to have a drink. Sweeney didn't hesitate in his acceptance. Apparently, a free drink was a welcome offer any time of the day.

Monahan checked his pocket watch before he followed them inside. It read ten forty-seven, giving him less than an hour and a quarter to figure out Buckshot Bob and hike another half mile up the pike to meet George Miller—good old George Miller!—for lunch at the Addams Hotel.

* * *

By twelve-thirty, Sweeney was halfway through a roasted prairie hen, and wondering if Monahan had taken leave of what little remained of his senses. He wasn't dining with them, preferring to take his lunch with his friend George over at the Addams, but he had filled him in on Buckshot Bob and his alleged thievery—alleged, because Sweeney hadn't seen one thing that made him think Bob had suddenly come in to money. He'd ordered the next to cheapest thing on the menu, and currently sat across the table, fiddling listlessly with a drying tortilla.

"So, you stayin' at a hotel?" Sweeney asked.

Bob shrugged his shoulders. "Don't know. Reckon it's too late in the day to start back now?"

"Might be. Why don't you come on over an' stay at the place where me and Dooley took us a room? Place is clean, anyway. Ol' Dooley's real keen on a clean place." Actually, Monahan had never said one way or the other, but Sweeney figured it served to draw out the conversation.

Not by much, though. Bob shoved back from the table, which disturbed Blue, who had been napping beneath it. His head poked out from beneath the tablecloth and whimpered, eyeing the bird left on Sweeney's plate.

The young cowboy stared the dog in the eye. "Ain't much."

Blue let out a note that started up high and traveled down someplace below the cellar before it stopped, and then he let out a long, needy sigh.

Sweeney made a resigned face and let out a sigh. "Right. Just let me take out the bones, first."

While he struggled with the tiny carcass and Blue licked his chops, Buckshot Bob sat back in his chair and lit a smoke. "That'd be real good of you and Dooley to take me in tonight, but I think I oughta be hittin' the road."

Sweeney tossed the first meat down to Blue. "No, I don't think so," he said, his attention back on the carcass. He was pretty certain the wing bones were too puny to hurt Blue, so he just ripped the little wing off and tossed it to him. "You be careful with that, now." He turned back to Bob. "It's gettin' too late to think about startin' back now. I think you'd best bide out to the Russell Hotel with us."

Bob slowly shook his head. "Nope. Think I'd better be gettin' on my way. It's a long piece out to the ranch for a man ridin' alone."

Sweeney glanced out the window, and saw Monahan and another fellow tying a horse at the rail. "Well, I guess I'll let you talk it out with Dooley." He tipped his head toward the window. "He's comin' right now."

Julia stood up from the kitchen table with a purpose in mind. She did her part with the cleaning-up chores from lunch, then excused herself and wandered outside. Everything was quiet at the stage stop—everything but her.

She scooped up her saddlebags—she'd put them out under the back stoop earlier in the day—and made her way to the barn where she found Parnell dozing in his stall. That was one good thing for Buckshot Bob—he'd let her take really good care of her horse since she'd been there.

But that didn't make up for what she'd discovered when she'd looked in her hidey hole this morning. There was a place in the girls' room, in the corner down by the floor, where part of the baseboard came up like a secret panel to expose a little nook where she imagined previous tenants had hidden their valuables from marauding Apache or bandits. It was the place where she had put her vouchers, along with the other papers she'd been given in Yuma. But the vouchers weren't there anymore. She had taken every last paper out of the hidey hole along with every last broken piece of toy and each scrap of torn doll clothing, but they weren't there.

She knew who had them, all right. As far as she was concerned, the missing vouchers had Buckshot Bob's name written all over them, if you could write on something that had gone missing.

It was then that she had made up her mind. She didn't know her way around, but she thought she'd learned enough about camping in the open to get her to Phoenix. At least, she knew beyond a shadow of a doubt that Phoenix was east of there, and that only one road led that way.

And so she saddled up Parnell and tied her saddlebags on behind. She took water and a couple of measures of grain, led him clear of the barn, and set out with nobody seeing her except young Robbie.

"Where you goin'?" the boy called to her from the front yard.

"Gonna go find your daddy," she called back. "Tell your mama not to worry, okay?"

Robbie nodded, she waved, and that was that.

The second she saw him go back inside the house, she urged Parnell into a quick canter that ate up the road, and soon left the station behind.

After lunch, Monahan, Sweeney, Buckshot Bob, and George Miller, who'd given Monahan a ride down from the Addams Hotel, all walked up to the bank where the old cowboy made certain Bob opened a savings account for Miss Julia, and then put her money—every single cent that he still had on him, anyway—in it. Miraculously, he was only about twenty dollars short. Monahan made up the difference out of his own pocket.

The clerk made up a passbook for Julia, and Monahan took possession of it, saying that he'd hold it for her. Bob tried to fight him on it, but when even George Miller agreed that Dooley should have possession, Bob gave up. It had finally become obvious to him that everybody was wise to what he had done—they were just too gracious to accuse him out loud—and that he'd best shut up about it.

Monahan had decided to set out west the first thing in the morning and take it to her himself. It hadn't occurred to him what Sweeney was going to do, but George Miller had signed on for the ride, saying he was going to California anyway. George was good enough company for him.

After a good dinner downstairs in the hotel dining room, Monahan, Sweeney, and Bob retired early. Night fell, and Buckshot Bob wasn't very happy about the situation. but Monahan figured there wasn't too much Bob could do about it.

Morning was going to come all too soon.

Out on the trail, Julia had long since stopped for the day, led Parnell off the trail, and made camp. The sounds of the desert spooked her at first, and she pined for the comfort of Monahan's company, and for that of Blue, who often curled up next to her for the night when they were out on the trail.

But she made supper and ate, despite her loneliness, and after a few hours, the sounds of the desert no longer bothered her. Well, most of them. She nearly jumped out of her skin when an owl hooted, and then punched herself in the shoulder for being so jumpy.

She hoped Mae wasn't fussing over her. She knew Meggie probably was, but it couldn't be helped. She needed to do this, needed to track down Bob and get her money back before he spent it all on himself. Or before he spent it on women besides Mae. Shame on him, anyway!

She fell asleep trying to figure out how in the world Buckshot Bob had found her hidey hole.

28

The men set out from Phoenix in the morning. They were all in high spirits, with the exception of Buckshot Bob, for obvious reasons. Monahan was enthused and grateful for the company of Sweeney, who was happy to still be tagging along, and especially George Miller, who had plenty of stories about the old spread up in Wyoming which he willingly shared at great length.

According to George, Monahan had been quite a hand with the beef stock . . . and with the ladies. The old cowboy flushed deep red when George told the story of Monahan and Miss Franklin, a popular schoolmarm with whom he'd kept company for some time. Sweeney practically fell off Chili, he was listening so hard, but when he pushed George for more details, George said, "You're gonna have to pester Dooley about that, son. I only tell what's fit to tell the preacher!"

And of course, Monahan remained silent on the subject. Sweeney figured Monahan was just as hungry for the details, but he'd probably not shared those with George at the time. It was a real pity, if you asked Sweeney . . . but of course, no one did.

No one knew what became of Miss Franklin, either. That was a real shame. The one person who would have remembered the most didn't recall a blessed thing about the incident. Why, George didn't even remember the first thing about Miss Franklin!

After a long and full day on the trail—and about twenty miles under hoof—they settled, at last, into a sleep. Sweeney took first watch to make certain Buckshot Bob didn't bolt, and woke Monahan at about two in the morning to take over for him.

They set out the next morning in good spirits, although Monahan was a little groggy. George Miller told more tales about the old cowboy's past, up in Wyoming. Sweeney listened, rapt, as George went on for hours about the beauties of the land around Yellowstone, and the smoking lakes and the geysers. He told the tale of Monahan and the grizzly bear (Monahan won), Monahan and the rabid lobo (Monahan won again), and Monahan and the lumberjack's daughter, which had a more questionable outcome.

George talked and talked all through the morning ride, and lunch, and then the afternoon and supper, until he was so hoarse he couldn't talk anymore. Sweeney, who was beyond thrilled to finally get to hear more of the tales of the old cowboy's past, had forgotten all about his earlier longing to get himself shed of Monahan, to get free and quit getting shot at. Well, his shoulder tried to remind him, but he regarded that as just a battle scar, something that marked his hide to remind him of his brush with greatness. He was certain there'd be more. At least, he kept reminding himself that the past repeated itself.

After all, he couldn't seem to get shed of Julia, could he?

They ran into her just before they stopped for the night. She had already stopped and was off to the side of the road. Her horse was stripped of tack and grinding blissfully at a nosebag filled with corn and oats. And Julia? She was across the road, holed up behind a patch of prickly pear with a rifle to her shoulder and an irritated look on her face.

She came out soon enough, though, and added her prairie hen to their rabbits and quail. They made a tasty stew—while George finished his day's tale of Monahan and lapsed into an exhausted silence—then ate it and stretched out on the desert floor for the night. George was run fresh out of stories about the time he'd run himself out of fresh throat.

Sweeney was standing watch first. Well, sitting watch, anyway. He had to admit—if only to himself— that running in to Julia again wasn't half as awful as he'd thought it would be. Besides, she had some salt in her saddlebags, which he and Monahan had forgotten to bring, and she did pull together a decent stew. Well, all right, he admitted with a sigh. It was better than decent by quite a bit.

He thought she had taken the news about Buckshot Bob's betrayal like a true stoic. She hadn't even been mad about it. Of course, it helped that she'd already guessed that he was a thief, and she was just glad they'd run into him in the city and got things handled so she didn't have to. She accepted her bank book from Monahan, quickly inspected it, and then, behind a clump of cactus, secreted it on her person. She was no fool, all right.

And she'd asked about his shoulder. *That was real nice of her,* he thought, *especially since nobody else cared in the slightest.* He'd told her that he was fine, thanks, and healing up just crackerjack.

She was asleep on the other side of the fire with Blue contentedly curled up on her blanket. She'd told Sweeney to wake her at midnight, and she'd spell him and Monahan, shortening their watch hours.

Actually, he mused, she was a real peach.

He settled down for the night, and tried to keep his eyes open. "Just until midnight," he muttered sleepily.

Later that night, Monahan sat in the predawn desert haze facing west, watching the sun breech the eastern horizon in the broken glass that lined the Old Mormon Trail. Everyone else was asleep, including the dog, who had wakened at around four when the old cowboy got up to relieve Julia, made a circuit around the sleepers, then returned to her blanket. He'd claimed it as his own sometime during the course of the night.

Monahan was awfully glad they'd run across the

girl, and grateful for her help on night guard, too. The half nights of sleep were harder on his old bones than he liked to admit. At least with her around, he had to spend fewer hours on guard. It surely did make a difference.

To help pass the time, he ignored his ready-mades and rolled himself a smoke, stretching out the ritual of lighting it and taking the first drag. There was still nothing like the taste of good tobacco the first thing in the morning.

He'd already completed his morning ritual of beating and pounding and grinding everything awake, but now that he'd settled in for the long haul, he was starting to freeze up again. He tried to remember what it was like to have no morning aches or pains, but it was too far back to recall. It just seemed like he'd been born into hurting. His cross to bear, he guessed.

He poured himself a cup of coffee, and his shoulder hurt. He moved back to his pallet, and his knee screamed. Seemed like there wasn't a move, either big or small, that he could make without some part reminding him that he'd broken a bone or ripped a muscle or gotten into a one-sided argument with a rank bronc or a crabby steer.

It wasn't fair.

But then, what in his life *was* fair? What in anybody's life turned out the way they wanted?

He puzzled over this for quite a long time—long enough that the deep morning shadows were erased and light flooded the desert, bringing with it the morning birds and the snakes. The latter he couldn't stand, especially when a rattler climbed out of the brush and stretched himself out on the bumpy surface of the road to warm in the pre-noon sun. Snakes had as much right as anybody to live, but not when they came so close to him. He dragged himself up off his pallet and shot it, which of course, woke everybody else.

Sweeney jumped immediately to his feet, shouting, "Holy Christ! Who's tryin' to kill us?"

Buckshot Bob twisted his head like an owl, George grabbed his pistol and aimed it out toward nothing, and even little Julia threw her arms tight around Blue's neck and stared wide-eyed.

Monahan took a long breath in through his nose and said, "Snake."

The camp deflated, as surely as if it had been a balloon that he'd suddenly popped with his one-word explanation. Sweeney dropped back to the ground, Bob's head stopped twisting, George's pistol lowered to earth, and Julia released the dog.

Blue bounded over the dying fire, then leaped to Monahan, whimpering with joy. His first instinct was to swat him, but the big pink tongue rapidly scrubbing his face and the happy sounds emanating from his 'attacker' got the best of him. Laughing, he fell down and back, taking the oblivious, joyously squirming dog with him.

They reached the station a day and a half later, and poor Mae, always left to worry, was thrilled to see them, particularly Bob and Julia. Although

Monahan had made his companions promise to keep their mouths shut in front of Mae, he took her aside later and explained his reasons for riding back with Bob.

He finished by saying, "I don't figure to know if there's anything funny goin' on betwixt you and your hubby, Mae, and it ain't my business to second guess. Now, ol' Bob feels pretty dang bad about this whole ruckus, I'm guessin', but you'd best keep an eye on him for a while."

Mae was crying, and the old cowboy took her into his arms and said, "There, there," and tried to comfort her, but she was so shaken—and embarrassed—by her husband's actions that she had no words. Monahan understood without being told, and he simply held her. He'd known her since she was a little girl of eleven—even though many of those intervening years were cloudy for him—and chasing chickens on her daddy's ranch in Texas, so she let him.

As for Julia, the first thing she did upon her arrival at the station was to find a new hiding place for her bank book. Having given it quite a bit of thought over the past few days, she had decided that no place in the house was safe—Mae and Buckshot Bob had lived there a good deal longer than she'd been breathing—and so she started searching the barn and the smaller outbuildings in search of a safe spot. She finally found one inside a saddle stand, wedged up into a slit where the wood was cracked, and left her bank book behind without a second thought.

Having taken care of Bob and Mae, Monahan found himself at loose ends. He knew he was supposed to be moving on—California, probably—but had no idea why. He wandered out to the front stoop and sat down with a smoke. Sweeney was already out there, leaning listlessly on the front rail and talking to George, who was out roaming around the front yard with his gaze downcast.

Looking for snakes, Monahan guessed. "He find anything yet?"

Sweeney shook his head. "Nothin'," he said. "What's next?"

Monahan honestly didn't know what to tell him, although he was certain he'd known before. "Dunno right now. Ask me later."

The young cowboy shrugged and went back to watching George, who was surreptitiously keeping one eye on the horizon where Buckshot Bob was out after cattle with his dog. Although he hadn't known Bob earlier, he was full of Bob theories and more than full of ideas about where he and Monahan would go once they had things wrapped up.

Monahan was still concerned about Buckshot Bob. He had got himself real embarrassed and Monahan figured he'd never try to steal anything from anybody again as long as he lived. He just wasn't the type. But the old cowboy fretted over things and people long after they needed fretting over. It was just the sort of man he was . . . or at least, he used to be.

George knew all about the old dream to go to Alaska. Monahan had been harping on it since they were up in Wyoming, and he'd sold George on the idea years ago. But he hadn't heard mention of it lately. Was it possible he'd already got himself up there and back, and found nothing?

George didn't think so. Monahan had been too certain-sure of himself and Alaska, and he was too pigheaded to fail at something he was so convinced of. Besides, George had been keeping tabs on news coming out of the frozen territory, and best as he could tell, there were still fellows striking it rich up there. Just not as many as had gone to California. Alaska was a forbidding place, all right. He'd heard there was snow on the ground all year-round, and that if you accidentally dumped a bucket of water outside, you could skate on it within fifteen minutes!

Of course, according to Monahan, all that was blown way out of proportion. Oh, it was cold, all right, but there were regular seasons of the year, and yes, summer, too. He'd had books and papers to back up what he'd claimed, all kept on a makeshift set of shelves beside his bunk. George wondered whatever had become of the books, all those tales of Alaska and its wildlife and its terrain. He shook his head. Monahan had probably just got up one morning, forgot he had them, and wandered off.

At his movement, George heard Sweeney call out to him, asking if he'd spotted something. He shook his head, turned back toward the house, and hollered, "No, nothing!" then went on with his, well, whatever it was he'd been doing. He wasn't sure quite what that was, but he carried on, just the same.

His eyes flicked out toward the horizon, where he spotted a distant Bob coming in with about a half-dozen cattle. His dog was with him, keeping the cattle bunched up and headed the right way. Except for her coloring and her smaller size, she was a lot like Blue. George would have bet hard money that she could have gone out by herself and rounded up those cows just fine. But then, he supposed Bob needed something to do, something to get him away from the house—and them—to think things over, and so he had let his dog take care of finding the cows.

Being younger than Monahan by about only a decade, George was beginning to slow down some. He was just as smart as he'd always been, but he could see old age was creeping up on him, and he wasn't half ready for it. He wanted something where he could make a good chunk of money in not much time so he could retire decently. More than anything, he didn't want to end up like other fellows he'd known, fellows who hadn't been able to set anything aside and had ended their days begging on the streets or mucking out stables, and buried in pauper's graves.

He wanted to travel with Monahan to the Alaskan gold fields. He figured there was one place he could still be a pioneer, and Alaska was it! There was time to get in, strike it rich, and get out again before the main wave of gold diggers came rushing in, like they had in California.

He was all for getting in and getting out fast. He just hoped Monahan was of a like mind—if he ever thought about it at all.

Bob and the cattle were almost upon him. He lazily lifted an arm and nonchalantly shouted, "Hey, Bob!"

The rancher acknowledged him with a wave, and that was that.

29

Time seemed to drag on. Sweeney had almost given up entirely and put Chili out to pasture, George was chafing at the bit, but managed to keep himself under control—just barely—and Monahan seemed more relaxed, more content, than Julia had ever seen him. She didn't know what impression she was giving the others and frankly didn't care, but secretly she was hoping the old cowboy had forgotten all about leaving her there and would pack her along once he got it in his mind to move on.

Even Mae and Buckshot Bob seemed more relaxed. They were almost back to normal—well, what was normal for them, anyway—and Mae was cooking great big breakfasts again. That, Julia had to admit, was her favorite part of the whole deal—Mae's cooking, especially those shoot-the-works breakfasts. Monahan always called them that, anyway, and she figured he'd just about nailed it. Mae always made toast, French toast, bacon, and eggs, and then rotated in ham, biscuits with honey, beans, chicken, fritters, leftovers from the night before, and fresh juice with each breakfast.

They were something to write home about!

She didn't, of course. The only way to do that—and have anybody read it—was to write a letter to herself, or maybe to Monahan. But he wasn't paying any attention to anything, except did he get enough sleep, and was General Grant getting enough grain. Anyway, it seemed that way to her.

The truth was, though, Monahan was thinking on leaving a powerful lot. He was consumed with it night and day, and if he didn't show it, well, he was self-trained to keep those cards close to his vest. Although he knew he had a purpose, he just couldn't recall what it was. He sat for long hours by himself out on the front stoop, smoking cigarettes and staring at the same knothole on the same post, trying to remember what in the blue-eyed world it was.

But not a blessed thing came to mind.

He even spent four hours out by the corral talking nonsense to General Grant, but nothing came to mind, except that perhaps he was getting a little heavy handed with the grain. The General looked to be putting on a bit of extra weight.

At least he remembered that! He stopped pushing the corn and oats so hard.

Three days later—and almost two weeks after they had arrived at the stage stop—George took the bit in his teeth. He was tired of waiting on Monahan and almost ready to go up north on his own, even though the prospect nearly froze his gizzard—literally—every time the thought occurred to him. But it was time he talked about it. He wasn't getting any younger.

After breakfast, he waited until Monahan got situated out on the front porch before he took a deep breath and walked outside, all casual-like. He calmly walked past him to the edge of the stoop, leaned up against a post, and lit himself a smoke. "Gonna be hot one," he said, shaking out the match.

Dooley grunted.

"Want to talk to you," George continued. "About Alaska."

Suddenly, something clicked in the old cowboy's head. He jumped to his feet and hollered, "Yahoo!" With a smile almost bigger than his face could hold, he shouted, "Why didn't you say somethin' afore this?!"

George's jaw dropped, but no sound came out.

Muttering and mumbling joyfully to himself, Monahan dug into his pocket like a man possessed, yanked out his wallet, thumbed it open and pulled out a worn clipping, then danced in a little circle right there on the porch, jubilantly shouting, "Alaska! Alaska! I'm goin' to Alaska, where there ain't no poison bugs nor sharp-fanged rattlers to pester a man who's lookin' for gold!"

Slowly, George slid down a porch post and landed with a thunk on the floor of the stoop.

Monahan didn't notice. He was too busy celebrating his amazing and colossal return of memory. Actually, while it was fairly amazing, it wasn't so colossal at all—considering all that he'd forgotten—but it seemed like the world to him. He just kept cackling and dancing in that little circle, dreaming of the gold and the cold.

Alaska!

Within the hour, Julia was scrambling to pack her saddlebags before they left without her! Sweeney was already out back saddling Chili, and George and Monahan were doing the same with their horses.

Sitting on the bed was Meggie, her head propped on her fists. She wailed, "But why do *you* have to go, too?"

Quickly, Julia folded her spare shirt. "Don't hafta. I wanna go!" She squirreled it away in her saddlebag, then started folding her spare britches.

"But why? Why can't you just stay here with us?"

"Because, Dooley is my family. Can't explain it better 'n that." The pants were stuffed in the bag beside her other clothes, and she stood up. "I'll be back sometime, Meggie, honest!"

"But—"

"Gotta go!" Julia bent down and brushed her lips across Meggie's cheek. "I'll miss you!"

Meggie didn't reply. She was too busy crying.

The truth be told, Julia did a little crying herself, but she always took care to wipe away her tears before anyone saw them. She got her bankbook out of the crevice, Parnell saddled, and accepted a gunny sack laden with food from Mae before she hurried out of the yard, waved a quick good-bye to Buckshot Bob and young Robbie, and galloped to catch up to the men.

They were almost on the far western horizon when she made it to the road. It sparkled ahead of her like two lines of giant, broken diamonds in the sun, and she rode between them as fast as she could, with her head down so her Irish setter hair mixed with Parnell's black mane. It flew and fluttered in the wind like an ebony and scarlet banner.

"Well!" Monahan declared when she finally drew up and fell into pace with them. Her horse was blowing from her hard gallop from the station, and she was a little out of breath, too.

"About time," Sweeney grumbled.

George tipped his hat a tad and said, "Howdy to you, Miss Julia."

"We're all glad you could make it, honey," continued Monahan. "You get your bankbook?"

Julia nodded. "You fellas sure cut outta there in a big toot! Where we goin' in such an all-fired hurry?"

Monahan's only answer was a half-mad laugh, but Sweeney said, "Goin' west, then north."

"To where?"

George twisted toward her, a big smile on his face. "To Alaska! Gonna make our fortunes."

Julia just nodded and said, "Oh, Alaska," like that was someplace that everybody and his Uncle Ned ought to see before they died. She was a child of the West and had heard of the place, of course, but also being a native of the southern clime, she couldn't see why anybody would want to go up there, especially on purpose!

But she kept her mouth shut, figuring some things either played out or disappeared over time. She didn't soon find out which was the case because they continued on in silence, then stopped for the night in much the same way they always had. Monahan's mood continued to be high—at least, according to his expression—and George was the same.

It wasn't until they had gone to sleep—and Blue had curled up on Julia's bedroll and sighed a deep sigh—that Sweeney whispered across the campfire. "Pssst! Julia!"

Reluctantly, she forced her eyes open. She'd been climbing into the arms of Morpheus, and was a little disgruntled. She said, "What?" more loudly than intended.

"Keep your tone down!" whispered Sweeney.

"I'd rather just turn it clear off. What you want?"

"Dooley say anything to you? 'Bout where we're goin', I mean."

Julia furrowed her brow. "Both him and George think we're goin' to Alaska, the loons. Of all the places!"

"We are. I'm askin', did they say anythin' else?"

Julia snorted out air, then lay back down and pulled the blanket up. This beat everything! If Sweeney thought they were going to Alaska, too, they probably were. She threw an arm around the still-sleeping Blue, and said, "I don't know a damn thing more than you do. Now, lemme go back to sleep!"

She yanked the blanket the rest of the way up to cover her face and closed her eyes. She supposed Sweeney did, too, because the next thing she knew Blue was snuffling at her face, and it was morning.

The following week, they were still spending long days in the saddle, but at least they had run clean out of west and were traveling north along the coast. It was just like Dooley had said it would be, Julia thought, and so she kept her mouth shut. She was still uncertain as to their ultimate goal, but she was learning to live with uncertainty.

They were riding along when Monahan suddenly thumbed them over to the east, until the ocean was clean out of sight, until they couldn't even hear the waves breaking anymore. Julia got more and more tense with each step the horses took. She figured they had finally come near their goal, and that any moment, Monahan would reveal it to her.

But they just kept riding northward, gradually up a seemingly endless rocky slope, and then over to the west once again without any sign from Monahan except for the occasional wave of his hand.

Julia was on the verge of calling a halt once and for all when she heard the first whispers of the sea pushing into her range of hearing. She perked up, startling Blue—who rode behind her on Parnell's rump, as he had been since the midday stop for lunch—but not saying a word. She held her breath and listened harder.

They were indeed approaching the ocean again, but at a much higher vantage point. The world seemed to fall away, and when she rode closer, she found herself high atop a steep drop-off. The ocean roared far below and met the steep rocks in crashing waves. She shuddered and reined Parnell away, choosing to ride about ten feet from the brink. She could still see the edge of the precipice, but was in no danger of accidentally toppling over it.

She fell in behind the other three, who had already chosen the inland path and seemed unconcerned by their proximity to the edge. Personally, she was still shaking inside.

They continued on for what seemed like hours, until it began to grow dusky. Their shadows grew long at their sides, and the sun began to lower itself below the far end of the ocean. Ahead, Monahan's arm rose up and she heard him call a halt. She was hungry and chilly, and therefore grateful. The first thing she did once she dismounted was to pull open her saddlebags and pull out her jacket. They must have traveled farther north than she thought.

She was right. They had managed to get themselves almost all the way to San Francisco in the past week or so—a joyful tidbit shared by Monahan over dinner—and would ride into its outskirts the next afternoon. He promised they'd have hotel beds to sleep in and restaurant meals to eat and hostlers to take care of their horses and real outhouses to use. It would be his treat! Well, for a few days, anyway.

She cranked up her courage. "And then what?" she asked between bites of quail stew.

"Well, that's up to you!" he replied cryptically, and George laughed.

She and Sweeney just sat there, silenced, she supposed, by their own stupidity.

She looked over at him and he looked at her, and then she suddenly found her voice again. "What'd you mean, Dooley? S'pose I choose to say that we all ride right into the Pacific Ocean?"

Monahan laughed, and George said, "Then I figure you're not half as smart as I thought." He turned to Dooley.

"That 'bout sums it up, I'd say." Monahan topped off George's stew, then held up the ladle and asked, "Anybody else?"

Julia and Sweeney held out their plates.

30

They rode into San Francisco the following afternoon and settled the horses at the Simmons Livery, then signed the register at the Dew Drop Inn. Feeling magnanimous, Monahan signed for all the rooms, even George's, and then announced he was taking them all to dinner, and they should all go clean up.

While the others set off with keys in hands, Sweeney lingered. The whole thing made him . . . uneasy. He'd never seen Monahan so happy and footloose. Admittedly, they hadn't known each other long, but they'd gone through enough together that it should make up for a lost year or two, maybe even three! Anyhow, he figured it that way.

And it bothered him royally that he still had no idea where they were headed. He'd asked George, too, but he was as slippery as Monahan.

Dinner was the time to press for the rest of the information. He planned to do just that. No ifs, ands, or buts.

* * *

Sweeney and Julia met in the hallway and walked down the stairs to find Monahan and George waiting for them in the lobby. George opened the door for everybody, laughing and bowing, and Monahan ushered them up the street. They walked about two blocks, with Julia terrified by the hustle and bustle going on, before he pulled them into a place called Morgan's Fine Dining.

Halfway to a table, Monahan stopped stock still. Almost running into him, Sweeney grabbed the old cowboy's shoulder to steady himself, and said, "What's wrong, Dooley?"

"You see that feller sittin' over there, by the window?"

"Yeah. What about him?"

"Don't know. Somethin' about him, though." Monahan gave a last glare to the table at which the man sat, then continued on after Julia, George, and the waiter. Sweeney followed, and they were all seated. Monahan stared at the stranger's table.

"Why don'tcha go on over there?" the young cowboy finally asked.

"Bad idea," Monahan replied, without bothering to turn toward him.

Sweeney was getting disgusted. It was bad enough when Monahan got spooked on the road, but in a big town, with folks all round who could hear him? It was plain embarrassing!

He ordered along with the others, and by the time their dinner arrived—still sizzling from the grill—Monahan was dividing his attention evenly between the table across the room and his own. Dinner itself? Well, that captured his attention entirely.

It distracted Sweeney completely, too. It was steak—a juicy tenderloin, thick and wrapped in bacon—and lobster which he was convinced he wasn't going to like. But it turned out that he was crazy for it, and swallowed down every last butter-soaked scrap of the sweet stuff. Who would have thought something that looked so much like a big old water bug could taste so flavorful and rich?

The lobster was clearly a hit with Julia and George too, although he waited until the others had eaten at least half of theirs before he tried his first bite. But then, he was off to the races!

They cleaned their plates, leaving only the empty remains of the cracked lobster shells.

Julia leaned back in her chair with her hands splayed out over her stomach. "Holy cripes!" she muttered. "That was *g-o-o-d* with a capital good!"

Monahan smiled wide. "Kinda makes you wonder how inland folks survive without it, don't it?"

"Sure does, Dooley," George said, and sighed happily while the waiter cleared the table, then slid a thick slice of lemon meringue pie before him.

They had ordered desert when they ordered their dinner, and each of them sat before the confection that had tickled his or her fancy.

Sweeney finished his strawberry shortcake first with Julia not far behind, spooning up the last of her ice cream. Monahan swallowed the last bite of chocolate mousse and pushed back from the table.

"We goin' already?" George asked around a mouthful of lemon meringue pie.

Monahan stood up and waved. "No, you stay on and finish your supper, George. I just remembered somethin' I've gotta do." He shoved his chair back under the table. "See you back at the hotel!"

Before Sweeney could think twice, the old cowboy was out the door and gone.

When Monahan told them he had remembered something, he wasn't fooling. He had finally figured out why that man seemed so familiar, and he had remembered the man's name. Len Dobbs was a little grayer of hair, but it was him, all right.

A quick look showed Len about two blocks up the street—right out in front of the hotel, in fact. Monahan scurried to close the distance, but Len had moved on to the livery where General Grant was boarded. *Len had best not try to steal his horse!*

Horse thievery was, of course, what Len Dobbs had been guilty of, and it was what Monahan had been blamed for when the horse thief had skipped town. That was back in . . . Monahan had to stop and think. *Cheyenne, wasn't it?* He remembered it was awful cold, and the horse in question was a gray Missouri Fox Trotter that just happened to be his! He snorted. It was just his luck to get arrested for stealing his own horse. Silver King, he remembered. That was the horse's name. It had taken him nearly a month to get hold of the fellow who had sold the horse to him and prove his ownership. Of course, by that time, Len Dobbs and Silver King were long gone.

It was kind of odd that the man was in San Francisco, but Monahan wasn't about to look a gift horse in the mouth, so to speak. He wanted a few choice words with old Len. At the least, he wanted to give him a well-deserved punch in the mouth.

It was the least he could do.

As he watched, Dobbs' figure vanished into the stable. *Damn it!* he thought. *That mushy-faced straw walker's up to no good again!* Monahan lengthened his stride to a half run and sped down the walk toward the livery.

He paused outside the wide doors, listening and thinking. All he heard were rustles of straw and hay, the soft sounds of livestock put up for the night.

He didn't trust his ears, though. So far as he knew, ol' Lenny was still inside, and probably getting General Grant ready to hotfoot it out of town! Slowly, he drew his gun. Holding it level with his waist, he stepped into the soft light spilling through the wide doorway.

There was no one inside. Not one blessed soul! He looked all around, shook his head, and then slowly slid his Colt back into its holster. He could have sworn . . . *Well, hell.*

He was even dizzier than he figured, thinking he'd seen ol' Lenny Dobbs in San Francisco! Now, that was a laugh. Dobbs would fit in with San Francisco Brahmins—or Barbary Coast denizens, for that matter—like Monahan would fit in at a retreat for Roman Catholic monks—which was, of course, not at all.

He made his way over to General Grant, who was half asleep in his stall with his knees locked, his eyes half lidded. "Well, how you doin', ol' son?" Monahan soothed. One of the General's eyelids rose a bit, and the ear on that side pivoted toward him. He smiled. "Didn't figure you was sleepin'."

As he held out his hand to rub the horse, he felt a sudden, searing pain at the top of his head and collapsed, unconscious, on the straw-strewn floor.

There was a rap at the door and Julia looked up. "Who is it?"

Although it was muffled by the heavy oak door, she heard the reply just fine. "It's me. Butch."

"C'mon in. The door's not locked."

The door creaked open, and she looked up from her cards. She was playing solitaire on the bedspread.

Sweeney stood in the doorway. "You seen Dooley?"

She shrugged her thin shoulders. "Not since dinner. You check his room?"

Sweeney shook his head. "He ain't in there. Ain't anywhere. I was hopin' you had him."

"It's early yet, Butch. He's probably off just doin' Dooley stuff."

The young cowboy cocked a brow. "Dooley stuff?"

"Oh, you know what I mean. Stuff that he doesn't

think we're ready for yet, or stuff that he thinks is going to be too hard on our tender eyes or ears, or just things he doesn't think are any of our business." She put a red jack on a black queen.

"Wondered when you were gonna see that."

"Yeah, like you could see it from over there."

Blue chose that moment to jump over to the bed from the armchair, and her neatly placed stacks and rows of pasteboards suddenly looked as if they'd been run through with a harrow. The dog seemed unconcerned, and smiled at her.

She made a face at him and muttered, "I was gonna win this one for real, you dirty ol' dog!" She looked over at Sweeney again. "What're you lookin' at?" she demanded. "He ain't in here, and I don't know where he is." She began to scrape the cards back into some semblance of order. "Move your foot, Blue."

Sweeney bent and scooped up a few cards Blue had sent flying his way and handed them to her. "Okay," he said as he turned to go back into the hall. "Sorry to bother you."

Why did he have to do that? Why did he have to turn around and be nice to her once she thought she'd put him in his place?

"Butch?"

He turned and stuck his head back inside the room. "Yeah?"

Suddenly, she didn't know what to say. Instead of stammering like a fool, she said, "Could you take Blue out? He ain't been since before we went to supper."

"Sure. C'mon, Blue." He gestured, and the dog sprang from the bed all the way out into the hall. He landed with his backside wiggling, and Sweeney laughed.

So did Julia, but she covered her mouth. "Thanks, Butch," she said, although it was muffled.

"I'll bring him back," he said, as Blue sprang up to lick him square on the nose. "Easy, boy! Might take him back to my room for a while, first. He's good company, 'specially when there ain't nothin' decent to read."

Julia looked up from her cards, intending to ask why he hadn't snagged a newspaper from the pile out in the lobby, but he'd gone off down the hall. She called, "Hey! Shut the door, will you?"

She heard the thump of running boots, then saw his arm snake in to take hold of her door's latch and pull it closed.

"Thank you!" she said loudly as the boots thumped back toward the front lobby.

She heard him call, "Hey, Blue! Wait for me!" then the muffled sound of a collision, then Butch saying, "Sorry ma'am. Excuse me!"

Smiling, she shook her head, then went back to her cards.

31

Monahan came back into consciousness. He was all alone in a strange place. Although he quickly recognized General Grant, nothing else was even slightly familiar. His head hurt, and he was pretty sure somebody had hit him. *The coward!* He quickly went through his own pockets and found nothing that contained a name, but discovered that he was practically rich. There was over a thousand dollars in his wallet, which stopped him from searching it further. One thousand dollars! A man could live a good long time on a thousand dollars.

Why was he carrying that much cash money? Was he a gambler? Or maybe a rancher who had just sold some stock . . .

Outside the livery, somebody walked along the sidewalk.

Monahan was well back from the door and most certainly couldn't be seen by passersby, but in case their eyes searched the dim interior, in case they knew to look for an old man squatting on the floor outside a bay horse's stall and rifling through his own wallet, he scurried back, hiding the wallet and himself. He stood up a few minutes later, when he was sure the coast was clear, and saddled General Grant.

He didn't actually recall the entirety of General Grant's name. Oh, he was certain about the General part, but confused as to the specifics. Lee? Sherman? Grant? Maybe Custer? He'd figure it out in time.

He was halfway up and into the saddle when the dog surprised him. It came from behind and landed square in the middle of his back, all four paws out. It was barking over the noise from the street.

He whirled and raised his arm, intending to do whatever it took to beat the dog off, but when he faced it, he dropped his arm immediately. He knew this dog, and it seemed the dog surely knew him! He pegged it immediately as a butt-wiggling, bob-tailed California Shepherd. He figured he was safe in calling it that, since he'd seen a little sign on the inside of the door that led him to believe he was in California. So far as he knew, he didn't have any sheep or cattle that needed herding, and no need for a trick dog either.

But he might have had in the past. He was pretty darned certain the dog belonged with him, anyway. He put a hand down and stroked the short, silky hairs on its head and ears. "You mine?" he asked.

When the dog smiled wide and pushed up against his hand, he muttered, "Well, you sure are, ain't you?" He chuckled softly. "I ain't doin' so bad. Hell, I ain't been conscious more 'n ten minutes, and I already got money, a dog, an' a horse." And then he got to wondering how he could remember the same thing had happened before, but not recall what came in the middle. His pounding head—and the lump on the back of it—told him somebody had walloped him, sure as shooting. But he didn't know why, or why they'd left him in the out-of-the-way stable without even going through his pockets! And how the heck did he know the stable was out of the way?!

Shaking his head and grumbling, he mounted the General—to whom he'd already tied all the saddlebags and paraphernalia he thought belonged to him—and ambled out of the stable with the dog at the General's heels.

"Sorry to do this to you, General, but I figure when just 'bout everythin' comes up cockeyed, it's in a man's best interest to get his tail outta town. His horse's and dog's, too!"

The dog woofed softly under his breath as if he were seconding the old cowhand's comments.

"Yes sir, we'd best be headin' out."

And they did, following the signs that pointed them out of town, then south, then west, until they ran clean out of signs and the old cowboy's watch read a few minutes past midnight. They stopped, and he made camp and a small fire, then searched his saddlebags for something to eat.

"Now, why in tarnation did I ever bring my backside clear to San Francisco?" he asked the dog over a couple of leftover biscuits he'd found in his possibles bag. "You're wonderin' how I knew we was in 'Frisco? I read it on the other side o' those signs we followed to get outta town, that's how!" He tore off another piece of biscuit and tossed it to the dog, who caught it in midair and swallowed it whole, and then looked at him expectantly.

The old cowboy chuckled then said, "Don't reckon you got much to say to that or anythin' else, do you, boy?"

The dog replied with a whimper that emerged high at first and then wound down at least four octaves to a low, creaking groan.

"My stars! You sing opera in your spare time?"

The dog cocked his head and the man threw him the last chunk of their shared dinner. It was gone in two chews.

"Well, let's see. Been most of the way through my wallet, and found out my name is Monahan. Dooley Monahan. Got to say I like the Monahan—good and strong, you know?—but I'm not crazy about the Dooley part of it. Well," he added, stretching his arms, "I s'pose I'll get used to it."

He leaned back on his bedroll and went on, "Guess we got you figured out, too, if that's your old bowl I found. Blue's what it says." The dog woofed happily and Monahan nodded. "Yup. I reckon that's you, all right. Fits you, anyhow."

He still hadn't figured out why in the world his first instinct had been to get himself out of town as fast as possible. He hadn't even thought about it.

A lone owl hooted in the trees behind him and

the dog leaned toward the sound, twisting his head back and forth.

Monahan ruffled the fur on the dog's head, saying, "Oh, that's just an ol' hooty owl. Don't you pay him no mind, now."

The dog sat back, and the man stretched out, squirming to find a more comfortable position. When he finally found one, he said, "Good night there, Blue. I 'magine we'll figure out more of the story come mornin'. Sweet dreams, ol' son," he added, and pulled his hat down over his eyes.

It wasn't more than a minute before he felt the dog sneak onto his blanket and curl up against his leg with his silky head and throat stretched out across his thigh. Beneath the brim of his hat, Monahan smiled.

The light had barely broken when Julia was aroused from her slumber by a banging on the hotel door, and she promptly rolled over, mumbling, "Go away!"

The person on the other side of the door set pounding again. He was putting everything he had into it.

She rolled back and pulled herself up. "Hold your horses! I'm comin!" she called as she took the single step toward the door and flung it open.

It was Sweeney.

"What in hell are you doin' out here!" she demanded sleepily.

"Where's Dooley?" came the answer, if you could

call it that. He stuck his head in the door without asking and looked around. "Where is he?!"

"Quit askin' like I got him hid in here or somethin'," Julia said. It was awfully early in the morning for being this angry, but he had made certain she was up for it, all right. And then she said, "Where's Blue?"

"My next question," Sweeney grumped. He stuck a hand in his pocket. "Last night, he run off while I was out walkin' him. Hell, I figured he'd caught Dooley's scent or somethin'! Figured he'd come on back to the hotel with the tail of Dooley's shirt 'twixt his teeth! Musta fell asleep whilst I was waitin', 'cause I woke this mornin' and couldn't find no dog, or no Dooley for that matter." He let out an enormous breath and practically collapsed against the door frame.

Down the hall, a door opened and a woman in a nightcap—pink and ruffled—stuck her head out of her door and stared at them. Julia gave in to gravity and opened her door all the way. "Come in, I guess," she said, hauling him inside by his collar.

She pushed him down in the upholstered chair over by the window, then said, "You ain't seen him at all since dinner?"

Sweeney, having shot his accusatory wad, just shook his head.

"How about George? He seen anythin'?"

Again, a shake of his head.

She sat down on the bed with a thump and mentally weighed the circumstances. If he was right, and if he had exhausted every single possibility, it could only mean that something had happened to Monahan—either somebody had pulled him into a fight and he'd taken off, or he'd gotten thumped upside the head, by mistake or accident. She took some comfort in that the dog was gone, too, although she would surely miss him almost as much as Monahan.

She looked up and asked, "You check the livery? To see about—" Sweeney cut her off. "I already been there. His horse, his saddlebags, his gear . . . they're all gone. Just poof! Like that!"

Part of Julia was relieved. At least Monahan had his belongings as well as Blue.

She asked several questions. Did they know anything in the office? They didn't. Had Sweeney noticed anything out of the ordinary the night before? Actually, he had, and related the story about the man in the restaurant.

Julia sent him off to wait out in the hall while she dressed, and then they picked up George and went to breakfast.

George, normally an affable sort, wasn't happy about having been awakened so early in the morning, but he wasn't happy about Monahan, either. He got right to the point. "All right, you two, just hold your damn horses," he said, holding up his hands. They were seated at a nearby café, and the waiter had already taken their order. "I only got one question for you. Who's goin' north with me?"

Julia just stared at him. She couldn't believe he was thinking about himself at a time like this! Sweeney sat beside her with his chin on his chest, doubtless thinking the same thing.

George took advantage of their silence, saying, "Well, it sounds to me like ol' Dooley's been took with one of his spells again. Ain't the first time, and I don't figure it'll be the last. You two best get used to it. He's just gone." George shrugged his shoulders as if that was that.

Julia heard herself say, "No."

"Now, I know you've had a tough go of it," George continued, "but it's gonna be even tougher iffen you can't just let loose of ol' Dooley's ghost."

"But—"

"No buts about it, girl. And he is a ghost, or same as, once he's gone and got his memory all fuddled. Ain't nothin' you nor anybody else can do to fix it. Why, it was a full-on, pure D miracle that I ran across him like I did, and he near 'bout shot me in the process! Now, you can go up to Alaska with me, either one or both of you, or you can go anywhere else you want, try to track down ol' Dooley, or whatever. I ain't gonna stop you."

Julia couldn't think of a thing to say, but after a moment, Sweeney said, "I reckon I'll go on up north with you, George. Guess I don't have no place else to go."

Arrangements were made for the mute and defeated Julia to head back south with a band of wagoners that day. She rode stoned faced in a Conestoga with Parnell tied on behind. As for Sweeney, he spent the rest of the day searching the streets for any sign of Monahan, but sadly came up empty. That evening, he left with George on a tramp steamer headed for Alaska, with a stop-off planned in Seattle.

By the time they left the docks, Dooley Monahan was almost to Virginia City. Night had overtaken him—and the dog and General Grant—in a little town called Ogden, and he had decided to spend the night. He signed the hotel's ledger and settled in to his sheets with no further memory of where he'd come from or what he'd come out of, or why he was carrying so much money. He simply decided to let it alone.

After all, nobody would be looking for an old cowhand and a blue merle cow dog in a wide spot in the road like Ogden, now would they?